ENJOYMENT

ENJOYMENT

A COMEDY

ALAN BROWNJOHN

Shoestring Press

Printed by imprintdigital
Upton Pyne, Exeter
www.imprintdigital.net

Typesetting and cover design by narrator
www.narrator.me.uk
info@narrator.me.uk
033 022 300 39

Published by Shoestring Press
19 Devonshire Avenue, Beeston, Nottingham, NG9 1BS
(0115) 925 1827
www.shoestringpress.co.uk

First published 2016
© Copyright: Alan Brownjohn

The moral right of the author has been asserted.

Photograph of the author by David Barton

ISBN 978-1-910323-58-8

ABOUT THE AUTHOR

For his work as poet and novelist Alan Brownjohn (born in south-east London in 1931 and educated there and at Oxford) received in 2007 the special award of the Writers' Guild of Great Britain for lifelong achievement. He has also gained a Society of Authors Travel Scholarship and a Cholmondeley Award. For many years he was a teacher and lecturer in schools and in higher education. He has published thirteen individual volumes of verse, several of which have been recognised as Choices or Recommendations by the Poetry Book Society, three collected editions, and a *Selected Poems: The Saner Places* (2011). Two major classic drama translations have been produced: Goethe's *Torquato Tasso* (National Theatre and Radio Three) and Corneille's *Horace* (Lyric, Hammersmith).

for John Birtwhistle

1

The moment when two large cakes unbelievably vanish from the man's hands. And Frank Winterfield witnesses the event from his seat in a No.22 bus in a tailback in Chelsea. The person carrying them is William Bridgnorth, who becomes, through a network of further coincidences, the most important person in three people's lives over several weeks of extreme heat in one of the Great Years early in the third decade of the century.

Things start with Frank, and then switch a little later to Merlinda and Jake, who are also both drawn into all this by Bridgnorth. Frank had only to observe William from the window of the slow-moving bus in those few minutes to sense that someone he had once known about a little, but never properly taken in and had no reason to remember, had suddenly returned to his life and become peculiarly real.

First the vehicle passed Bridgnorth, then it was overtaken by him walking steadily on in the same direction. And then it passed him again. This was repeated several times – and then the something inscrutably odd happened, and it worried Frank very much indeed.

How had Frank known about Bridgnorth? Not long before this they had both been declared redundant by separate departments of the same large authority, but all Frank knew about this distant colleague was that when people referred to Bridgnorth they would do so with a degree of respect, and shake their heads and smile. Bridgnorth appeared to be liked; but he had a reputation for some kind of immense eccentricity, of dress, manner, and most of all of the way in which he addressed you.

The sight of him striding along out there on the pavement beside the bus showed that he was still alive and active, still a fact. But somehow his reappearance there at once seemed to render him more significant.

2

Frank hugged to his diaphragm the heavy litre bottle of low calorie tonic water he had bought, wrapped in a flimsy Lifelong Bag, as the bus edged very gradually westwards along the King's Road towards the desired neighbourhood of his home. This was during the traffic chaos of the latest Great Year. He held the bottle that way so that it could be kept upright and still, and might not explode wildly when opened; and he appreciated its coolness against his body. But the repeated lurching as the driver applied and relaxed, applied and relaxed the brakes in the mile-long tailback shook the liquid, and trembled its owner. Finally Frank gave up and put it down on the vacant seat next to him; so it fell out of the bag onto the floor as the bus pulled forward again, and rolled down the aisle. He had to leap up and go and rescue it. Frank now began to think it was that sort of day.

Once he was back in his seat with the bottle a mass of seething bubbles, he saw for the first time a figure he identified – yes, it had to be the curious William Bridgnorth. Bridgnorth went past as the vehicle paused again, very tall and broad and upright, marching slowly and with dignity along past the shops, carrying in his hands in front of him two vividly white, square cardboard boxes, one on top of the other. They could only contain round, freshly-baked cakes.

He walked with care, as balancing the boxes involved an effort of precision, and he kept both eyes fixed on his next few paces. It would have been completely unsuitable for Frank Winterfield to tap on the window and wave, even if he had known Bridgnorth well enough to do that. That would have distracted the man in his task, perhaps caused him to stumble and release his load. A pair of ragged dogs ran past ignoring him. Then the bus went on and left him behind.

After about thirty yards' progress the driver braked abruptly and brought the bus to another trembling halt. This allowed Bridgnorth to catch up and slowly pace on beyond the vehicle, lost from Frank's sight for several seconds because of a large truck immediately in front of it. Then, with another acceleration, Frank was again passing Bridgnorth, and this time he could see, mainly in profile, a kind of resolute and pleased expression on the man's face. It looked as if the two cakes in their separate square containers had only minutes before been placed inside, warm and fresh from the oven. Bridgnorth seemed to be carrying them with a serious purpose.

When the bus stopped yet again, allowing him to overtake it in the same measured fashion, Frank thought he sensed something three-dimensionally extraordinary about Bridgnorth. It was as if he was proceeding, with large regular paces, towards some sort of ritual; and Frank would not have been surprised to see him either followed by a short line of ceremonial attendants or met by a display of officials who would step up to receive the cakes and set them down on prepared stands. All this might happen to a fanfare of music and with a hand of greeting extended by someone wearing a mayoral chain or comparable emblem of rank. But they had already passed the former Town Hall.

All the same, when the bus stopped for so long that the driver, who had switched off the engine, could be engaged in rueful talk and laughter by the driver of another bus caught alongside him in a tailback headed in the opposite direction, Frank momentarily forgot him. The buses were there so long that the fizz in his tonic water subsided a little, and there were other figures on the pavement to look at. For example, why was that sixty-ish individual walking towards him on the pavement wearing a collarless yellow sweater, and jeans which left a three-inch gap and a bare navel between the two garments? On the sweater was a slogan or exhortation in black block capitals: GET ON TO US! Beside him a wife or woman companion of about the same age wandered drearily past windows which occasionally caught her gaze but never gripped her attention enough for her to stop. More and more he was finding people very hard to explain.

But now the bus had restarted, and charged eagerly ahead for some hundred yards, and they were once again moving parallel to Bridgnorth. Except – it was a large "except" – there was now something wrong, something alarming. Frank saw the man's unmistakeable tweed-suited back pacing along the pavement ahead at the same speed – but he was swinging empty arms. He was no longer carrying anything at all.

Frank's reaction was first disbelief – then almost panic. Was this the effect of many months of pressure, strain and resentment, loss of sleep about the betrayals committed by his colleagues, deep fears about his health? Did it connect with his nightmares, his waking up to the dread that as he switched on the light in his large bedroom in "West Chelsea" (a space that had developed eerie echoes since he had lived alone) he could easily be losing his nerve, his grip on – on anything? He had never until now experienced delusions, or hallucinations about odd persons from his past. Was this the way in which such illnesses began?

He was bound to take this as a case of hallucinating. He had been curious enough about the appearance of Bridgnorth, known to some at work as "the odd character in Environment", to turn his head and look at him when the bus had at last left him behind ten minutes ago. He was certain that he had been carefully carrying two white boxes of the kind that always contained cakes, and that those had vanished. The sight of the swinging arms produced palpitations, the pains of a sudden fear that he was going crazy. The cakes had been there, and they had gone. Obviously not eaten, and surely not given away to passers-by on a summer pavement in the King's Road in the last sixty seconds. Or had they never been there? Figments of his stressed-out imagination? What is a "figment" he wondered? If so, what has caused me, he wondered, to hallucinate, above all things, about cakes in boxes? Not office e-mails? Not dismissals on complex conditions only "made clear" to me in clauses and sub-clauses online?

As the bus passed him for the last time, he turned his head to try to catch Bridgnorth's eye when it reached him. He did not manage to do that. Bridgnorth kept up alongside for a second or two, then was irrevocably left behind as the bus found an empty section of the road ahead and speeded west towards a darkening sky.

3

Frank Winterfield went slowly up the steps of his block to his own and everyone else's front door, stepped inside, and blinked in the first deep darkness of the corridor on this afternoon of punishing heat. Then he walked very slowly indeed up the several flights of indoor stairs to the first floor, where his own apartment occupied a corner at the end. It had windows facing both the street and a yard with a view of the rear of other houses, and the brightest thing in that prospect was a vivid yellow drainpipe on the back of another mansion block about thirty feet away.

Inside, he set the heavy litre bottle down on the top of the fridge, and went into his lounge. Last winter this had become more spacious and echoing, and more costly to heat, than when Sara's furniture had filled the corners. But it was cooler in here this afternoon and he sat down to think what he would do to-night with the Great Year and the Fun dominating the media and allowing him little to watch on television. It was becoming thundery and was now prematurely dark. He stretched over and switched on the table lamp without getting up from his chair.

There was another incentive not to try the television, because he heard the voices starting. Frank looked at his watch and the sensations were the same as usual, beginning around the time people came home from work, if they worked. There would be a door closing in the equivalent flat upstairs, a shouted greeting and a response, and following that, always a dialogue. It would go in a kind of regular rhythm, as if the two persons involved, female and male, were reading exchanges from a script, even rehearsing them. If one voice faltered – more often the male speaker's – there would be a curt prompting so that the other would resume. Very few actual words could be made out, but the fact that Frank, if listening carefully, could occasionally catch some of them was due to the rooms being large and echoing, probably not having carpets. Every walk taken above could be heard step by step.

When there was a row going on, more walking about would be done, more words used, sometimes whole shouted phrases could become audible. Had these rows become more frequent? Or had Frank just realised how angry and bewildering they were – especially late at night – as the empty spaces in his own life opened up for him ever more widely?

"I think – this has—be-come ri-di-cu-lous!" was the first complete, understandable, phrase transmitted to him today, in a furious and yet very controlled female voice. The last word was enunciated with heavy, ironical slowness, as if she wanted every syllable to be clear to someone unlikely to understand. He could hear it very well because their window was open as well as his, so the words didn't have to reach him through the ceiling.

That last sentiment seemed to leave her partner in the conflict wordless, because no response came. Then an object was dropped on a surface with a loud sigh of resigned disgust. There was a kind of scurrying around, and an impatient dropping of other things, soft or sharp, light or heavy. This was followed by heavy footsteps going to and fro as if in frustration and anger, with a slapping sound. Their perpetrator must be wearing sandals. Finally came a man's voice saying something angrily without the same rhythm and emphasis. And a door was opening, or rather being yanked open, in the corridor above, and immediately slammed. Footsteps were going somewhere.

There is such a thing as ordinary slamming, when a door needs it in order to close properly, and there is slamming done to make a point. This was the second sort. What was it that raised Frank Winterfield from his lonely armchair and sent him out into the lobby to open his own front door and listen? There was an element of concern in his action, lest someone should run out and do something impulsive, even self-harming, in the corridor or the street. Many people would recoil in caution from domestic disputes like this, but in Frank Winterfield at this period there was much more curiosity.

Where would the footsteps go?

Through a gap of a couple of inches he could hear them walking the corridor above, the slammed door being opened again, a man calling out "Anna!" and then closing it.

"Anna" must have paused for a moment, but not to say anything that Frank could hear; and then she began a very audible descent of the stone stairs.

When the footsteps reached the landing on his floor and turned to walk along his own corridor, he could not see Anna because his door did not open in her direction. Only when she must have passed three other doors coming towards him did he decide to close his own in case she thought he might be spying on her private movements. But he did not close it at once, because he was paralysed for a moment by an intriguing possibility. In fact, he opened his door more widely, and dared to look round it. He saw Anna in her sandals rapidly approaching, and he stood there with the dimness of the corridor in front and the storm-darkened flat behind, in a state of great uncertainty.

Anna, it turned out, was the figure he secretly called "the woman on the stairs", who about once a week became "the very attractive woman on the front steps" or "in the street" or "in the launderette". Smiles and nods had begun to pass between them. They were near-neighbours recognising each other. There had never been any words exchanged. In this big anonymous block he had never before worked out which flat she might live in.

"Do you have a high-energy light-bulb?" she said.

"I'm sorry?"

"An old-style light-bulb that gives out some light." There was a slight stress on every other syllable as she said that.

"I don't know… I might have."

He turned back into the flat and went into the cramped kitchen, where he kept bulbs in a dresser drawer. Without being asked, Anna followed him and stood looking over his shoulder as he searched, as if they had always been acquainted. She took from his hand the yellow packet with the single bayonet bulb, looked at it, and shook her head.

"No. I need one that screws in."

He looked round at her and smiled, and she smiled back. If they had not known each other before they did now, without any preliminaries such as an exchange of names or an acknowledgement that they lived within feet of each other, below and above.

"He's no good in darkness," Anna told him quietly as he rummaged in the back of the drawer.

"It's not dark," Frank replied uncomfortably, not trying to understand her remark, which he thought he might not have heard properly. His mind was on finding for this physically appealing neighbour a suitable light bulb, nothing other than that. Yet immediately after this absent-minded response he did start wondering with amazement whether she was in fact imparting some very private information, and why.

"It's as good as dark," she suggested. They saw lightning, a flash striking in the silence that intimates a storm about to break very near.

He searched hard among the messy contents of the drawer, bringing out bulbs in single or double packets. Most were energy-savers, free gifts from the power people, dim illuminations Anna would not have accepted.

"Is it going to rain?" she wondered.

"I don't know," he replied, adding, "Is tonight the Fun Equestrian Event? Floodlit?" He surprised himself with that much knowledge of the Great Year. He was giving up the search for what she needed. "Looks to me I don't have an old-style bulb among these. But I have another thought."

As she followed him into the lounge he heard a door upstairs closed firmly, not slammed this time but surely the same door that had been opened and slammed ten minutes before. It reminded him that he had not shut his own door, so he went out and did that. The first thunder came.

"He's abandoned hope and gone out," she said. Frank may have looked puzzled or anxious because she added. "Don't worry. He does not know where I've gone…" Then, after a pause, "Where he goes has no rel-e-vance for me." She laughed at her serious, slow statement, made with that small emphasis on alternate syllables as if she had remembered a quotation.

Anna's relaxed air meant that Frank did not say, in that larger, emptier room, "Please sit down!" in one of the big shabby armchairs he had retained when Sara had gone. He felt it would have formalised the atmosphere. Anna's ease had awakened in him, he realised later, an ability to think of things he had not been able to initiate for years. It had been for so long that he might have forgotten such moves altogether, and revealed his forgetfulness with some blatantly self-defeating action: a sudden violent embrace, for example, and a move towards the equally well-worn sofa which would unbalance both of them, Anna pushing him aside with embarrassment and anger. He had nodded to her in this same white blouse and tight-fitting black trousers well inside a hundred-yard radius of this room. But what, literally what, was the next tactic he should try now it had come to this? He would surely try something, because she had favoured him with excuses to bestow her attention on him in order to escape from the crisis which he had accidentally overheard.

She was smiling now, her manner implied all this was such a delight. Fancy having to come down and ask the reserved-looking but rather appealing, bald but agreeable, guy whom she often saw around the place, and knew lived immediately below her – to ask this guy if he possibly had a bright light-bulb because Jeffrey liked to see her when they made love, and energy-saving bulbs, besides being useless, made Jeffrey feel dizzy.

"Uh! – that's going to be hot," Anna said as Frank switched off the bright table-lamp he had switched on ten minutes before. This left the lounge as good as dark now. The loudest peal of thunder yet clattered along the yard outside.

"You're right," he said. He went back to the kitchen and returned with a duster. "We'll let it cool down before you take it."

His hand with the folded duster fitted awkwardly into the small aperture of the cylinder. As he clutched the hot bulb he was saying to himself, "First I hallucinate, about a former colleague carrying cakes which vanish into thin air. Then I believe the neighbour whose body has attracted me when I see her around the place has called in to seduce me."

The bulb would not move. It was stuck, probably rusted into the socket. He was worried in case it broke. He had known before this the task of pulling and prising the shattered remains of a bulb from its socket with pliers and sharp-pointed kitchen knives.

"It won't turn," he said.

"Don't worry."

"I don't think I can help you."

"You tried."

Anna was unmistakeably hanging around as if there was something further to do.

"I'm sorry. I could do no more," he still said, and shrugged with a smile. He knew that he was deliberately not dismissing her. And she continued to wait. He picked up the duster for one last attempt, not wanting to be defeated but also hoping to give Anna a reason for staying; although she had done or said nothing to suggest she was proposing to leave. She was standing and smiling.

"I'd say don't worry. You have done your best."

Each word was pronounced very distinctly, and she ended the sentence with a laugh and a hand placed on his wrist to draw his hand away from the lamp. He looked at her sincerely.

"Dear Anna", he said, as if naturally permitted to after years of experience and familiarity. Next thing, they were hugging, and Frank was looking over her shoulder at his reduced array of furniture, which looked new and different to him in these circumstances. He could feel her eagerly pressing herself against him with the full length of her body, and he realised that because he had turned away from the table a bit clumsily the two of them, locked together, were likely to fall over now just as he had dreaded ten minutes before, unless they steadied themselves. So they might have been fated to overbalance anyway, he thought.

The scene outside was all at once vividly illuminated by more lightning, and the yellow drainpipe on the back of the adjacent opposite block at the back became an image he went on remembering. For the time being he thought, "I am having a very strange, momentous day. I had an illusion that William Bridgnorth appeared carrying some boxes containing cakes, but if he did, he was not –" this proving more relevant to Anna and himself than he could possibly know yet – "and now I am beginning an affair with an upstairs neighbour I have found sexually attractive ever since I moved in." But suddenly they were collapsed onto the sofa, from which Anna immediately got up and pulled him after her by a hand he at once took when she offered it.

"Is your place like Jefffrey's?" she laughed. "Bedroom first right, second door?"

She was leading, pulling him along the short corridor past the kitchen.

"I didn't make the bed this morning," he protested.

"I never make a bed."

"Not for visitors?"

"Never for visitors."

"I change the bedclothes for guests."

"You haven't for this one."

Anna was speaking rapidly, he was thinking, with none of the measured, prepared enunciation of syllables uttered as if she was acting a character in a Shakespeare play. Yes, Frank Winterfield thought a couple of weeks later, I actually did believe on the first of those days we spent in my bed that she sounded as if she was reciting everything on a stage.

She was undressing him and managing to remove her own clothes at the same time. She stretched out one foot after another and flapped her sandals so that they dropped on the floor, doing that as she undid his belt. Frank was complaisant in all of it: the dragging up of his shirt from inside his trousers, the pulling of trousers and pants down together so that he willingly stepped out of the heap and pushed it aside with one foot. At some point, he didn't take in when, she removed her own blouse and trousers and was kneeling down and asking him to raise his feet so that she could deal with his socks.

"I'll tidy this," he said.

He always slept restlessly and was glad to be out of bed and bedroom as soon as possible in the morning. Sheets and blankets were usually tangled together, the work of an impatient insomniac.

"No – don't tidy it."

Anna now knelt on the edge of the bed, cleared a space for them to lie on, tugged him down close to her. When they were both stretched out she brought back some of the confusion of bedclothes to half-cover them – unexpected, but perhaps for decorum's sake, or out of a fear that they might be overlooked from higher buildings opposite. They lay on their sides facing each other and clutching and didn't notice at first the rain entering the window opened during the night before to let some air in.

Frank went on to experience what he had known each of the four times in forty-eight years of life when making sexual contact with someone for the first time – a sense that there must be an acknowledged method, or convention, or set of rules which he had never fully known. The partner knew what you had to do, and he complied with her movements with a respect for her command of the procedures. Everything Anna did he reciprocated, every action he copied as if she was training him in how to do it. When observing, admiring and wondering about her figure on the stairs he had never made her an object of lustful conjecture or fantasy, so there was a complete utter newness about the movements of her legs and hips; and all this was done without the preliminary kissing and stroking which he took to be the usual way of beginning eager intimacies.

Eventually they were calm enough to hear and see the rain, so he got up and shut the window. Rejoining her, he actually straightened the very light blanket and drew it up to just below their chins as they lay apart looking at the ceiling.

"What time do you think you are expected home?" he wanted to know, "home" sounding a strange word to use because it was not a distant place to be reached by a train or car journey, not even elsewhere in the street. It was ten feet above. He asked the question with some triste because he absolutely did not want her to go, and besides, he was finally beginning to feel they might have blundered into something well beyond solving.

"There–is–no–reas-on–why–I–should–re-turn," Anna said slowly and firmly.

4

My name is Merlinda Cassell, I am in my early twenties, and one day I agreed to go for a coffee with Jake, a slim, plausible guy in, I guessed, his early forties. But I told him I couldn't be more than a few minutes because I had an appointment to go and see William Bridgnorth over in West London. I gave William's full name right away just in case Jake had heard of him.

It was true I was visiting William, but I was going (the second time) on the following day and I only said it in case I needed to get away from Jake after the one coffee, which we were having once we'd escaped from the auditorium in New Cross. There were plenty of vacant seats, but he'd come and sat himself down right next to me in the little theatre. The Laughter Studio got away with paying people peanuts to go there because they were desperate for the money. The publicity told them it was more like pleasure than work, and anyway they thought they'd be able to see themselves on t.v. But not really enough people ever turned up, even though "Come and laugh" flyers were distributed by other underpaid persons all over London. I doubt whether they ever came twice just to sit and laugh in this shabby auditorium – no Superluxe this! – and imagine they'd had a great night out with famous entertainers.

The day I met Jake I don't think it was more than forty per cent full, so we all had to come down to the front and bunch together looking happy in the first sixteen rows. Before that, at the start, there were seven empty seats between me and the aisle in the row where I sat, but Jake came in and placed himself alongside me with this ingratiating smile; though he was not the sort of person you would expect to be there, and totally unlike other members of the audience. He was stylishly-dressed (at some cost?) in the latest casual stuff, and looked bright, though I had a theory he hadn't been to uni.

"Hi, I'm Jake," he said.

I know that's the way people introduce themselves, but it always sounds to me like they're expecting you to have heard of them already. Like saying, "I'm the famous So-and-so." If I'm not sure of the person saying it, I sometimes reply, as I did this time – a bit boldly – "Jake who?" – not rudely but as if I haven't quite caught the name.

Young people will usually say to that, "Oh, 'Pete' is enough', or whatever. Jake looked almost offended, though, and paused, like he had to think about it before he replied: "Jake Coleman". But he recovered fast and asked me, smiling, "And you?" "Merlinda Cassell," I told him. "How're you doing, Melinda?" he asked, not hearing my name properly. "How'd you hear of this place?"

I said I didn't hear about it, I'd been unemployed for months after graduating and sent on an assignment to assess them as a client for my possible employers, Hemingway and Faulkner. So I was actually working by coming here. I wanted to establish that. He looked slightly nervous and serious on hearing these facts, and he immediately got going about himself to explain being found in such a weird set-up.

I'm wary when men tell you about themselves in case they're trying to go on and draw you on your own life. But I listened, thinking the show would be starting soon and he'd have to stop. Apparently Jake's father had had a large store, a family business. Jake hadn't gone into it himself. He was not suited to it, so he sold it. At this point we all had to move and occupy the rows in the front, but he went on speaking.

"It's a long story. As it happens, I don't need the 'salary' we get for coming here. I do need the laugh. I've had some problems I could do with forgetting about."

As he said that his face quivered. This too was nervous, but it was not a twitch, it was more an intentional grimace expressing something definite and bad. But actually he didn't start on any details. They will come later, at William's place, on his big day.

He produced a smile.

"I was given this by someone in Oxford Street yesterday" – he uncrumpled a flyer he took out of his pocket – "and I thought it could be entertaining. And I'd got nothing else to do. Nothing. And who knows who you might meet. So what sort of assignment is this you're doing, Melinda?"

"Merlinda," I corrected him, thinking it was about time. He smiled again and shook his head with a deliberately puzzled expression.

"That's an unusual name. Something magical about it."

Yes, he tried that one. People will always think you haven't heard comments or jokes about your name, whereas you've had them all the time. I'd heard this one often before. But I still smiled and gave the answer many people had heard from me in the last year: "If I could magic myself into a job I would have done it by now."

"But you say you're here working?"

The fact is I was still thinking my consultancy activities with Hemingway and Faulkner, or HandF Consulting, were hardly "a job" – yet. I'd been so relieved to land the trial, after the most peculiar interview experiences it's possible to imagine, that the provisional engagement felt like a reality.

"I have had to turn up here the first time unknown to the Studio – except they know I'm coming sometime – and deliver a report to the consultancy on how they could improve."

And it was just then, before I could explain my presence to Jake's satisfaction – because he looked very bewildered – that the house lights went down and new, brighter lights focused on rows A to P, where we were all crammed together. And onto the stage in front of the screen came Clive Sangley walking in his own spotlight, an older version of him than I remembered from those dire afternoon shows for infants at home with their mothers. Myself at home with my Mum, come to that.

What had brought Clive down to this? Still hoping some of his modest fame would be recalled, and would stick to him? Today he had an air of trying to appear like a famous tv personality condescending to do this job while resting from really glamorous stuff. In fact he was making a faded attempt at being his old self.

"Ladies and gentlemen (last time I'm going to be as polite as that!), I'm Clive Sangley – welcoming you here to the Laughter Studio. Thank you for coming. Those who've done this before will still be tickled pink with it and dying to repeat the pleasure. But if you're new to it today – I'll explain to you what our loyal regulars already know.

"We've got you here for this generous fee – did I hear someone chuckle? – to get you really laughing!" (We, his audience, stayed absolutely silent and I started to feel sorry for him). "The episodes you'll be seeing have been filmed at TVBritain – but you have to imagine you are the actual audience – watching the show and responding to the action with some laughter.

"There's something I should say right away. Some of our audiences here think they should shriek and guffaw – ooh, isn't that a funny word! – guffaw! – as loud as possible. But please – don't go OTT – Over The Top. Laugh naturally. Laugh when you can laugh. Let yourself go a bit – but don't go too far. Have we got any good basses and baritones here today? Hands up? Because it's good to have variety in the laughing. You, sir? Let's have it! – Great! A good deep laugh sounds great itself and gets others laughing. Gets people at home laughing. Any nice altos and sopranos?"

People around me were catching on now. A few more hands went up and some tittering started. "Now that's lovely. But now – ladies and gentlemen, everyone – I know it won't offend you if I say this: Go easy on the hysterics. If you think it's really that funny, don't hold it in, let it come out. But don't pitch it too high and go on and on. Any dirty laughs with us today? Male or female?"

Clive Sangley raised his grey eyebrows in this sort of lubricious leer – and a middle-aged guy two rows in front of us gave a deep, dirty chuckle, whether genuine or acted for Clive's sake I couldn't tell. Had he been planted there to get us going? Could be. Whatever, it was a pretty good attempt, and it produced a small wave of laughter from the rest.

Clive looked across in his direction with an expression of comic shock and said, "Now that's great! That's really great. But remember the golden rule – don't overuse it. Don't laugh like that at everything, it will sound as if it's faked." (What else could it be, I thought. Like all the other things in the Great Year?) "Any good gigglers? Excellent! Now – there's another particular thing about what we're going to show you today. It's summer outside. It's July, isn't it. We're having a heatwave. But these are Christmas shows. Because, naturally, everything has to be made well in advance. Actually these were made two months ago, in May. So please imagine you're watching this entertainment in a festive spirit. You've done all your shopping, you've had your dinner, you're ready to relax and see the funny side of things. OK? All right, we'll start, Jason."

Jason was sitting somewhere waiting for Clive's signal to switch on the recorded show on the screen on the stage. I hadn't made any notes on what I had seen so far, but I reckoned I had a fair idea of what was wrong. People had come out of the heat into an auditorium without much air-conditioning – any air-conditioning? There hadn't been much of a welcome. A cup of something and a biscuit offered at the end, yes, but why not at the start? Clive's intro had been, like, OK. But he'd gone cold on them when he had to tell them the shows would be on telly at Christmas. He could have made some jokes about that, surely. He hadn't.

There was flickering on the white screen, some spots and shadows and so on, then it went blank again. Next we got a bit of pointless "ident" stuff as they call it, giraffes leaning over to graze leaves from tropical bushes or something. Lastly came the titles, and the well-known music that always started the show, and the sound of some clapping we hadn't done ourselves – bigger applause than this small audience could have provided. I couldn't see the camera that must have been somewhere shooting us all the time. It was there in the dark somewhere, invisibly surveilling us, like any one of the millions of cameras out in the streets. Could Hemingway and Faulkner have been following me here on camera to be sure I was carrying out their instructions?

Father, bald, clumsy and long-suffering – and apparently with a reputation for infinite, blundering tactlessness – was dressed in a red Santa Claus cloak that was too small for him, and came into the kitchen where mother was at the table making something. You couldn't see what her hands were doing. Beside her was a large fruit-cake which looked very heavy and unappetising. The actor playing Father was used to getting a laugh with his first entrance onto a screen or stage, and people among us who knew him gave him a short, perfectly adequate laugh of welcome. I'd heard of this actor but never seen him, so I couldn't join in. I thought of an obvious point for HandF: get more people into this laughing audience who would already know and like the show being done (except you'd have to pay more to find them than if you just collected people from the street).

"What – you still making the icing?" Father exclaimed. There were a few friendly chuckles.

"It's nothing to do with icing – I'm making your bloody beard," Mother protested, holding up a football-sized mass of cotton wool. It turned out to be stuck to her fingers because she'd accidentally dipped them in the paste, and during the dialogue that followed she was pulling most of it off Father's face as soon as she'd applied it. The show was as bad as that, and yet parts of this action were quite well-timed, so that a lot of the audience produced a bit of quite authentic mirth. But myself, I couldn't laugh. Next to me Jake did laugh, but had to open his lips and force the sound out of his throat and oesophagus in a series of jerks. It was all an effort. As it seemed likely to be for us throughout this show. Suddenly I could understand why the people laughing during tv or radio comedies sounded mad: after a time they were feeling actually desperate and hysterical, the strain of trying to laugh was driving them mad. Would this thin, hypocritical mirth come across like that on the sound track? If it did, would it matter? Would the families at home notice?

As I watched, I was thinking how a guy like Jake Coleman and I were totally unlike the others we were sitting with: out-of-work women with homes in the nearby streets and children at school, pensioners with nowhere else to go (several poor-looking old couples), young people a bit like myself, probably in the same situation as me. But I got from Jake a sense of loneliness and isolation that wasn't totally different from theirs, wasn't totally different from mine come to that. Therefore curiosity, as well as a feeling that I would be able to shake him off if I needed to, led me to accept his offer of coffee later – "Something we can look forward to." I hadn't had a coffee that morning. We'd run out of it.

The comedy on the screen developed just as I'd expected. The favourite son of the family, Matt, was coming home for Christmas with his new girl friend Ayshea, and Mother and Father had no idea how far the relationship had gone. Mother's unmarried cousin Lucy was also coming, and Lucy was very prim and respectable. So when Matt and Ayshea turned up early and immediately parked themselves in Matt's old single bedroom – with jokes about his single bed, etc. Ayshea being a good-looking but sizeable young woman, there were going to be hilarious complications.

The main theme of the "humour" was that Matt, now in his late twenties, had been receiving gifts from Father as Santa Claus well into adult life. The custom had never been dropped and why should they stop it now? In fact anybody staying in the house for Christmas had to hang up a stocking and be asleep (or pretend to be) when Father in his Santa outfit crept into their rooms. For all their sharing of Matt's room the substantial Ayshea was a shy girl, rumoured to be a vicar's daughter. But Father was a bit of a one for broad humour and had obtained a vibrator for her stocking – for a future daughter-in-law. As broad and tactless as that. Then there was a lot of confusion about the presents, because they were all done up in the same wrapping paper so some looked exactly like others. A grandma also lived in the house, and the vibrator intended for Ayshea ended up in her stocking, and so on. This brought some hooting laughter from the audience, if not from me or Jake. Despite some more pranks and muddles and near disasters about plans for the Christmas dinner, everyone of course ended up happy and smiling, appearing as themselves before the camera to wish us all love and good wishes for our own Christmas with our own families. It ended on a Christian note with the camera panning past the twinkling lights of their tree and, after a scan of jokey, sometimes risqué, seasonal cards along the mantelpiece, focusing finally on a traditional manger scene with a soft female voice recommending we all watch the next instalment on New Year's Eve.

I could have found an excuse to change my mind about coffee, but as it was a reason for abandoning this entertainment as soon as we could, we apologised our way along our row of seats and ran away up the aisle before Clive Sangley could launch into a speech about the second hour-long show we were all supposed to laugh at. Out in the main road we found something I thought unlikely in New Cross, a kind of student eaterie with rough tables, low prices and walls covered with posters about campaigns and causes, past, present and to come. I took in a couple of posters referring to the Forgotten Nation – a play, was that, or a film? The heat meant we gave up the whole idea of coffee and had juices.

"You were telling me about your assignment". Jake was obviously eager to assess his chances with me, but I could cope with this for about ten minutes, and it was kind of good to voice my true feelings about it and not boringly pretend how great it was, which I partly among the friends I lived with. One of them, Aurelia, was rapidly climbing out of the student life and making her way upwards in a hard and not very caring world. Jake was definitely not like them.

"I am a consultant," I was proud to explain. Very awkwardly, though. "Or rather, as I said, I work for Hemingway and Faulkner, which is a New Spring consultancy." I was really just starting, on a temporary basis, but I kept that back for the time being.

"'New Spring'?"

"It's what they call businesses starting up, or restarting – maybe rebranding – when we're through the current crisis. My company mainly specialise in advising them."

"Not a steady old firm then?" This seemed to me a funny reaction at the time, but when I thought a bit more about what Jake's job had been in his early life, I saw why he'd at once thought of secure old businesses. I thought first he was being ironical about anything called "new". Which was very understandable.

"No," I said cautiously, hurt in case I was in for a put-down about the only job I'd landed after all the months of trying.

"So you're ready for when the latest recession ends?"

"Yes". I gave a small laugh, not believing it.

"And today, Laughter Studio has been consulting you?"

He said it without any trace of a belittling smile, and I answered it with, "No, not yet. Next, I go back to my directors and say—"

But there I hesitated, because I did need the evening to work out what I would be saying to Hemingway and Faulkner, if anything, after this experience. Then,

"I could say I could advise them not to do what they're doing already, but something else. But, for one thing, not to have electronic laughter because it would sound dehumanised and that wouldn't be right. Maybe they should get someone in to inspire some real laughter, like a good stand-up comedian, and record that, and fit it into the shows at the right places…"

"You're saying you needn't show anyone the programmes? And Clive Sangley couldn't make them laugh in a thousand years."

But the more we talked our way around it the less chance there seemed to be of finding an answer.

"There's a great shortage of laughter despite all the Great Years, and the Fun, and Enjoying Yourselves. I just wish there was more to laugh at," I said.

"They could laugh at existence," he suggested.

We were both silent for a moment.

"Have you really got to rush off somewhere?" he asked. I hesitated before saying "Yes", because I knew that a notion was forming in my mind. His using the word "existence" had reminded me of something. I looked at my watch, still pretending and cautious. But I accepted his offer of a second juice, saying I'd need to leave in another fifteen minutes. The fact was I needed to have someone to tell about my going to see William Bridgnorth and getting involved in his idea.

"Recently," I began, "I answered an ad. On a website: 'Your Language is your Existence,'"

I could hear myself sounding convinced and enthusiastic. I had been completely intrigued by William Bridgnorth when I rang, immediately arranged a meeting, and when that happened it lasted for almost two hours. I didn't let on about any of this to Aurelia and Sonia and Rick because I didn't think they would understand. Or maybe Rick would, except that he seemed to be busy with so much else. So I hadn't told anyone that I was likely to be going to Bridgnorth for tutorials. But I needed to tell someone, because you like to share your enthusiasms.

Was I a bit mad? I was now telling Jake Coleman about William and his cause because I had an instinct he might be interested. When I mentioned William's fame in his own world, and his appearance on a Newsnight programme he looked very thoughtful and started to ask a lot of questions.

5

"How dare you! I'm talking to someone," Anna shouted at Frank when he walked into his spare room while she was using her smartphone to make a personal call that was nothing to do with him.

But before this moment, which occurred two weeks after she moved in –

If it seemed odd that Frank Winterfield had never mentioned Bridgnorth and the cakes to Anna – they talked a lot about everything else during her days sheltering in his flat – maybe it was because he went on fearing it might have been some heat-induced optical illusion.

Alone for some while, penurious after a divorce settlement and an enforced retirement at an early age, could he be in the grip of something worse, schizophrenic in nature? Of course, if he had spoken of it to Anna, and named the man seen from the No.22 bus, everything would have been settled very easily. As much happens in life because of coincidences that fail to occur as happens because they take place. She had her own connection with Bridgnorth, which might even have kept them together – a shared interest; although it hadn't preserved her relationship with Jeffrey. Sometimes she would say, "I was having to leave soon" as if making it clear that she might not be staying long where she had ended up at the moment, although Frank in his astonishment at her arrival failed to appreciate the hint.

If the dread of madness occurred when he was lying on his back, side by side with Anna, and she was revealing fears of her own, he would reach across to her farther breast (the closer one being too near to touch comfortably) and assure himself of its reality by covering it so that its alert nipple rested under the palm of his hand. Anna was happy with this, but less happy with other action and gestures which – Frank was soon told – were too reminiscent of Jeffrey. In this she suffered from an affliction which had proved an appalling burden for Jake Coleman: a distress at small actions which only too vividly recalled other people.

About some specific examples of Jeffrey's behaviour as a partner she said today, "I told him I would not put up with it!" – speaking the words in that determinedly rhythmic way Frank had detected when listening to the two of them in conflict upstairs. (The special matter she would not allow in that case was Jeffrey's enthusing about firearms and his possession of one such, which he was priming for use – with no specific purpose, she thought, simply for the sheer pleasure of making it useable). Because she couldn't risk being heard she only whispered the words, fiercely, in case Jeffrey was at home in the room above. On another subject, sexual aids, she breathed hoarsely one one occasion, "I ask you – please!– a Lat-vi-an loo-fah." And laughed, and capped her mouth with her hand. "It wasn't just light bulbs – oh, electrical things, that reminds me" – not stressing the syllables now – "I need to get my hair-dryer out, in case he changes the locks or something. I reckon he's capable of doing that so that I don't take away anything of his."

What Anna had been doing was complete her abandonment of Jeffrey by visiting his flat daily when she was quite sure he wouldn't be there, pretending that she was calling in from much farther away. She had required Frank to go out and buy her a packet of stationery and some stamps because she was sending Jeffrey letters making out she was settled in with someone else on the far side of London, Catford in fact – no address given him, naturally. "Won't he see the postmarks?" Frank wondered. "Postmarks don't give you places any more," she replied, correctly – he had not noticed that. Mainly she would write notes at the kitchen table here, to say she had been in to collect cosmetics, clothes, credit cards and similar property, most of which now occupied Frank's spare room.

It was crucial for her, she maintained, to be seen as rarely as possible in the corridor upstairs. Or on Frank's floor near his flat, or on the stairs, especially carrying things, in case anyone guessed she was in and out of Jeffrey's all the time, and it would get back to Jeffrey and he would trace her. For the same reason, to be seen too much in the neighbourhood, in nearby shops for example, would be equally dangerous. There could be the awkwardness of having to pretend she was no longer living where she used to but simply happened to be in the area. She and Frank should absolutely not be seen together.

Everything compounded Frank's alarm. He had no idea what Jeffrey looked like. Which of the neighbours occasionally spotted on the stairs (as he had spotted Anna) was Jeffrey? Anna would not describe him to Frank in case Frank began looking at him and it made Jeffrey suspicious.

Anna now knew that starting an affair with Frank because of a low energy light bulb and having nowhere to go except Frank's had been a bad mistake. After a week like this, Frank was saying,"I almost certainly am in love with you," and Anna would reply with "Oh Frank darling!", which was equivalent to "Yes, but you shouldn't be, because this can't go on much longer". Or she would merely set her lips on his and stroke his back as if she was comforting a sorrowing child, kissing it better. Except that sometimes she tried humour to relieve her guilt about this absurd and complex situation and said something like:

> "I dread the thought of Jeffrey finding out,
> Coming down here and knocking on the door…
> You open it and find him standing there
> With a great canister of shaving foam
> He either hits you with – or it's a spray
> Of lethal poison. And he's good with guns."

All of which she uttered in a low tone in case her voice should be heard; and this meant that Frank himself began to talk quietly, so that the few persons telephoning him would wonder why he had taken to whispering. Anna would jump every time the phone rang, from the fear that it could be Jeffrey having realised where she was.

She started saying, after another fearful trip upstairs to leave a letter and extract another plastic bagful of articles, that she had to spend some more time in Frank's spare room sorting out her things because after all the time with Jeffrey she needed to get rid of some. "It's terrible what you accumulate!" When she said that, with that emphasis, she wondered why she'd never told Frank about her classes with William Bridgnorth and her doing that job for him with the flyers, standing and handing them out in Oxford Street. But she supposed she thought it wouldn't have interested him. Besides, she had made again a resolution to keep a bit quiet about herself. Jeffrey knew much more about her than he should, and she might be committing the same error with Frank. The situation she had landed herself in made her irritable. The claustrophobia she felt – though the rooms in these flats were not small, the present heat required the windows to be kept open and Frank was there all the time – led first to tensions and then to rows. She knew she had to go. But go where? To find a job (some hopes of that!) and accommodation in another part of the country? The company that took on several of her colleagues at Mandelston's when that chain went into administration had itself gone bust.

While she was sorting her large mound of belongings she insisted on closing the spare room door. On the eighth day of their co-habitation there was something Frank needed from a cupboard, and he automatically strolled in. He found Anna seated on a pile of trousers and sweaters on the old single bed he had managed to retain for "guests" (there had not been any before Anna) when nearly all of his best furniture had been removed by his divorce settlement. She was talking on her phone, which had been a recurrent nuisance during their hours on the agreeable kingsize bed in his own bedroom. (There had been several times during their lovemaking that she maintained she had to take a call when she could see who was calling, and when she insisted Frank did not withdraw himself from her because the call would not take a second – and then it took several minutes, and she appeared to have forgotten what she had abandoned so as to attend to it). This time she was conversing normally, though quietly, having closed the window as a precaution. He saw she was smiling at what she was hearing, but at once she covered the device completely with her spare hand.

"How dare you! I'm talking to someone."

Frank was too surprised at this shriek to do anything except stand and look at her. For a second he was thinking, "I've done something more complicated than I thought, letting her stay here." But immediately he began to try to think what sort of apology was required at this point, and make amends for causing her to lose her temper because the wonderful unexpectedness of their relationship was giving him a lot of unusual delight and he was frightened in case she left him alone again.

In a moment she went back to her call and was flapping a hand at him with a loose, shooing movement; which was somewhat more friendly. Therefore he did retreat, but left the door deliberately open as he went back to his lounge, so as to be able to hear when she had finished. Did he leave it too long? When he went back, knocking with satirical abruptness on a panel of the open door and going in as she called out "You may enter!" she was vigorously arranging garments in two separate mounds and she greeted him with a laugh. He would not ask her who she had been talking with. No need. It had been a wounding episode. But the relationship was re-established.

In the third week, in the middle of a cooler evening, "I want to go out," he said.

"O.K."

"Don't you want to know where I might be going?"

"No. It's private, isn't it?"

"Yes. But perhaps I'd want to ask you something before I went."

"Perhaps you would?"

"Yes. I want to go and see a film, and I wondered if you felt you could come with me?"

Did he see a tempted look in Anna's reaction? But she sighed.

"Ah – I can't."

Frank thought there was a low, grieving sound in the way she said it, and he believed that at that moment she was as near to tears as she ever came in his presence.

"I dare not," she said. He was wise enough not to ask why.

"Well I thought I'd really love to take you, if you wanted to risk it. We could leave separately – it'll be nearly dark by the time of the last showing." He was not really sure of that.

Anna seemed to be considering it, for a moment.

"How long would we be out?"

"Oh – two hours. Less, if we miss the commercials." She looked up at the ceiling as if doing a calculation. Then, disappointingly, she shook her head.

"No – it isn't worth it."

"We've been together over two weeks – nearly three – and we haven't really done anything," he suggested. Later he thought she might have corrected this bad mistake, and spoken of their lovemaking. She hadn't.

"I'm expecting a call from someone," Anna said. Frank nearly responded by saying, cynically, "I'm sure you could take that during the film." "And I'd say it might be going to rain," she added. It was as thundery as it had been for days, the way of this summer.

"We could hide our faces under our umbrellas," he offered. Her own bright umbrella had been in a last large bundle of goods she had brought down from Jeffrey's during the afternoon.

She mutely refused this notion, so he said, somewhat impatiently,

"Will you mind if I go?"

"No. Why should I?" She smiled. "Yes. You go. I can get busy on all sorts of things I have to do. Please – you go." She was becoming insistent for some reason.

Unwisely he forgot to take his own umbrella. Rain was beginning to fall as he entered the Multiscreen, a walk of fifteen minutes from home – he had to hurry to avoid it, ran for the last fifty yards and arrived out of breath.

He thought he had timed his arrival to see this picture precisely enough to avoid commercials and trailers, but he had not.

"Has the film started?" he asked at the box office counter.

"No, sir. There's the Great Year Feature before the main feature, sir."

"Which screen is it?"

"The Superluxe, sir. Where would you like to sit, sir?"

"Er – somewhere in the middle."

"G6, sir?"

"Yes."

"Young lady will show you to your seat, sir. Ilona – Screen 7".

With this small smiling woman of apparent schoolgirl age in the corporate uniform he walked in the silence along a soft purple carpet past Screens 1, 2, 3, 4, 5 and 6 to a double door opened by huge handles in the shape of the company logo. A large "7" shone on the wall.

"Which seat, sir?" It seemed this was the necessary form of address for anyone showing customers to the Club Standard screen. He handed over his ticket and she shone her torch on it. Paying with his credit card, he had not noticed that he had been charged £25.

The seat was large and comfortable, as he would have hoped. There was ample leg-room and the arm-rest on his left offered space for any refreshments he might have purchased in the foyer; he had taken in nothing. He didn't blame himself for thinking that Anna's declining to join him had saved him twenty-five quid, possibly more if, despite a decent meal at home, she'd wanted things to eat and drink here.

The Great Year Feature, one of several variations playing in cinemas everywhere, was what he had expected. It began with a preview of "the Great Events", cutting in a flood of nano-second images from football to swimming to pole-vaulting to bowls; and then the coming pageants, processions, pyrotechnics for the latest Great Anniversary. But it finished with a difference. The recognisable voice of one of the corporate celebrities who had jointly sponsored the film and most of the celebrations turned solemn and read out the script slowly over images of frowning police and soldiers.

"And for your personal safety in this Great Year, wherever you may be among the happy millions of the British public and foreign visitors attending these historic occasions – or going about your business in the streets of any of our towns and cities by public transport or private vehicle or on foot – there will be the police and the army there to help and protect you because danger is ever-present." (Frank looked at the firm but friendly-looking constables and smart ranks of the military. And here they cut in a very brief shot of a control room in which people sat at table after table of screens working in surveillance of central and suburban streets and individual buildings, and even small towns and villages; as if no citizen could ever escape the watching eye.) "And at sea," the voice went on, over images of small armed vessels patrolling among yachts,"and in the air (military jets and circling helicopters) we shall be on the look-out for any threat to anyone's safety and leisure in this, your latest Great Year."

No mention, Frank thought, of the street closures, the security restrictions, or the accompanying compulsion to rejoice. But there you were.

Then it was time at last for what he had come to see.

It had been impossible to avoid the publicity for *The Lowdown* during the last three months, least of all the ever-deepening bass voice in the commercials on TV and BBC Popular, mouthing its echoes "in your basements and along your corridors". Frank endured several fast flashes of violence and arcane sexual peculiarity in split-second early shots intended to anticipate later incidents. Then he did become briefly intrigued by the simple notion of the plot: that all the development of basements under well-to-do properties in London was governed by one vast criminal enterprise which had simultaneously created an even lower world further down, connected by a network of passages with their own transport system. At a sudden signal, all access to their basement luxuries – all those nurseries and saunas – from the houses above was suddenly sealed off, and London came to be ruled by an evil subterranean power controlling all its services, holding it to ransom and submitting it to terror and rape and blackmail. By this time Frank's credulity was well-stretched, and as the action collapsed in a mish-mash of unexplained and incompetently assembled images which confused all the themes and characters, he became bored. Yet he saw it through to its end, hoping for a redeeming conclusion which never arrived.

Outside, when it was over and the lights had gone up to reveal that he had been sitting in the Superluxe alone, the rain was falling much harder than when he went in. No, there was not the taxi he could anyway not have afforded, or the bus arriving conveniently at the unsheltered stop outside the Multiscreen. He set out to walk.

All his clothes were soon soaked. It was difficult to extract his key from the drenched right pocket of his trousers and push it into the lock of the downstairs door. It was dark now, and this street was not well-lighted. There would have been little risk to Anna on the walk home.

Having dripped all the way up the stairs and along the corridor to the corner, he opened his door to find – and it was not later than ten, was it? – his entire flat in darkness. Anna was not in his bedroom or his lounge, and he called out her name, much more loudly than she would have liked. It was the first time he had ever done that, because he had obviously never doubted that she would be there. He half-ran round into the spare room – in which, he was sad to admit, Anna had slept for the last two nights alone on a bare mattress under his ancient throwover. It was clear that she had gone, utterly and entirely, without even leaving a note on the blue notepaper he had bought her (the rest of that had also disappeared).

He had to peel off these soaked clothes and dry himself down, and went to the bathroom to do that. On the edge of the bath was her hair-dryer, still plugged into the electric point where his shaver went. He removed the plug and started to wind the coil around the dryer, which he discovered was still warm.

6

Jake Coleman could not sleep for all that drilling going on in the street. What was it for? Would it never end? This was a Saturday and it was still going on unremittingly as it had all the week.

It was to do with an endless succession of roadworks out on the main road which no one in the neighbourhood understood. The wooden barriers and cordons gave no indication of who was undertaking it or what it was for. When he glanced down at the holes along the side of the road he could see no cables or other signs of services such as gas, electricity or water. By the side of these excavations heavy, morose men in very hard bright hats, who never smiled – Jake could understand that, given the weather and the conditions in which they worked – constantly shouted out orders or reproaches to each other.

Today he thought he would try asking one workman what it was "all about", in those very words in fact, and with a friendly smile. But this was a mistake from someone dressed like Jake. It could have looked like interference, or irony, or straightforward complaint. The man he proposed to address was standing still, casting occasional glances at two others shovelling dirt up from a large hole into a growing heap. Jake assumed he was taking a moment's rest.

Keeping his body language informal and his voice friendly, Jake caught the man's eye and said, "What is this work all about?" The man looked back at him for two or three seconds without changing his neutral, weary expression. He could have been thinking up a helpful reply but then, abruptly, he turned his head aside and looked up to the far end of the site, where a fourth man in the team, wearing the same lime-green hard hat, was seated on a low wall staring down at a telephone. The first man showed no sign of responding to Jake and moved away in this second man's direction. Jake believed he could be inviting him to follow and possibly obtain an answer from the workman they were approaching. Perhaps the information on the man's mobile would provide a plan of what they were doing.

Jake picked his way past more piles of earth, over muddy patches between holes, around almost invisible strings presumably marking the boundaries of where they had to drill and excavate. When they reached him, the man with the mobile looked up and shook his head in puzzlement, then handed the 'phone to the first man. Both of them ignored Jake, who wondered if he was expected to repeat his question to the second workman. He was clearing his throat and swallowing before doing that, when the first man suddenly bellowed, impatiently, at the second, in a language Jake did not recognise (it had no resemblance to the north-eastern European tongue spoken in the town of the sex therapy clinic where he had stayed in the winter).

As the man shouted, he pointed repeatedly at the image on the tiny blue screen with his large forefinger. Jake now saw that they were looking at a chessboard and having an argument about it. The dispute continued for about a minute before the first workman turned aside with a shrug, and spoke to Jake for the first time.

"He no fucking good!" he said, in thick, grating, but comprehensible English. "He challenge his brother. His brother chess champion of place he live. I tell him he no good against a real player."

He gave Jake a look that could only be described as one of despair – and moral contempt, because he also crossed himself. There seemed no way of pursuing the inquiry. Besides, only a few feet away, spraying dust and splinters of stone in their direction, someone began drilling at the pavement without warning, making any further interchange impossible.

Beyond the end of the site were the shops. When Jake reached them the sound was still loud; probably suitable for this young woman's purpose. She was dressed with businesslike style and her short smooth haircut would not have been disturbed by the wind when she was working out of doors, bareheaded of necessity, making contact with the public and reporting back to the studio. Any headgear was out as far as interviewers were concerned, except possibly in extreme conditions when most interviewees were wearing it.

She had a small yellow-headed microphone in her hand and was moving from one shopper to another with a cameraman in train. The wish to know or say something caused Jake to pause – he had time enough – and make contact with the media in case she was asking about the roadworks. The interviewee she was finishing with had a bewildered expression, as if she had not seen any reason for being stopped and questioned but felt it was flattering to be asked. If someone poked a microphone at you, you had to answer.

"And how old are you"? she asked Jake, pointing the mike towards his lips. "Charlotte from TV Britain."

Jake hesitated because of the directness of the question, and it might have looked as if he was having to think to remember his age.

"Oh – thirty-seven."

"And are you local?"

"Yes – certainly."

He was greatly hoping she was going to ask about the disruption caused to his daily life by these months of unexplained drilling. She did not.

"And your occupation?"

"Well – I don't have one at the moment. I was in the retail furnishing business."

Inevitably there came back to him those last long days among the beds on the second floor in the store, his heart-to-heart dialogues with a father who, despite Jake's expressed reluctance, still hoped he would take over the company when he died. There was no-one else. At his father's insistence, and because he had to live, and father saw the likelihood of his becoming fixed in another job if he found one immediately after his A Levels – there were fewer problems about that in pre-recession days – he entered upon his "training years" in the firm. Father believed in keeping his employees happy by moving cheerfully himself from one floor and department to another and serving a few customers; and Jake, who was soon brought onto the Board, was expected to do the same so as to learn what it was all about. He felt he owed this to Father, but it resulted in month after month of boredom.

"And now?" The little yellow ball came back to him from the faithful servant of TVB like a small sweetmeat offered him by a rather pleasing hand. He began to link her in an instantaneous fantasy with the beds in the store, but then he pulled himself back to the present.

"Now I'm – I'm not in anything particular. I'm going to take a class in –"

"So would you say 'unemployed?'"

She was, he was sure, hoping to fit him into one of the age-groups and categories she was required to represent.

"In a way, yes." He was not going to tell her about his private resources.

"But you are seeking a job?"

"No."

"Drawing benefit?"

"No."

"But seeking a job?"

"Er – Yes."

The answer was No, but that was too complicated. Now would come the questions about his genuine willingness to find work, how he actually managed to live and so on, he was certain of that.

"All, right then. May I ask your name?"

"Jake Coleman."

"Great. I would like to ask you a few questions, Jake. You are a job-seeker without much spare time on your hands. But are there things you're hoping to do to enjoy the Great Year?"

He had realised the kind of thing she would say before she said it, so he was prepared.

"Well I know there are the Events, and the Occasions, and the Fun Parade and the Sporting Opportunities Programme. But so far I am enjoying nothing – apart from talking to you"

Something went wrong with the interview at that point, he thought, because she turned away and gave the microphone to someone else. TVB did not broadcast any of their conversation.

He had thought he had plenty of time to get to Merlinda's place, but now he felt less sure. Last night he had circled round several times to find a place to leave the car. It took him a while to remember where he had left it, and further time wasted in order to get there. But eventually he identified the street from the closed futon shop on the corner – once a lively business – and saw his vehicle away up at the far end. When he reached it he had to scare away a small group of stray dogs gathered around it and sniffing; which gave him a sad sense that things were going wrong in this part of London at least.

Driving off with Merlinda in mind and with, if he admitted it, ominous recall of the failure of his treatment in the foreign clinic, the futons that used to be in that corner shop brought back the memory of the beds he used to sell in Father's store and the bed he had acquired from it for his first personal flat, the only one he ever rented without owning – a bachelor apartment he had moved into at the age of twenty-six, so different from where he lived now. In the long tailbacks of London today, driving towards an establishment where young people were living – Jake had time to reflect on that stage of his unsatisfactory life.

In that bedding department he had his own cash desk and till in a screened corner, virtually a little office. There were two comfortable chairs fitted in there at his insistence, because spending several hundred pounds on a new double bed often justified long and candid face-to-face discussions. Most of the time, though, he needed to be out of this corner, to encourage likely customers taking a casual look at what was on offer. Wearing the required serious suit he would be parading slowly and smilingly up and down the aisles between the beds.

He was not without flair, and he acquired some responsibility. After what seemed several years of this, Father trusted him with the task of dealing with reps and buying beds, and he told himself he had learned a lot about the trade. He believed he had developed an ability to judge customers, know whether they were going to want an ornate bedhead (younger, better-off people usually) or prefer a lavishly padded version on which insomniacs would be glad to rest their heads and shoulders while they read books or watched tv into the small hours. He knew who would need beds with deep drawer space underneath, compartments for duvets and blankets. He knew exactly when to mention that the moderate price in large print on the card was actually the cost of the mattress only.

"'Sell it to the lady' was the old principle he practised when – this was most often – a couple and not a single individual came to look at big beds with serious intentions. He would praise the comfort and convenience of a particular bed, try to assess how serious their enquiries were, and if they seemed hesitant lead them to a cheaper, less glamorous, example. If they went silent and thoughtful he would bring out some favourite introductory phrase like, "Of course, for something special and prestigious there's always this." While he uttered this kind of thing he would be all the time catching the woman's eye if he could, and hoping for a smile or even a little laugh.

And when an eligible woman walked into the department by herself… He would then speak more quietly, confidentially, even try a question such as "Is your partner as tall and/or slimly-built as yourself?" even when that description was not exact. He would even venture one particular suggestion or offer, tactfully stepping aside when things reached this stage, and say, "You're perfectly permitted to lie down on it and try it…" This worked, very occasionally, by selling the bed because a sense of obligation was created if the idea was taken up, or by delivering the customer to him as a lover. Jake had a liaison with Carolyn, who lay down at once on the bed he was showing her, with a lot of giggling. No, I have no partner, she told him, I have space for a larger bed and might have one. Yes, a bed, I meant, I didn't mean a partner. Or did I? Carolyn did not purchase a bed, and in general it was only the non-purchasers who accepted his advances. It was as if they had only visited this floor of the store in vague search of what they associated with them rather than the beds themselves. In these purposeless years, as Jake saw them, an average of 2.5 women a year yielded to one or other of his methods.

That was sadly quite enough to set up the hesitations which changed into the fears that were converted into a specific terror – and illness – lesser words would not have been sufficient. It was a deep dread that almost anything at all about a woman with whom his experience had been less than perfect would recur in his memory to destroy his confidence about another. It was a terror lest the words, the smiles, the small actions, the preferences – but, well, even the appearance of a new candidate for seduction – reminded him of someone in the recent, or even the farther, past and destroyed all sexual desire. For a long time most of Jake's sexual adventures had culminated in failure. There was little about them that he actually liked to remember. It would go like this: something well-meaning that Lisa did or said before sex would remind him painfully of Alexandra; or Vicky wore the same brand of bra as Alison and that completely turned him off before starting. Even matters as small as a sudden tone of voice or a habit of posture would deliver disabling recollections of someone else. As his range of experience increased, the chance of momentary satisfaction, let alone lasting happiness, became more and more remote.

As far as his purpose in life was concerned – he became increasingly convinced that he could not and would not take over the firm from Father. He had created an epiphanic moment for himself late on a Friday afternoon in early autumn three or four years before he ever met Merlinda Cassell, or William Bridgnorth, or Frank Winterfield. A lone individual was moving slowly and with the faintest of limps along the aisles and into the narrow spaces between beds, prodding at the mattresses and feeling them. Jake had learned the virtual impossibility of pleasing the hesitant customers who would detain you with endless questioning and go away shaking their heads with polite, valueless promises of coming back. This man, dressed with grey, gloomy respectability, hatted and cravatted, looked as if he was about fifty-five (and feeling his age; but then what could you expect?) He had glanced at Jake but didn't move in his direction. Presumably he could be left alone, it would be wasting time to approach him? So Jake thought of returning to his office. But Father liked to do a friendly daily tour of the store and so far today he hadn't done that – he might turn up at any moment with his son nowhere to be seen. "And I am doing this at thirty-four years old," Jake thought.

The customer suddenly symbolised the dismal entirety of Jake Coleman's failure. But almost instantly he realised he had come to false conclusions about him.

"Do excuse and forgive me." The man shuffled awkwardly towards him. "May I possibly cite my problem and request your advice about it?" He spoke in a rich and delicate accent Jake took to be from Oxbridge, tones he thought he would never command himself.

"By all means go ahead, sir." He rarely addressed new customers as formally as this, but there was an intention vaguely shaping in his mind and he sensed that a little preliminary courtesy would be appropriate.

"I am a martyr to a backache of an indefinable kind to which no orthodox – or for that matter unorthodox – medical remedy seems to apply. I have in fact tried virtually everything without relief."

Jake heard himself listening with fascination to the cadences of this address and the scrupulous exactness with which the customer developed his account, unnecessary when all he needed to say was, "I've got a bad back, would a different bed help?" But – "I sleep very badly, so I am driven to speculate – and my partner shares this view – whether it might not be the elementary case of needing another kind of mattress? " Jake became all deferential attention. "I have heard, on the one hand, that one requires a softer bed in these circumstances but, on the other that a hard bed allows the vertebrae and muscles to resume a firmer, less indulgent, position and to correct themselves".

Jake nodded sympathetically, but had not changed his mind about what he had decided to say next. He tried to clear his throat in a polite, inaudible way.

"I have one simple piece of advice to offer you, sir," he said. "Forget about soft beds or hard beds, and don't waste your money on anything you see here."

The man's mouth opened a little wider in a second of surprise. His eyes doubted if Jake was being serious.

"I assure you it isn't remotely worth it, sir," Jake continued.

"I see... Well, that's very candid of you. I'm grateful..."

"Do you by any chance use duvets at home, and have a spare one or two?"

"Well, yes – we do."

"Put one under your lower sheet – without a cover on, of course – and turn it over every time you change your bedclothes – that's enough."

"Is it really?"

"It's quite enough, sir."

"Well, well."

His small, puzzled smile and sideways inclination of his head as he thanked Jake and turned away suggested that (as he later remembered in telling the story) "not every day can be counted upon to vouchsafe such welcome surprises."

Father died suddenly that week-end. Jake inherited the business and sold it without hesitation or compunction before the year was out.

Both front windows of the car were open. At a traffic light where the road beyond the yellow box was ominously blocked he pressed a button for the radio and pressed it to turn off when he heard the words "the Event of all our Lives". A young man with a bucket and a rubber-blade wiper in his hand offered to wash his windscreen but Jake refused, only hoping the youth would not turn persistent, with the usual hint of threat in his voice and expression. He did not.

The strange things I do for girls, Jake was now thinking yet again. He supposed that most men and women in the early stage of a relationship – if that was what this was going to be – found that they would have to show interest in, or tolerance of, an activity they had never experienced before. They went along with it because they wanted the company of the other – or a lot more than mere "company." And here he was, about to embark on an afternoon of –

He crossed the lights at last, and took the left turn the satnav gave him into the street where Merlinda shared a house with her three friends and was providing the snack lunch which she said was all they needed before the two of them went together to see William

Bridgnorth. He was aware, because Merlinda had prepared him, that there might be several young people to greet him, but how many he didn't know.

At his ringing the bell there was immediately movement inside and he heard voices, feet on some stairs, and a female laugh. Someone approached the door. It was not Merlinda who opened it, but another girl, in khaki shorts and the thinnest of t-shirts, no bra, who called out, rather softly but clearly "Mer – lin– da!" and showed that she had been expecting Merlinda's guest and no one else. This one immediately stepped aside as Merlinda appeared from the farthest door visible from here, possibly the kitchen.

"You found it!" she exclaimed.

"With no trouble."

"This is Aurelia," Merlinda said. "You met Sonia at the door." There were seconds of a silence they could almost touch as this quartet stood awkwardly in a narrow hall. Merlinda had to break it.

"Well – Sonia and I were at Uni together in Suffolk. And Aurelia went to New Leatherhead University. Oh – " she flapped her hands around – "this is Jake."

"Hullo – Jake," Aurelia said, with an emphasis almost putting in his place this man with a new name, different from anyone else who came here.

This was the first time ever that Jake had stepped into a house of "young single professionals", as Aurelia called them. An unfamiliar atmosphere of shrill energy left him uncertain and to some extent shy, very unusual for him. With introductions over, the young women busied themselves with what they had been doing before he arrived, preparing a lunch to be eaten in the garden. There was a lot of embarrassed laughing, they pretended to blame each other for not having enough salad spoons, they came out into the garden overloaded with bowls and plates, tripped on the crazy paving and said "Fuck!" They were showing off their sophistication, even Merlinda, whose friend Jake was, after all. "You can see it's chaos here, Jake," Aurelia said.

"What else would I expect!" he said. Although Aurelia's eyes smiled, the corners of her mouth turned down and he believed he had not hit the right note. But now they were all seating themselves and giving him reassuring grins.

"Rick baked the bread and I made the salad," said Merlinda. He had heard about Rick, the one man in this set-up, from Merlinda when she invited him. There was no sign of him. Jake felt his absence.

"Ham, pate and olives from Consumerama," Sonia told him. Aurelia smiled again, and Jake realised that her facial imitation of a small mask of tragedy was how her face was naturally shaped, not a performance. It was how she smiled. They helped themselves and made conversation and he had to be careful to take in Sonia's legs with general glances across the garden rather than with a direct gaze. He asked them what they did for a living and they told him. In the course of that the other two congratulated Merlinda on her new job. Jake covered for the fact that he himself had no job any longer and no need to go after one – and followed no career (he saw Aurelia give a momentary perplexed frown) – by saying that he was taking some time off to reassess his life, a resolve none of these young people quite appreciated because their own lives were only beginning.

"I like your car," Aurelia said, in another sudden silence. It told Jake that she had been watching from an upstairs window as he arrived, because he had parked outside No.7, in a bay only just visible from the door of No.18, and had immediately crossed over to their side.

7

Yes, rather late, and I was getting to be anxious, Jake had been there ringing the doorbell and Aurelia, who was looking for a rather special car to turn up, ran across the landing and down the stairs helter skelter calling out, and she was on the way so it wasn't a question – "I'll go? I'm nearest."

I was in the kitchen and I shouted "No!" But although I was annoyed at the way she took the initiative whenever anybody came to the house, I caught myself laughing, for several reasons. Partly it was at Aurelia's typical cheek, but also it was nerves. And then I admit I had a sense of triumph at a man arriving for me in a car like that. I was also showing Jake I had support, which was the point of bringing him here. I wasn't simply alone and available.

But neither Aurelia nor I made it to the door because Sonia happened to be just inside the lounge, in the front, and went without a word. When she opened the door and belted out *Mer-lin-da* I felt in fact that it was a bit rude. You might do that if it was a delivery of something: *Merlinda – your parcel's come!* But not when someone's friend is making their first visit, and Sonia knew he was coming. It showed Jake that we were all a bit tensed up and expecting him as a big deal. But I forgave Sonia because we've always got on, and her behaviour hadn't got an edge on it, like Aurelia's has. Besides, Sonia and I had had practically three years when we were friends at Uni and living in lodgings together.

Sonia stood back and let me greet Jake, who was actually about twenty minutes late but didn't explain.

"You found it!" I said, a bit sharply. I suppose I'd been worried in case he didn't turn up at all. He did that suave smile I came to know well.

"With no trouble."

He had hardly put a foot in the hall before Aurelia announced her importance by joining us anyway and offering him her hand. Then

40

there was one of those terrible silences when no one has the faintest idea what to say or do apart from stand and not do anything. So I did the introductions, and although I'd already said all this to Jake when arranging the visit I went on about Sonia and I being at university together, and Aurelia somewhere else – well, New Leatherhead, but I didn't think Jake knew enough to realise that place was, like, the smart choice at the moment. Aurelia was going to be the smart person of the group if she'd been a student there.

Probably I don't really mind Aurelia. Why else should we all have taken No.18 together (apart from the fact she saved the day by making up the numbers to pay the rent at the last minute)? But she does pull class a bit about New Leatherhead and go on about the minor royalty due to go there and the woman long jump champion the nation had to pin its hopes on for future Great Years. She somehow missed out the academic side, never quoted the saying – if she'd ever heard it – that "Leatherhead's where old post-modernists go to die", but she loves the fact that Lemmy Litmus, the lead guitar in the Sordid Syndrome, the crappiest of outdated boy bands, was an ex-student, that really gave it status, didn't it. That really mattered. It mattered to New Leatherhead, because they'd made him an honorary Doctor of Music.

Sonia had done the shopping, while I had spent most of the morning doing the salads. I had to hint to Aurelia that she'd done nothing towards the lunch, which she really only stayed for out of curiosity to see this older guy I was bringing in "to flutter the equilibrium of the house," as we'd said before about any male visitor not a father or uncle – not many of those came to your first post-Uni homes by invitation.

We shuffled out into the garden somehow, and because I didn't want to get onto the subject of university and jobs, I got us at the beginning into a little bit of conversation about the current Great Year activities. The problem was I thought Aurelia might be going to monopolise this topic because of her job, but Sonia cut things short by talking about the way they were ruining everyone's daily lives in getting to work and so on, and I got on with bringing the food out. As soon as we started eating, though, Aurelia stared hard at Jake and asked him what he did for a living.

She received the answer that he was doing nothing at all apart from pondering his future and looking around for activities that entertained him, hence going to the Laughter Studio where he said he'd had the good luck to meet me (that was "chivalrous", I suppose, but disconcerting). I could see from her expression that Aurelia was partly puzzled, partly contemptuous of the Laughter Studio, which she knew about from my account of it. But she said nothing before Jake could turn the subject on to her.

"What do you do then?" He was looking at Aurelia with a smile that seemed to say, If you want a contest, O.K., let's have one.

"I'm getting into television as an SRA – Sport Relations Adviser," she said.

Jake nodded as if he understood, but I don't think he did.

"You hope to make a lifetime career of it?" His reply wasn't intended to be the nicest possible putdown, but it was, and I don't know that Aurelia heard it that way. But she came back with a typical defence.

"Yes I do hope to make it a lifetime career. It's part of all our futures." At this, Sonia grinned to signify her friendly boredom with the prospect that Aurelia would faithfully recite phrases from her company's mission statement yet again. "As my friends know –" and now Sonia and I chanted it with her – "Sport Is All Our Futures! And –" we carried on, with Jake slightly bewildered at a world and a private joke he couldn't recognise – "not just this Great Year, but Next Year will be an Even Greater Year! Hurrah!"

Before Aurelia could follow up our laughter and elaborate on this – which she certainly would have done – Sonia cut in to veto a topic of which we heard daily and said, "I'm just starting as an industrialist in Whitehall."

"She means the Civil Service. She's a rising official in the Culture Industry," I explained. I would have said more on Sonia's behalf, but Sonia wanted to complete these revelations by consoling me with congratulations on my getting at least something after nearly eighteen months of graduate unemployment.

"And Merlinda has just landed a Real Fun Opportunity to apply her skills to a hundred different businesses," she declared.

All I could do was cover my face with both my hands and shake my head. I was wishing it would come true. Jake, of course, knew about this already.

"No – Come on Merly, you're doing fantastically," Aurelia said, making that a very big word, maybe to raise my status in Jake's eyes – but she took it so far it sounded almost mocking. "Not just the Laughter sessions – there's the restaurants – and the dogs."

"I'll know I'm doing fantastically when I've done it all for three years, not three weeks," I said.

So there I was, being not despised or pitied by my friends for having no job on leaving university, but worse – patronised with overpraise when I at last had something different from child-minding or house-cleaning (I'd done some of both). Immediately I knew this wasn't right, I was downsizing myself in front of Jake when I wanted to impress him (or I supposed I did).

I think the two of them – even Sonia, lately – knew they were overdoing it, and maybe my expression showed it, because they both suddenly lapsed into silence. I was thinking what they must have been thinking: they were onto a ladder rising into the sky, and I was still scraping around at ground level trying to find a first rung.

Not that the garden was silent on that sweltering Saturday afternoon. Anything we talked about as we sat and ate the salad was nearly drowned by the grating roar of the devilish machine overhead.

"A gysh," Sonia said.

We all at that moment looked up at the machine. It had droned in abruptly and deafeningly from nowhere and was circulating with an ear-splitting buzz overhead, in absolutely empty and beautiful blue air. It could easily have been looking specifically and on purpose – for training purposes, or on some real "mission" (one of Rick's most hated words)? – at everything down in our garden. It could have been making a record of what was there, and who were there, and whatever was going on. And verifying whether we were enjoying ourselves.

"I like your car," Aurelia said.

"It was nice meeting Sonia – and 'Aurelia'?," Jake said to me about ten minutes after the two of us left together, when he was driving us along the urban motorway going west from near the Sherlock Holmes end of Baker Street.

We'd been chatting about nothing very much and I was waiting for his reaction to the lunch, which I had also been glad to give him in return for dinner three nights before. I was still thinking as formally as that about our friendship, or whatever you'd call it.

In the first tailback, "Was lunch O.K.?" I asked.

"What? Oh yes. Lunch was great."

"As great as my friends?"

We were moving again, unexpectedly. He turned his head for a moment, eyes off the road as he manoeuvred in the dodgy second lane, not very sensibly.

"Both friends and lunch were fantastic." Making a joke of it, obviously referring back to Aurelia crediting me with doing fantastically in my crazy consultancy job. For which I didn't have a contract yet, only some words in a letter assigning me various tasks pending a contract and a salary. We took the downhill approach to Shepherd's Bush at speed and I wondered if he felt tense about anything, and if so, why?

"Look…" He paused. Paused to position the car for the complicated roundabout near the Westfield shopping mall, then went on, "Merlinda, I'm twelve – thirteen – years older than you and your friends, right? But as far as having a future they're twelve years on from me."

I paused myself now. This sort of situation was new to me, although I'd had forewarnings of problems Jake was having at our very first meeting. As soon as you've got into an intriguing bit of – of friendship, the guy comes out with his vulnerability.

"What do you mean?" Playing innocent, and trying to help him already! About what, I couldn't tell.

"Very small things like – things you know and I don't know them, and I'd like you to tell me. For example: Why did you call that helicopter a 'gysh'?"

"Great Year Security Helicopter. Do you know PPP?"

"No. I don't know PPP."

"Police Protection of Pleasure", I explained. "In the first place it was the police lines allocated to crowd control. But it's become the special riot police trained in Kent to protect spectators and tourists from terrorists – and ordinary protestors. They say that police spies will mingle with crowds to spot those who aren't enjoying themselves. Or go to pubs and listen for people dissing the Great Year."

"Yes… I see."

I wasn't sure Jake was seeing; and I hadn't seen for myself until Rick told me about it. Told me about the entire network of surveillance and control put in place to ensure national optimism and enjoyment in an era of permanent crisis. But I thought Jake had begun to get the drift.

"The next thing you're going to tell me," he went on, "is if you think the satnav's correct and we go straight opposite off this roundabout and keep on until we hit the New King's Road."

"Yes. It is correct. We do."

The thing I was doing with Jake was take him to see William Bridgnorth as a possible participant in a group for his scheme. But was I close enough to Jake to trust him with this role? I suppose you could say I was, because I was only introducing him to an idea he was free to decline if he wanted to. Yet you could also say that I was curious to see how he would react to something I was interested in myself. I wanted someone else's opinion. If it finally turned out that Bridgnorth was merely mad, there was no farther to go. If he had something, it would be worth exploring it further.

"The next turning on the left is – correct," I said eventually. "And we can park here on a Saturday afternoon, as he said."

Leaving the car ahead of Bridgnorth's block we needed to walk back about thirty yards. The front door was close to the corner of his street and the New King's Road. There was a panel of numbered buttons, 1 to 24, and if you wanted a flat on a higher floor you had to enter, very precisely, a 2 and a 3, say, and press the "Call" button for the inhabitant to let you in. But all we had to do was press 1 and "Call" because Bridgnorth lived on the ground floor.

I pressed an ear close to the panel to listen for Bridgnorth's instructions, but I needn't have. There was an emphatic buzz to tell us the lock was being released, and a very commanding voice saying: "Please enter! It's the first door on your left."

He said that with the steady rhythm we came to know so well, and which he could use in a huge variety of tones, even quite softly when he was relaxing. These first words, spoken to us in the flesh, had the essential beat he would train us to use, a regular pentameter: Please en-ter. It's the first door on your left. We entered the hall.

When his own door opened, though, the first person to appear was a woman, someone I recognised from a previous meeting here. She must have been having a session with William Bridgnorth before us.

He introduced us with due formality.

"We met," I reminded him, but he'd either forgotten or wanted to refresh my memory.

"This is Miss Anna Armitage, who's been – coming for, what is it? – some four months now?"

"No – only three months, William, I think", Anna told him.

"Well then, your progress has been excellent. But now I should give way to my new friends – and ask, good Anna, which day did we fix – for our next meeting?"

Anna had a hefty black bag on her back, which she swung round to her front to rummage in it for her diary. Which gave her the answer: "Exactly three weeks from this afternoon."

"The day the Fun Parade takes place! We'll need – to be in touch and choose another date."

I was transfixed listening to this. I hadn't expected to hear examples of William Bridgnorth's verse technique demonstrated in the course of saying good-bye to someone at his door. I looked at Jake. He had both an impressed and a pleased expression. Neither Bridgnorth nor this Anna had said anything that sounded unnatural, and the way they said things was neither artificial nor pompous. But they were speaking in verse. "Good Anna" was a bit old-fashioned, but it sounded to me ordinary and courteous in a voice such as Bridgnorth's, a humorous-friendly way of getting Anna off the premises. Now he turned to us.

"Well now. Come in, please. May I offer you/ some tea or coffee? No? So. Let's sit down / and speak perhaps without recourse to verse / at our first happy meeting, as to why / you've come here."

I couldn't take my eyes – or my ears – off William Bridgnorth as he gestured with open hand at a three-seat leather sofa and settled into his own similar, yet grander, armchair. Maybe it looked immense just because he was sitting in it, but there's no other word I could use.

William must be about six foot seven inches in height, with a huge broad chest and shoulders. They look powerfully gentle rather than strong, if that makes sense. He'd have large lungs – his voice and breath-control suggest that – and the rest of his figure goes with his torso: the big face with piercing, and yet mellow and good-humoured, brown eyes, the head of lavish grey hair which would have suited a seventeenth century portrait of an earl or duke, and legs long enough for stretching them out in front of him to be dangerous – because anyone else in the room could trip over his extended feet.

On his feet on this occasion – but he always did wear things like this – he wore shiny brogue-type shoes of ox-blood colour, and glaring yellow socks. The trousers were crimson corduroys, the shirt a red, outdoor, rural-looking garment, the sort you would buy in the St James's area as a pretence of having been down to the country for some active pursuits; you wouldn't be able to get it in a rural place where people actually worked. Over that, for all the summer heat, he wore a stern but well-worn woollen cardigan with four pockets that looked as if it had been sold to him in the same shop as the shirt. This might have lasted forty years provided you took care not to wash it very much. Bridgnorth didn't give an air of cultivating a "gentrified" look, if you can use the word for people as well as localities – you might have taken him for a country gentleman by birth. It impressed Jake all the more when he later told us he had been to "a comprehensive school in Hertfordshire" – he asked us only to note that that phrase was an iambic pentameter – and most of his working life (until they made him redundant) had been spent in the Environment Department of an inner London borough.

That fact, Jake said later, combined with this talent – genius?– for speaking in a manner he greatly admired as soon as he heard it, gave him high hopes for himself. Jake, as he subsequently revealed, had his own private income, and was really quite wealthy… If he could only overcome the sexual problem which shattered any confidence he had in himself and in life, he would turn his mind to the changes he could achieve in his own personality.

After those few preliminary words in verse William changed to prose as promised, and asked us about ourselves, stopping tactfully short of asking how I had recruited Jake as a possible class member. But social conversation was brief because William was too eager to expound.

"To get down to business," he said suddenly. "In this country we inherit the language of the great – of Surrey, Shakespeare and Dryden, Pope and Wordsworth – and we do not (consciously) use it. Our ears are closed to the resonances and the grandeur – but also to the convenience and the usefulness – of its rhythms. We do not employ what is there waiting for us to use, lurking just below the surface of our everyday speech."

He got up from his armchair, with surprising ease and speed for a man of his size and weight, and went over to a small table behind us where he switched on a device which would project images onto the bare wall behind and above where he had been sitting. He pulled on a cord to close the curtains and we sat looking at ten lines of print with italicised syllables.

"Iambic pentameters. Miss Cassell may know already what they are from her education," he said, resuming his armchair and sitting with his back to them. "But perhaps Mr Coleman will appreciate acquiring a little knowledge which is just very slightly technical. Take the first phrase on the wall behind me:

Is Earl's Court Road the second on the right?

It is a common enquiry. But, like all others of the kind it is a very simple example of an 'iambic pentameter.'"

He went on to explain the number and the pattern of the stresses and the way the count of syllables might vary but the number of stresses remain the same. Jake was silent and looked enthralled.

"Now – if you listen to the sound of the lines you can read on the wall, you will notice they are all iambic pentameters –- but that each of them has been taken from everyday speech, or from the media: television, radio, newspapers, the labels on foods or on medicines we consume hour by hour:

> Should Man-ches-ter U-ni-ted pull it off,
> It would be something of a miracle.

How often have we not heard that opinion! And how rarely is it acknowledged that the speaker is expressing it in verse.

> The tighter fiscal rules are here to stay.

And there again we have a daily fact, or injunction, not normally associated with verse.

> Now on to Scotland: There should be some rain,
> Which by the morning might arrive as snow.

Do you listen to the meteorologists with attention to the stresses? I shall not comment on the remaining examples – you may observe for yourselves:

> Do not apply to wounds or sunburned skin.
> You say you're anxious – what is it worries you?
> I'm rather partial to asparagus
> And four more bottles of that Chardonnay."

After he had pronounced all of those loudly and proudly he smiled and patted his knee with every stressed syllable of what followed:

"And so, if you are truly serious,
Start now. Say something simple – anything –
In that same cadence. Let the words come out
In that most natural English form and shape,
The fine blank verse our greatest poets used
– The iambic pentameter. Don't feel
You need to feel Shakespearean. Try it with
Some small or casual everyday remarks…"

I looked at Jake. Who did not look at me. He was staring at William Bridgnorth and his lips were quivering. His nervous smile, not his suave one, revealed that he was struggling to say something in response to Bridgnorth's challenge. I couldn't believe it. I was very relieved that I hadn't conned him into putting up with lunch with my friends and driving me here for nothing more than the embarrassment of putting up with a madman.

Then Jake spoke, very quietly and slowly as I drove my nails into the palms of my two hands, out of sight:

I spent – last win – ter in – a free – zing place
Hav–ing some treat–ment for–a strange dis–ease
I don't – wish to – discuss – or not – just now.
I can't – say it – was much – of a – success.
I – I –"

William Bridgnorth had pulled himself into an eager upright position while listening to Jake, and now motioned with an extended right hand to urge, without speaking, "Keep it up – yes, splendid – go on, don't stop. Please – please don't stop! And practise, practise now you have begun.

But Jake dried at this point and laughed, amazed at his achievement. Finally he looked at me, begging and spurring me to continue.

William spoke before I could try:

"I feel that was extremely promising!
You see – it comes quite naturally, you
Began to think there was no other form
In which you could express your darkest qualms
About your negative experience."

To my horror – but what else could I expect? – they were both now looking to me to sustain the momentum. I was shaking; but I started, because I couldn't have forgiven myself if I'd copped out at that stage.

> "I myself spent last winter as I spent
> All of that autumn, and the summer too,
> Scraping around for some small humble job
> To pay for living here – to justify
> My education in Humanities
> At Yarmouth University – three years,
> A good 2/1 in English Literature,
> And then, thrown out into this corp'rate world
> Where, after many workless months I've been
> Employed by a consultancy which gives
> Businesses doing badly wise advice
> On how to do better – no doubt for huge fees
> Of which I get a tiny cut. This is
> A truly Great Year, isn't it!"

In saying all that I'd been, like, walking barefoot along a narrow breakwater. Or so I conveyed in a batch of clumsy blank verse lines I am too shy to quote, or only a few:

> "A high tide lurched and gulped on either side,
> While up ahead was only the full sea
> And out there, the horizon – a cruel line
> Drawn under all my hopes – beckoned me on."

Except, I only thought those last lines, didn't say them. Suddenly I was getting worried in case this game had taken hold of me and I myself was incapable of stopping, not needing encouragement to continue.

William's eyes gleamed with approval as he nodded and nodded, line by line, during my oration. He was silent, Jake was silent, as I finished. Then William said, in the plainest prose, "Do you know, I think we can see a way ahead which might please all of us. But for the moment let us just celebrate."

He left us alone in the room puzzled as to what was coming – while he went out, presumably, to his kitchen, because we heard cupboard doors opening, plates being taken out. Jake and I said nothing to one another while he was gone. Later I said, "We were like happy kids too surprised to know why we were being treated." Then he was back, carrying three white china plates balanced on a square cardboard box which could only contain a cake.

We sat back and ate, and discussed practicalities like which days we could fix for future meetings.

"There is just one matter which requires to be considered", William said eventually. "I have discovered through what I call my two essential ex-es – experience and experiment – that one best acquires a good command of this art when working in a group of the right size – in threes rather than fours, say. A quartet chaired by myself is what my experience suggests. Five or more would be far too many. Would you be able to recommend a third student with whom you could work happily? Someone you get on with and preferably known to you for some time? (I had not told him of how, and how recently, I had met Jake). "Enthusiastic, obviously, and able to give time to 'the cause'?"

Jake told me afterwards that he racked his brains for a suitable person and – as something of a loner anyway – could think of no one. Nor could I. I couldn't imagine Aurelia, or Sonia, or Rick suiting the role. They would think I had gone crazy. "She/he was always a bit odd" was a phrase Aurelia used frequently about others. This would leave her speechless. Who on earth could we find who would understand?

8

Frank Winterfield did not know the name of the manager and sole waiter in TheEndemic Restaurant where, in the early evening, he could always expect to eat cheaply and alone to the quiet drone of unidentifiable music. But he thought of him as Godneau.

Sitting one night at the window table to which he was always shown, Frank asked, "How is it the restaurant is called 'TheEndemic'?"

He believed he would get no answer beyond a shrug of despair from this melancholy figure in the short white coat. But there were no other customers to attend to so there came a long explanation. An unknown company based far abroad (on a Micronesian island, for tax reasons) owned seven separate and dissimilar little premises scattered over this area of inner West London, and had leased them all to a separate restaurant concern trading from another far-off foreign place. A representative of the latter business, employed on a temporary consultancy basis, had advised them that converting the seven into a small chain franchised to individual managers who could develop them independently but retaining one overall name would be a brilliant idea.

This consultant came up with a title for the chain: "TheEndemic". This branch was "TheEndemic: North East Fulham". So why such a name? It would be very "distinctive" for a small set of smart restaurants operating in a well-defined, rapidly gentrifying region of London and offering an identifiable range of excellent, original meals. "Brand identity" was all-important. Consultants said that people who came to spend money in the stores and famous markets of the area would come in before or after their shopping and remember "TheEndemic" chain for making families welcome and yet preserving the charm and peace of old-style inexpensive estalishments. In TheEndemic restaurants there were tablecloths, not glass-topped tables decorated with artificial flowers. There were equally no glossy standard menus for the entire chain, but an emphasis on the individual menus offered by the different franchisees. The consultant marketed this vague idealism to the individual owners as a recipe for success.

But it did not produce what was called "footfall". Godneau longed for customers and noise. He switched on his little string of fairy lights and kept the music low. Despite having little to do he bustled around with his pretence of a smile and made sure he was always visible from the street. But few people came in. The peace here was the silence of a failing business. It was what drew Frank in. And sent in Merlinda to advise about its difficulties.

Godneau confessed to Frank one evening in the winter that he was doing so badly that one week before, at dusk, he had faked a power breakdown to save electricity and brought out romantic candles to compete with the glaring striplight of his nearest competitors, several streets away. It was Valentine's Night. His ruse attracted two couples that evening (and between one pair there had been a violent quarrel). No-one else at all came on the following two nights. The place looked merely dark and abandoned.

"Why you think I sit you here?" he asked Frank in his window seat.

"Do you think I like a view?" Frank suggested, and at once regretted it in case he sounded ironical; it looked across to boarded-up shops opposite, victims of the latest downturn.

"I do it because I take advice and they say, people in the street see people with smiling faces, they come in. You have a smiling face, the public see you enjoy your dinner." He pushed his hair back to give an unwelcome impression of Frank's baldness and did a humorous imitation of a Frank Winterfield grin, which was disconcerting to him. If that was how he looked to people –?

"I suppose it makes sense." Frank smiled as humanly as he could.

"It make good sense. Look – now!"

The door swung open at that very moment and a couple entered. Godneau showed them to a table further inside but still quite visible from the pavement.

Then on another evening the boss was deploring his inability to give the restaurant a name of his own choice.

"I not like 'TheEndemic'. One customer say he think it "TheEpidemic". I want, like, to call it something like "X-Quizito". But these days so many restaurants close round here with the Crisis, people say, 'Shall we go have a meal in a nice restaurant?' He grinned, and Frank knew a joke was coming. 'The other person say, good idea, yes.

But where?' And the answer? 'God knows – they all close down.' You think 'Godneau's' spelt like it's a French name is good idea? I want to have it in big letters, yes? And bright lights? Then people start coming. We go on a list and soon people can't get a table – they go on 'Waiting for Godneau'. But they not allow me to call it that. Philistine cunts!"

A third occasion when the boss introduced this subject he came up with a proposition for Frank.

"You come more often, say you come once every week, I give you a deal: Fourth time you come, I give you one course free, starter or dessert for nothing. If you have this seat in the window and smile. And some time, I give you company as well."

Company?

"Two people happy, smiling, better advertisement than one. I find you young lady – gentleman – which you prefer?"

Frank was not completely sure about this offer. He continued taking long strolls for exercise through the district, not always passing Godneau's in case he was drawn in when he did not wish to be. But he developed a habit of observing the people in other restaurants and noticing how often they were sitting close to the windows and grinning. If there were pairs of people, they too were grinning as if they knew each other. He wondered if they could have been simply strangers, acting. Or actors taking advantage of deals? Gradually he came round to Godneau's proposal.

He wondered how he would manage an act of sociability with the arrival of a fellow-diner who had also been forewarned of his own participation in a plan. He had made his three visits inside two weeks, and would qualify for a free course on this fourth occasion. With company. Anna's departure had left him desiring it. He made the condition that it be female company.

The time, 6.45 p.m., was fixed a week in advance and Frank kept scrupulously to that hour, sitting down in the window seat and opening his free evening newspaper as the minute hand on the clock above Godneau's bar counter clicked onto the 9, fifteen minutes short of seven. The boss was being lavishly attentive, producing "covers" of olives, savoury biscuits, dips.

And now it was already four minutes past seven, with no-one else having arrived. It was bad for a Friday in summer. Godneau checked his watch unhappily. Frank thought he could see him summing up the poor quality of his decor – except that he was no doubt proud of the lustreless Mediterranean seaport scenes and the dusty hanging bottles that looked as if they could have done service, unopened and unrequested, for years on end.

"I think I take your order now? She not coming. You very kind to wait."

What would "she" be like?

Frank had almost memorised the menu in the twenty minutes since he had sat down. The two dips provided for him and his unknown companion had acquired an unattractively settled surface.

But now a young woman came in and closed the door behind her very carefully.

"I am so sorry." Frank saw her gesture despairingly, and heard her say quietly, "It was the traffic jams – everywhere."

"Yes, yes, the Great Year," Godneau remarked, excusing her lateness out of relief at seeing her, and guiding her towards Frank's window table. Frank wondered if he should stand up to offer a greeting; and after hesitating he did that. It was correct.

Godneau said, "This –" waving his hand – " Mr. Frank!" The proprietor was good at remembering names, or the part he had been given. But perhaps he had not learnt the name of the newcomer, because Frank was not given it. And she was not offering it herself. Thinking it probably courteous and suitable, he shook her hand, reflected that they came younger and younger, and resumed his seat when she took the one opposite to him with an equal view of the street. He stared at her longer than he needed to, then stopped. She looked to him like an attractive, straightforward, no-frills girl somewhere in her twenties, wearing a cool blouse, a thin pastel-coloured jacket, jeans.

"This lady is the 'student', Godneau said next.

It took Frank only a few seconds to recall that in the menu Godneau offered a 25% reduction of charges for students on proof of status. So she was not necessarily a student at all, only a representation of one.

"Do you get a discount then?" he said to her when Godneau had gone to fetch her a menu.

Then she in turn seemed to remember the student concession.

"Oh well – no. In fact – my meals are going to be paid for. It's work. I mean, I've got a placement – from a company."

"You're like – an intern?" he wondered.

She was not going to continue playing down her role as she had almost allowed herself to do with Jake.

"Well, it's better than that," she maintained. "I get to go round with responsibility for sending in reports so my company can advise their client companies what to do."

"Sort of consultancy?"

"They are consultants."

"You go to other restaurants?"

"All TheEndemics, for three weeks. I've started e-mailing my reports."

"You get free meals every time?"

She didn't respond. She did have some fears about her expenses.

"It is a proper job?"

She paused, not wanting to let her employers down, but wishing to be truthful.

"No – but a job might be quite poss-i-ble.—"

Was Frank hearing things? Or was it becoming a general habit for people to speak with a kind of deliberate stress on certain words – just now he had heard several little beats on certain syllables: "might be quite poss-i-ble." He had momentarily been back in Anna's company, trying to devise replies to remarks she made, questions she asked, in that similarly emphatic manner of speaking.

"What other places do you go to?" he ventured. Godneau asked them if they would care to select some of his wine, and they agreed. By the glass, they thought. And with tap water. They raised the wine glasses when he brought them – by implication, to the oddity of the venture in which they found themselves.

She smiled, half-embarrassed at being too hungry to respond to Frank's question about other places. When their main courses came she took a larger sip of the wine and found the courage to tell him about her trips to the Laughter Studio (though not about Jake Coleman yet). He listened with incredulity.

"So do you have 'solutions' for the laughter problem?"

"I shall advise the consultancy to recommend that the Studio employ someone who can make people laugh at existence. At our simply being here and living with the bodies we have and with each other."

She felt slightly bold. Frank stared, with knife and empty fork stationary above his plate.

"Is that funny?"

"It's hilarious… Isn't it?"

"I don't know." He seriously doubted it. "Is this funny – what we're doing now?"

"Yes." She was trying hard, and knew it. It wasn't really, but she laughed. Frank Winterfield laughed. They giggled. They ordered a second glass of the wine. They were getting on. Two people outside on the pavement were reading Godneau's menu displayed in the window beside them, and saw them laughing. But then they walked away. They voiced a sudden theory: Perhaps you shouldn't be seen laughing too much in restaurants.

"Last week I was doing dogs," she said.

"Funny dogs?"

"Stray dogs. Don't you notice them?"

"All the time."

This afternoon he had gone cautiously past the band of strays worrying round the bins in the entry alongside his block, where rubbish was dumped to be carried away after collection from the chute. He had seen similar packs elsewhere, and noticed that some of the animals were quite respectable, could even have had pedigrees. He assumed that many had been abandoned when their owners hit hard times, teaming up with more experienced mongrels and prospecting for food along the streets.

"What do you do with these animals?" he wanted to know.

"Advise on how to cast them for a film… No, you won't have heard about it – unless you've heard the working title."

"Should I have?"

"*Canine Terror?*"

"No."

"London in the near future is terrorised by dogs who've developed a new dog-to-dog viral infection humans can catch. And it's not fatal for dogs, but it is for people. Maybe human terrorists are spreading it. The dogs breed and the people are dying. Also it's a sort of dog-aphrodisiac and the stray dog population is increasing, and they're all vicious because the infection drives them mad."

"Like the birds in that film?"

She didn't know it, so was intrigued to hear about the film, even though Frank wasn't sure he had the details correct. He liked going to the cinema but hadn't a mind for remembering many facts.

"How did they get the birds to do that?" He did not have an answer. "Are there goodie birds who don't join in?"

"There might have been one kind pigeon." It seemed a nice thing to say to a young woman.

"I've got to provide advice for the consultancy to give to the film company on all the dog aspects in the film – best ways of getting dogs, training them, feeding them, delivering them to locations. One dog has to start as a baddie, and reform with the help of the human hero – who's a vet, and his marriage has broken down, and the reformed dog helps bring them together again. But they mainly need a lot of bad dogs."

"Doesn't the good dog catch the virus?"

"No – I told you – he's a good dog."

"There is a beautiful scientist who has been testing a vaccine on her own dogs. There's a problem, though. She's been having an affair with the vet's wife. I'm not allowed to tell you how everything works out."

"You've told me a lot already."

"Only what's been in the publicity." He hadn't noticed. But there it was again – the way she pronounced the alternate syllables.

Now one of the rain storms of this summer was once again about to shape Frank's future. Heavy spots had begun to fall on their window. Godneau remained at the cash register behind his bar, the picture of despondency as the summer sky darkened and people hurried on past not stopping to look at what he was offering or the customers trying it. When there was a sudden short-lived, glow of sunlight over the street he was reluctant to come over and settle the bill; which they agreed between themselves he should give them so that they could leave while it wasn't raining. Their departure would leave his restaurant empty.

Neither wanted coffee while the evening sunlight shone on the wet streets and there was a chance to get away.

"You'll come again soon?"

"Yes," Frank said. And looked at his new companion. She smiled, but wasn't promising anything to the boss, who was not aware of her real purpose in being there.

"May I take you to your bus stop?"

"It's several minutes," she said. But the tone was encouraging.

Of course by the end of this street the steady warm wind had brought heavy clouds back and the sky had darkened once more. All at once it was raining even harder than before and by now they were too far away from Godneau's to hurry back. There were no convenient shop entrances where they could stop and shelter. As they walked faster his hopes were realised: his home was going to be nearer than her bus stop.

They were both completely soaked. In the circumstances it seemed to Frank civil and sensible and practical to say, "This is where I live. Would you like to come in for a coffee – and maybe dry out?"

He was very happy to find that, after a moment's hesitation, she agreed, and therefore trusted him; and he was elated to be going up the stairs with her. It felt both courteous and adventurous. At his door in that ill-lighted corner he found it difficult, not for the first time recently, to extract his key from a trouser pocket which clung damply to his thigh. This was how the climate worked these days, Frank told himself. Only as he entered and saw his inadequate home with the eyes of a visitor, did he wonder whether they would both need to take most of their clothes off and how exactly would that be negotiated? None of Anna's garments had been left on the premises, so it would not be possible to offer to lend any. It would be a case of indicating bathroom and bedrooms to her, so that she could accept a towel and a dressing gown, take off her thin jacket, and blouse and jeans, and drape them over a chair or something in front of his old electric bar fire. That would make his lounge impossibly hot. He had better not start thinking in terms of a bedroom, though.

In his old dressing-gown she came out of the bedroom he guided her to faster than he expected. The coffee was only half-made and he was still positioning two hard-backed chairs in front of the clicking, glowing old fire as she appeared with her wet clothes over one arm and something else in her other hand.

"You can't stand there like that," she said. "I've had a good idea. Where can I plug this in?"

She told him later that she had foreseen the embarrassment of Frank himself having to undress somewhere while she sat there naked except for a dressing gown and watched her own clothes steaming while they drank coffee. So she was offering to dry him still wearing his wet clothes with Anna's hair-dryer, which she had found in the bathroom.

At the start even, the heavy rush of heat from the dryer turned up to max. didn't seem to make much impression on the soaked upper half of the summer suit he was wearing. Then gradually it was making a visible difference – the original fawn colour darkened by the wet was turning light again. And wonderful, he could feel his skin drying underneath it. He was enjoying the newness of the experience. The rush of warm air aroused his feelings, he could not deny that. He was happy for it to go on and on. The room was becoming hot and itself slightly steamy. But his clothes were drying.

"Turn round."

She took an arm and had Frank Winterfield facing the window and the view of the yellow drainpipe in the yard while she trained the dryer on his shoulders. The same: he could feel with great pleasure the dampness retreating and the warm air penetrating the garment and reaching grateful skin. Soon all of his back felt contentedly covered with warmth, with reassuring dry clothes. Nothing clung damply to him any more. Then she lowered the dryer to cover the rear of his trousers, the backs of his legs, and – getting him to turn round again – his ankles and shins up to his knees. You can do the rest for yourself," she suggested. He thought of asking her to finish it off, having got so far. But he did not say as much.

"I'm sure I can manage that," he offered reluctantly. He was almost entirely dry and content himself; but what about her?

"I'll see to the coffee," she decided for him. They had been smelling it while she worked. She could find the kitchen by tracing the aroma, so he didn't direct her. He admired her tact in leaving him to go and pour it out, into cups she could surely find somewhere, while he dried the front of his trousers.

As she pulled Frank's spare winter dressing gown closer round herself she rapidly assessed the implications of the last half-an-hour. She knew that her clothes should be dry enough for her to go in about twenty minutes; if the bar fire didn't achieve that, the hair-dryer could. There was the coffee to drink – it suddenly felt quite welcome because she had felt very wet indeed and getting dry (getting both of them dry) had left a sense of achievement.

There would be more talking in the time remaining for her to stay, because she did intend to set a limit and leave. She resolved to drink the coffee sitting discreetly across from him in a separate armchair, not on the sofa where he could take up a position alongside her if she let the conversation stray into anything vaguely personal. To prevent that, she was thinking, she would have to guide them towards some other topic – the topic? – to keep them going until she left. Dared she risk it? As she turned out of the kitchen, the two cups in her hands, keeping the door open with her foot, she knew what she would talk about in case her host seemed a suitable candidate. She could always speak about it and not try to involve him, after all. But if he turned out to be eligible... She looked at Frank, who took the coffee from her in his dried and lightened suit, and realised after a few minutes that there would be nothing to lose.

But she needed to ask him something first.

"I re-a-lise I don't know your whole name!"

"Frank Winterfield."

"Merlinda Cassell. Hi!"

9

Jake had been so intrigued by his hour with William that he could hardly speak as he dropped Merlinda and drove away afterwards, and it made his driving a little more forgetful than usual. From the moment he entered the young people's household early that afternoon he had a renewed sense of his own inferiority. He was much older and much wealthier than any of them, or he would not have been the owner of this Mercedes. But they might all of them, he thought, end up much richer than he was because they were all, surely, climbing very fashionable and lucrative ladders. And they were all more intelligent. He could not tell about Aurelia (was it?) and Sophie? – no, Sonia. But Merlinda was unquestionably brighter than either of those two; and something told him that Yarmouth was a better university than New Leatherhead. Merlinda knew much more about many subjects than he did himself, and was quicker on the uptake. He would not have phrased it like this – but during the afternoon the blank verse had come out of Merlinda like out of a tape measure, one of those consisting of a metal strip projected from its case at the press of a button – measuring him, and finding him inadequate. Her performance emphasised and strengthened his yearning to be able to do the same sort of thing and achieve a better kind of life. She had something which appealed to him in that peculiar English of the non-purchaser, a few years ago, of a bed helpful for backache problems.

Jake would be going with Merlinda to William Bridgnorth's classes – she was arranging that – and probably committing himself to the advanced regime proposed. "If Bridgnorth accepts me," he suddenly heard himself saying to Merlinda as he prepared to drop her off. She was sure he would, and he realised that this was one of the rare evenings when he had no interest in sex, therefore no prospect of expense, indulgence, disappointment, trauma, and could be happy. He was not going to be preparing a cleaner bed for a visit from Merlinda, but felt that she was friendly and pleasant, and undemanding in herself, and represented things to which he aspired. In sum he had many positive things to think about as he left her at a bus stop, noticing that she gave him the relieved, slightly exaggerated smile, and small wave, of a girl who was not impatient or hostile towards him but all the same glad to be out of his company.

Yet some special traumas lay in the wake of such a stimulating afternoon, because…

As always this summer (it had started with small delays and frustrations as early as March) any journey anywhere in this city, by private or public means, was going to be difficult at any time of day. He was thinking too distractedly to notice the traffic block ahead of him far too late to turn off and "seek an alternative route" – not that that would be simple because so many rat-runs had been converted into adverse One Ways that he might become seriously lost and even fined heavily for entering a Temporarily Restricted Zone (TRZ) You never knew, from one Great Year to the next, where the Highways would be installed; these not being new roads but marked-off lanes on existing routes which motorists or cyclists entered at their peril. Their effect on traffic was monitored each time, so confusing alterations and modifications would be introduced to land you into trouble during the Autumn Event where you had not experienced any a few months before – as "Spring" or "Summer Closures". Jake was now sitting behind the wheel with the engine switched off alongside a GYL (Great Year Lane) and with a large overhead sign spanning the thoroughfare and saying EXPECT 18 MINUTES DELAY.

As he looked at it, the figure changed to 17; but almost immediately reverted to 18, and ten seconds later 19. If Jake had been so minded, which he was not, he might have seen the next hundred yards and the buildings on each side of this broad road as emblematic of his modern world. In fact it's only possible to say he was furious with it and merely anxious to get home.

Take the two cars just in front of him and the one alongside going in his direction: In the farther vehicle of the two, a real boom-box, he could see movements which convulsed and shivered its whole body. Five persons, each of them very large, were crammed into it, jerking and trembling to the rhythm of a rock number that drowned out any other nearby sound. Meanwhile, from the nearer car a mother had emerged with twin boys of around three years old, to exercise them before bedtime and have a smoke. Both twins wore GYCHAS (Great Year Charity Hats) and were quarrelling on the edge of tears. The car alongside Jake had a left-hand drive. The driver was in his twenties and wearing headphones, his eyes closed and head nodding, hands drumming on the wheel. Beside him was a brunette with unbearably long legs and the man was seemingly paying no attention to her at all. Only Jake, not even any overhead security camera, was in a position to see where her hand was. The sight temporarily restored his interest in sex, and he exhaled in anger to see 13 MINUTES and 15 MINUTES registering on the sign above them. But still the traffic was stationary and the heavy rhythmic beat blared in every open window around, in cars, or in shops in a nondescript parade, or in houses. An exception was a tall block of what he took to be offices, completely wrapped in some off-white material, presumably to protect it from the weather and conceal what was being done with it.

A limousine with black, closed windows passed them on the Highway going very fast indeed. Immediately it was gone two obese males of unguessable age left the car emitting the rock beat and slammed its doors. They went on shaking as they crossed – illegally – the Highway, and entered a shop. 16 MINUTES. "Well, if they made it, I could," Jake thought.

He checked his wallet for a prescription and a credit card, restarted the Mercedes for a moment, pushed buttons to close its windows, got out, locked it with the key and set out towards the pharmacy which he had been looking at half-an-hour ago and had been thinking about all that time. He was only just able to avoid being run down by two outriding motorcyclists who preceded an even grander though much slower limousine bearing a foreign flag he couldn't identify and carrying a stout uniformed person frowning at a smartphone.

There was a queue in the pharmacist's, but two people were serving at the counter, a young man and a middle-aged woman he thought might be Indian. Through an open door Jake could see a third, younger, perhaps Middle Eastern, woman assistant shaking tablets into a small bottle and sending bright, dark-eyed glances out towards customers. His watch told him he still had thirteen minutes, but unfortunately the sign over the road was not visible from the shop. Some nervy dispute was going on at the top of the queue. Were these really the capsules the doctor prescribed? They looked different from the last lot, and they didn't work.

With that settled, Jake was next. He put the prescription and the credit card into the male assistant's hand.

"One moment, sir." Why, Jake wondered? Seeing his look, the man assured him, "We'll see if we've got it, sir." There were too many "sirs", and the assistant seemed uneasy. He handed the prescription in to the woman in the dispensary. She scanned it, and sent him that riveting brown-eyed message of her overwhelming attractiveness he had noticed two minutes ago. Then she came out.

"Have you had this before?"

He believed a little hesitation was somehow appropriate.

"Well – yes."

"What other medications do you take?" The low, slow voice could have reminded him of someone else from the past, but the impression was not immediate, and he fought it back. Quickly he recited the names.

"Can you spare a minute or two to speak about it privately?"

Was he to say "Not really", and miss an opportunity? He was beginning to be seriously anxious about his car. Not that a few minutes in a cubicle in a busy main road pharmacy would be more than a start, but he told himself not to appear so definite. He replied, "May I keep the prescription and come back on Monday?"

"Yes, you may come whenever you wish."

But with that small, engaging phrase uttered in a suddenly deeper register and with a tiny smile that somehow filled her entire face and brightened her eyes even more, YASMINA/PHARMACIST", as her name-disc revealed, destroyed any desire of Jake to return. The last beautiful use of those exact words, with that kind of smile on seductive foreign lips, he had heard on the scene of a sexual calamity so comprehensive and humiliating that he felt he could remain no longer in the company of any woman who used them in whatever connection. They turned him off, or rather, turned him back to a scene of disaster…

He recovered the prescription with trembling fingers and left the shop – where, his watch now told him, he had spent twelve minutes – to see his Mercedes swinging in mid-air above the spot where he had left it, gripped by – what would you call them, metal talons, claws, jaws? – about to lower it exactly onto the flat back-portion of a very long truck. And it was this sight that, not unnaturally, set him off so quickly and dangerously across the Great Year Lane with his right arm raised and his forefinger pointing up towards his car while his throat tried desperately to produce a shout to carry through the sound of traffic roaring past where he had stopped, everyone speeding with cynical relief at being released from the tailback. He therefore did not see or hear the large and shiny car which hit him.

The extreme alertness of the driver, who had been travelling along GYLs for almost a month and was used to people stepping out blindly into apparently empty and safe road space, saved Jake Coleman's life. The official vehicle swerved far enough, with brakes howling, for a wing only to catch an extended leg, "a trouser thickness", as the orthopaedic registrar described it. "Another millimetre and you would have been dead. Or as good as dead – for the quadriplegic remainder of your life." Nevertheless, the survivor of this impact went staggering back onto the pavement distantly aware that what you did in this situation – however it had come about – was recover your footing and balance yourself, because this was some irrational occurrence it would only take a second to emerge from.

But once at the pavement Jake must have tripped on the kerb because he spun round dizzily and fell, and hit his head, and also registered a drastic pain in his right ankle before he lost consciousness.

$$* * *$$

"Lift it up for me," she said, as she picked up the other one from the carpet.

Raising his foot, he was sent back for a moment to exactly the same words and the same experience three days before, sitting on the edge of the previous bed in the hospital and pushing his toes into his socks with the aid of guiding female hands. It was not the first time Jake had thought that these girls had a lot in common with nurses. Twice in this last year women had confessed that nursing was their day job.

He was also aware yet again of the way his memory delivered the past to him in all-too-thorough detail, although this time it was not a painful, disabling sensation. He had not felt sexually attracted to the young nurse who helped him put his socks on at 7.30 a.m. after his night in Accident and Emergency, and here a few days later at "Embraceable", drawn by the offer of "Brendella, Our New Girl", he had taken off his socks himself and was only having his still tender feet restored to those garments as a parting kindness that went with the thirty-minute service. He had been able to receive that without any tremors of fear about the associations which any resemblances or act or word might compel him to make. So matters had gone well.

No, everything about the New Girl had proved splendid, which was a rare but possible occurrence. Brendella was absolutely new, and reminiscent of no one and nothing else at all. As a courtesy, but genuinely curious, he asked her where she came from. He didn't understand the answer, and thought she was supplying the name of a town rather than a country, unless he hadn't ever heard of a country called that. She was very willing to repeat the word, but he still didn't recognise it and thanked her again, and smiled, as she nimbly loosened his laces and took his shoes and socks off.

"A man's heart is in his little toes," she said, in what he would later have described, when he knew a lot more about music, as a deep alto voice. No, he had never heard that dictum before. Never. He hoped he would never hear it again from someone else and have a future sexual experience ruined by its reminding him of this one. And then, a little systematically, but with arousing charm, she pushed the little finger of her left hand into the gap between the smallest toe and the fourth toe on each foot in turn.

"You are left-handed," he said, pleased with himself and his promising interest in everything she was doing.

"No – I like difference," she replied, and ran the right hand up to his knee and beyond. But it will not serve the purpose of this narrative to explore the detail of Jake's experience during the next twenty minutes or so. That is his private matter, and it is only relevant to say that he left Brendella's premises feeling pleased and renewed, and able to contemplate returning.

All the same, his leg had jumped with remembered pain as she first touched it, and he had had to explain why and tell her quickly about the accident, from the second he knew he had damaged his ankle up to the point when he knew he had recovered enough to manage the accelerator on the Mercedes. This he had redeemed the day before from the Car Pound on payment of £450, a penalty increased by a contribution to the Great Year Fund, a "registered charity", whatever that was.

"You tell me next time it happens. Except I hope it won't happen again," she instructed him. "I have a friend with access to the Car Pound. You can get out for nothing next time – you pay him something, of course, but not four hundred and fifty pounds!"

It had made an enormous difference that Merlinda and Bridgnorth had taken seriously his very first ventures into blank verse and welcomed him already as almost an equal in their attempts to meet life with an enhanced imagination and deeper dignity. More than that, Bridgnorth had been altogether emphatic that Jake belonged with Merlinda to a potential best trio of students – if a third could be found.

That night, after his visit to Embraceable, Jake decided he would go to the Public Library nearby and find some blank verse. He would sit there among other students and read under his breath to acquire a better sense of the rhythm. Then he would go along to a small restaurant and practise ordering a meal in verse; also seeing how much small talk with the staff he could manage in the same form. The second thing he would do would be to consider this challenging proposition that Bridgnorth was putting to Merlinda and himself – and to the third person yet to be found – that each of them, in separate sessions, should come and narrate a detailed autobiographical experience in blank verse entirely. Notes on the content of their stories they could prepare and bring with them, but there should be nothing in such documents to assist them in achieving iambic pentameters when they spoke, let alone any composition of drafts of the verse itself before they arrived. Jake might begin to-night to write down some of the elements of his experience in that clinic last winter, in a country which would never dream of marketing a Great Year. His mood of contentment with this plan, and with his world in general, after the successful meeting with Brendella, promised a worthwhile evening.

He knew that he was correct in believing that the Library would stay open until eight o'clock. He had checked the notice of opening times in the window on a previous evening in this district, and had promised himself a visit after his half-hour at Embraceable. "I am already rearranging my life because of Merlinda and William Bridgnorth," he told himself with a smile. Would I have framed this next thought the same way as I do now as little as three weeks ago – "'It's somewhat cool, we might be in for rain'"? It was an utterly natural pentameter.

At five minutes to seven on a cloudy, somewhat cooler evening there was a good hour still available for his research. He made his way carefully, still testing the ankle, up the path across the gardens to the Library entrance with a contented physical pleasure in his mental resolve. But the heavy glass Automatic Doors cancelled all that. They did not slide open. Then he realised there was no light in the foyer, where there had to be sufficient for people to read the Great Year and Fun Festivity posters. Beside the Library Opening Times in the window was a small extra sheet of information which did not draw attention to itself with any heading. He read:

We regret to announce that the Library will close permanently at 8 p.m. on –

Jake read and re-read the day, month and year with disbelief, even instinctively and stupidly checked his watch. Yes, a permanent closure had happened last week. And in this month and year. The notice went on:

> We thank our customers of many years for their patronage
> and wish to inform them that they will be welcome at the
> Central Library in the Upper High Road, which will remain
> open pending further improvements to the Library Service.

The disappointment affected Jake deeply. It was as if the world was making a calculated attempt to halt him in his progress towards another life. He felt undermined, almost dejected again – but not entirely, because he had acquired a degree of determination to carry on with his plans. It was the sort of strength that possessed him on the day he recommended that individual not to bother about investing in any of his beds. He was also hungry by now, and ready to eat anything.

The waiter who came to serve him in the restaurant held out no more than a standard menu but remarked, carefully and steadily, in a strong bass-baritone, "I do not think there will be rain to-night."

"The forecast, as so often, could be wrong," Jake replied.

"You may need longer to make up your mind?"

"No need to hurry. May I suggest you try –"

He tapped an item with a polite finger and named it, and Jake let the menu fall on the table. Was he hearing correctly? Were the principles of William Bridgnorth's teachings already altering the way he was hearing people speak?

"Which of the omelettes do you recommend?" he wondered.

"The omelettes are all excellent to-day," came the response.

"Then I shall have the Special Omelette
With Cheddar Cheese and Herbs and Trimmings in
The Old Venetian Style, with Fresh Pommes Frites".

The waiter noted this down carefully on his pad and then,
"Yes, thank you, sir. And may I ask if you
Would like the Salad with it?"

"Yes, I would."

While eating, he opened the tiny notebook he had bought on the way there, and wrote:

"I start my story on a train. Outside,
Snow covers the winter landscape –"

Then he recalled that Bridgnorth had forbidden the previous writing down of actual pentameters in preparation for the narratives his students were to give. So he simply jotted down a series of notes about the journey to Dr Erznik's clinic, the welcome he received, the curious forms of address he had to become accustomed to in that country – though not yet the dismal outcome of his visit.

10

What was he doing with a hairdryer when he was nearly a hundred per cent bald? There were things that were going to have to be explained about Frank. But maybe there were things to be explained about me as well?

Frank first, though. When I came out with the name "William Bridgnorth" as we drank coffee that evening he gasped with amazement. He knew him, though without knowing that much about him. It turned out that they'd both been fired from the same local council (but different departments) around eighteen months before. There was no telling whether William would remember Frank if they met now, but on the whole Frank thought he wouldn't, as they'd never worked together. After hearing how I'd come to know him myself, he pondered for quite a while whether he'd be interested in taking a look at what William was up to now. And finally he decided that – out of pure curiosity – he really might. But it remained very much to be seen whether Frank would take to William's idea as much as Jake…

It took quite a bit of arranging to find a date and time that suited all of us. But eventually I managed it. Frank and I met outside Sloane Square station and took a No.22 bus – the one I could have caught to start my journey home in the other direction from TheEndemic Restaurant that night – to move very slowly indeed down the King's Road on a sweltering Saturday afternoon.

"I'm nearly back at my place now," Frank said abruptly just after the old Town Hall building. Yes, he was, and I could have suggested I call on him there and we walk to William's. But I wanted to use half-an-hour to get him used to what he could expect from William (and also not run the risk of any delay if I had to pick him up from his flat).

When we at last got down no more than fifty yards from William's door Frank put on a sudden thoughtful expression.

"Yes… I didn't realise we were coming exactly here", he said suddenly; and stopped as if he didn't want to walk any further, so that I'd gone several paces ahead. This threw me. All I could do was turn back to collect him and say, "It's where William lives."

"It is?"

He was standing there absolutely still, and I began to be worried. It was as if something had been revealed to him, and I couldn't understand why. There was nothing remarkable or impressive about William's street, or the fact that he lived in it. Was there?

"He's expecting us," I reminded him, and that seemed to wake Frank from whatever he had fallen into. We made our way to William's door.

Always absorbed in his own concerns, William gave no sign of recognising him when we arrived. Out of caution, I had not mentioned their connection when speaking about the visit on the phone to William, though I had given him Frank's full name (to which he did not react). When the two of them were face-to-face I watched William carefully to decide whether he might be concealing any past knowledge or recognition, and came to the conclusion that he wasn't. Frank, for his part, made no attempt to establish any former association.

Anyway, there I was introducing Frank as a prospective student on a first visit, a fortnight after Jake's in this sitting room with the old-fashioned projector, down near the World's End, one Saturday afternoon, our host sitting there in his unchanging clothes (were all his shirts the same colour, or did he only own the one?) And with a possibility now that we could make up, with Jake, a special group of students speaking verse in long seminars under the tuition of William Bridgnorth (while the rest of the country, London most of all, got on with enjoying the Fun of the latest Great Year).

William was formal and courteous in a style which suggested very long experience in this sort of thing. "Merlinda has been here some several times," William began, "and will have heard my guiding principles." He repeated those for Frank, and produced the white panel on the wall which would give us his ten examples of pentameters we would hear in everyday life. Except that when these appeared they weren't like the ones at the optometrist's, where you might memorise the shrinking lines of black capitals after a couple of visits, and cheat when you read them for your next eye test – if you had any reason for cheating. This time William had devised a different set:

1. There are some matters which we might discuss
2. Technology is the new ignorance
3. Most education happens out of school
4. Our lives are simply sub-prime mortgages
5. Which platform takes me to Austerity?
6. Weren't you before me? – But I'm sure you were
7. People with heavy backpacks should pay twice
8. Tell me, do you think we are still in love?
9. May I sit here? – Yes… Well, I think it's free
10. Property being theft, I'll steal some back.

He went on to explain in the same way as before that one of the great virtues of verse speaking was the variety of uses to which it could be put. It was, as could hear around us all the time, the natural rhythm for expressing ourselves in English, for example when asking simple questions (No.5) or posing very serious ones (No.8). It was also ideal for uttering maxims and propositions of any kind, particularly original or controversial examples: Nos. 2, 3, 4, 7 and 10. But we should never forget that the pentameter was also the finest form for relaxed, informal and practical modes of speech. Take No.6. Here we suppose that someone has courteously assumed that the other person at the shop counter has the right to be served first. The other has, with words and gestures of equal courtesy, denied that, and the first speaker insists that he is correct, completing his own pentameter whether or not is or her interlocutor has responded in the same way. The pentameter encourages subtleties we are in danger of forgetting in day-to-day intercourse. Blank verse is about politeness and decorum as well as emphasis and aphorism. But look at No.9. Notice that the respondent to this frequent polite question as to whether a seat in a train or a cafe might be available has completed the pentameter unconsciously initiated by the other party and thereby paid that person a compliment.

"So – thus far – would you say you'd followed me?" William now enquired of Frank, looking down at his watch as if he had suddenly realised he had been expounding for too long. I was now expecting Frank to be tested as Jake had been, challenged to produce some spontaneous pentameters of his own in response to this first hour of William's tuition.

Frank did not immediately reply. He seemed to be fixed on No.10, a line which appeared to be causing him some thought. But then he gave a brief, shaky smile and made an answer which delighted his questioner, producing a pentameter without, I believe, realising he was: "As far as any first time student might".

William was gratified by these words but did not seem disposed to continue, so – "Is there a time you would not use blank verse?" I asked him, expecting him to deny that there was any occasion at all in which it would be inappropriate.

"There are cases in Shakespeare," he replied, to my surprise couching his advice in prose, "when the line of one character is completed by another with a phrase that chides or even insults. I would not recommend trying this technique in response to any aggressive observation or question from a police officer, tempting as that might be. You should forego the opportunity," he concluded with a smile, in excellent rhythm, rising to show us out.

As we left, clustered awkwardly in William's small hall, the doorbell rang suddenly and insistently, and William's smiling impatience with the demand on his response suggested he knew very well whom to expect.

On seeing the woman for whom he opened the door – this suavely-dressed, very self-possessed person of about forty years old, Frank exclaimed. It was not a word, let alone a greeting – it was an inarticulate noise expressing astonishment and a kind of fear; the kind of noise someone might make if they thought their eyes were deceiving them, or they were dreaming. Frank and the new arrival had clearly met before, and knew each other so well that no greeting was required, only an exclamation of strangled surprise followed by a peculiar little dialogue between them. Obviously it hadn't been here that he had met her before this.

"Jesus Christ!" he said.

"No – Anna Armitage," the woman replied, showing hardly any surprise herself. "So how goes it with you, Frank?"

Frank appeared to have no response ready for that and said, "What are you doing here? Is Jeffrey with you?"

"No!" She laughed at that. "Are you still living in the same place, Frank? Should I drop in some time?"

"No," Frank said. "Yes, I mean – I'm still in the same place, but—"

The rest of us were waiting for him, William standing at his open door wishing, I suppose, to see us politely away and get started with this next student, if that was what she was.

"Where are you living now?" Frank asked this Anna.

"I don't know. Nowhere especially. I didn't know you were such a friend of William's. Maybe I'll see you here. Bye."

"Yes…" said Frank.

Anna said something else before breaking off the conversation and going on into William's flat as Frank – I saw this – followed her with his eyes and looked concerned and bewildered at the same time. It was, "Did I leave my hair-dryer in your place?"

To which Frank nodded, and said, "Yes. You did."

11

Frank Winterfield, on a bright day cooled by a respectable breeze, went in through the huge glass automatic doors and walked slowly down the first shining avenue of the New Mall trying to be unnoticeable. He wanted to look like any other late middle-aged man, bald if he had to be, ordinarily dressed, among all the wandering shoppers dazed by the decorations put up for the Great Year.

His visit to the New Mall today, he said to himself, was a Voyage of Recovery. Not to commit shoplifting sins again, but to recover the feeling of what it was like when it had been his squalid obsession. He wanted to regain that sensation of stealing for the excitement of it, the pleasure of the small rewards. He needed to remember the impulse, the opportunity, the method, the sensation of walking away, quickly or casually, with the stolen item in his pocket, and setting it down on the table at home. He had no fear that the temptation to pilfer small items would come back; although he needed to be careful in case the exercise of recalling a once familiar routine led him back in that very direction.

On the other hand, the effort of memory was going to be difficult. So much had changed. As he had crossed the large courtyard with its fountains and lavish greenery and decorative pots, he could not fail to notice that nothing was less like the proper, but distinctly friendly, department stores that still existed in his boyhood and in his twenties. The goods in them had had some interest – and pleasantness – whereas everything in Consumerama looked like brightly-packaged mass junk. Consumerama itself had already existed at that time, but as a chain of fairly modest supermarkets competing doggedly with the big concerns. At some point the company had expanded, acquiring larger premises which offered tempting franchises to other traders. But by the millennium it had disposed of most of these sites, often very profitably, and seized the chance of concentrating the franchising activities in huge purpose-built hypermarkets spread across many acres of New

Development, called "Malls" or "Experiences". For all the glitter and artificial excitement, they were cold and impersonal. Here, for example, the words FOR YOUR SAFETY began a notice which went on to describe the 24/7 surveillance which had been installed for "CUSTOMER PROTECTION". Its text should have read WE'VE GOT OUR EYES ON YOU ALL THE TIME (to catch you if you nick anything). Another warning came in the form of a picture of a young woman with a smart, very modern appearance – mascara, bright lipstick, huge earrings – with the words A STORE DETECTIVE LOOKS JUST LIKE YOU. Frank looked around him as he walked on and imagined other customers ruling him out of that category for looking too conventional, too unlike the poor, clothed in whatever they could afford.

But he was here to imagine the psychology of theft, the mental experience of stealing, and hiding your pilfered loot somewhere on your person and making – not too rapidly – for the nearest exit. And because that was his train of thought, he momentarily saw everyone else as potential thieves. Their gaze at some item small enough to drop into their plastic bag became a preliminary to stretching out a hand, turning the article over to read the price or the ingredients (in this Delicacy Department), then stealing it. He watched carefully, but none of them did that. They seemed simply mesmerised by the goods which caught their attention.

He walked onto a narrow escalator to carry him slowly up to the first floor, the only passenger on it apart from a young woman with a large purple Consumerama bag a few steps ahead of him. Searching for something, she raised a grapefruit from the bag's depths, held it in her other hand for a moment, then dropped it. It fell one step below her and rolled down from one step to the next, a yellow ball luminescent in the strange lighting of this New Mall. When it reached him, Frank put out a foot to stop it bouncing down any farther. In five seconds they were both at the top and off the escalator, and he was handing it back to her with a smile.

"I used to play cricket", he said. It was not true. It was not appropriate. It was something to say.

Her return smile of thanks struck him as either shy or – uncomfortable? When she put the fruit back in the bag he briefly saw – as he described it to himself later – only some goods very free of wrappers and barcodes, mainly fruit and vegetables without anything attached to them which might set off an alarm at the exit if they hadn't been lawfully purchased. He then thought, and why he couldn't yet explain, "I might follow her."

She walked away in what he also thought later was a deliberately casual manner, past a man you couldn't have mistaken for a store detective in disguise – because he wore thick black trousers and a t-shirt with a line of letters saying "Security England" above a larger message: HAVE A GREAT DAY! The sight of this individual, all the more fearsome because he could have been in his early sixties with a lifetime of criminality under his belt, reminded Frank of the excuse he needed to answer the question, Why aren't you buying anything in this section of the store, named "FreeSpace: Women"? All right, he could say he was looking for a nightdress for his daughter's birthday (he did not have a daughter).

Two sounds intruded on his consciousness in these few minutes. One was of the tuneless junk music piped into this room changing suddenly to the current anthem, the Happy Song as rendered by a lately-knighted pop vocalist:

"Wherever you are – here or there –
It's a great – great – unforgettable year!"

The second sound was the noise of drilling, drilling going on and on, on the floor above, boring into the banal melody.

He passed a tableau of six dummies with featureless faces half covered by Your Holiday Hats and with shiny wax legs. Then he sauntered between rows of costumes on hangers clustered on stands, and turned as the woman turned, nervously he thought, towards a series of wall racks with stockings and – very oddly – gloves packaged up and hanging from plastic hooks. But this she passed, and at the end found a table display of loose knickers and handkerchiefs in piles in shallow wooden trays. Out of sight from the counter where cash was being taken by assistants exchanging remarks about anything except the tedium of the work, the young woman stood and looked at these articles.

Frank did not wish her to see him when he had registered that she was turning over the handkerchiefs and possibly looking to see if there were barcodes on the labels. He put two further rows of clothes between himself and her and began to look for nightdresses.

He could not see any, lost his way, and turned a corner to see first that about fifteen feet away from him the woman was quickly slipping two, or perhaps three, small white handkerchiefs into her bag, sneezing as she did this. Second, he noted that from a similar distance beyond her, Security England was moving purposefully in her direction.

Something told Frank he also should approach her. He thought it was sympathy, or even fellow-feeling, a sense of affinity with another shoplifter – if indeed she was that. He also knew, as he neared the two of them and saw the terrified look on the young woman's face, that he was going to do whatever he could to save her from trouble.

"Would you mind showing me what you have in that?" Security England was saying. There was a sickening tone of conviction and triumph in the voice. Frank was standing a few feet behind her as she pulled the sides of the bag apart. He would let her respond to this individual before he tried to intervene; though what he would say he was not yet sure.

"You've just put those in there, haven't you?"

"I bought them in here about ten minutes ago."

"Oh come on, my dear. I saw you putting them in."

"I didn't," Frank said.

Had Security England seen Frank at all before that point? Because he needed some seconds to take in Frank and say, with routine aggression, "I'm not needing your help."

"I'm not offering you any," Frank replied. "I'm wanting to help the young lady."

He was careful to say it in a good-humoured way, as if this was all a joke, he even managed a smile. He nearly tried a compliment to the man's vigilance, "Quite right you're keeping your eyes open," or something. But he stopped in time. The individual tried a more threatening tactic.

"Are you together by any chance?"

Frank actually trembled. He was glad he was not carrying anything that could be searched.

"No. We are not together," he said, though the intended tone of contempt sounded to his ears less than certain. He checked the impulse to mention looking for a nightdress for his daughter, who could have been about this young woman's age – which was wise. He said, "I happened to be behind the young lady in the queue in the

Delicacy Department and saw what she'd got before she bought the grapefruit and – the other things."

"You have your receipt, madam?"

She put the bag down and opened a purse and produced a slip, which she unfolded.

"I see." It was all he said, taking a quick look it and closing his lips firmly. Then he handed it back, favouring its owner with a hard look. For the first time Frank thought that the man probably had the option of threatening her with a showing of what had been recorded on the all-seeing cameras, so a receipt would not be essential. But no; or not yet. Frank now began to wonder whether he could read, because he hadn't scanned in any detail the slip she had taken back from him, with its list of a dozen or so items and prices.

"I'm saying to you," he went on eventually, "I know a thief when I see one." He was looking at both of them, but longer at Frank; which would have scared him if the man had not been patently backing down. "And I know a terrorist when I see one. I've seen plenty of them, I can tell you." Was he truly associating this student-age English blonde with terrorism? Especially the Islamics", he finished.

His eyes achieved a fixed, threatening light as he pronounced the middle syllable of the last word. Frank and the woman looked at him, each of them speechless at this sudden turn of the talk, uneasy in case Security England's aggression on this topic should be transferred to them. It was physically frightening. It looked as if it might be uncontrollable. "I tell you this," he went on, "there's a team of us working in this Experience. We're from all over this country and we've been together since the army. We've seen two embassy sieges, and we've been kept on to make sure no fucking Islamics – or anyone else – spoil our Great Year. Do you follow me?"

"Yes I certainly do," Frank Winterfield said, because he thought it was advisable.

"And when it's over, all the NES" – Frank assumed this was the New Enhanced Surveillance they were hearing about – "will still be there for the future. We'll be watching everything. Got that? Goodbye."

He was announcing the end of their meeting with a gesture of courtesy converted into a threat. No doubt at all on instruction, for public relations reasons, his hand went out to each of them to be taken and shaken, and (he couldn't tell what the young woman did) Frank instinctively stiffened his own grip in response to his; which was the hardest dismissive handshake he had ever known. As soon as the grip loosened for each of them, they turned and walked away, slightly apart for the sake of caution but agreeing with glances to come together again when they were well across the leafy forecourt of the New Mall.

"You had a receipt. For everything?" Frank asked her when they were out of sight of the building.

"Yes," she said. He was very surprised. "From last month."

"So –" he could hardly believe her candour, and hesitated before finishing – "you had nothing for today?"

"I had nothing for today. This came out of a bin last month."

"Do you think he could read?"

"Yes, but I think he was morally dyslexic."

Frank did not understand what she meant, except that she thought the man immoral. But what was she?

And what was he himself, come to that? He had been accessory to an act of larceny.

"But you took things, didn't you? I'm not a store detective, by the way."

"They haven't proved I've taken anything."

No. And they hadn't proved anything against Frank. Which was a relief. But he thought they had better get away.

"Would you like – a drink? Or coffee?"

A reasonable place was not easy to find in the surrounding streets.

"We should have had coffee in the Mall," she suggested, and smiled.

In the end they settled for a fast food cafe called the Mighty Snack. That deterred customers by putting large coloured pictures of its meals in the windows. Here they sat down at a table with benches below one end of the high counter, the young woman with her back to it. It became difficult to find anything to say, with no real option of returning to what had brought them together. The purpose of his own visit to the Mall had not been fulfilled, Frank thought.

Half-way through her coffee she shook, in extreme agitation. And shivered, despite the heat.

"Are you all right?"

She managed a courageous pretence of a laugh, then slumped sideways onto the bench, alarmingly pale.

Frank was round the table to lift her as she struggled to stay conscious, and a man who appeared to be the proprietor was with them at once, fanning her face with a free newspaper. The headline was OUR GREAT YEAR HEALTH DEAL.

"I'll be all right. I get this sort of thing," she said. "I'll go home."

"Is it far?" She told him, and he had vaguely heard mention of it from someone else, even recently. But he could not place it exactly.

"That's by tube for you?"

"I take two buses. I'll be fine."

"It'll be one taxi," Frank assured her.

"No!" She shook her head and meant she couldn't afford it. He understood.

"It'll be on me."

Would he go with her, he was wondering? He didn't want to stand in the street handing out money to her and saying good-bye, and knew it was the best way of saving her from being overcharged by the kind of new taxi outfits that operated among the shoppers round here. He assured her he was intending to accompany her.

"No!"

"Yes!"

The Great Year traffic slowed them down to a crawl through central London streets and inner suburbs to places beyond Frank's recognition, and the meter clicked up towards a total he began to fear he might not be able to meet. They were wordless and embarrassed, unsure how – apart from settling the fare – they would make the break at the end of this. It had become a journey he wished he had not undertaken. But he could not have let her go home alone under threat of a fare she couldn't pay.

As they turned the corner of her street she had apparently recovered, and fingered the depths of her purse to add the last of her small change to Frank's last forty-five pounds in notes. The driver was taking her advice about landmarks and numbers and getting his vehicle as close to the door as he could manage, with Frank greatly relieved that he had almost been able to pay for the journey.

He insisted on carrying her bag to the door, heavy with the looted vegetables and fruit, preparing the words of a speech to go with the delivery (to her parents, or boy friend, or husband? He hadn't found out) of a young woman taken ill in a cafe where he had been having coffee – no, there was no explaining it.

"That's so kind", she said. "Don't wait. He'll go." She meant the taxi, which was lurking in case Frank wished to travel on somewhere else.

"He's going already," Frank said quietly as she looked for her keys.

But before she could find them, the door was opened by someone who had seen a taxi arriving but not worked out who might be inside. Someone watching at the window.

"Sonia!" Merlinda said. "What's the matter?" It was as if she hadn't noticed Frank yet.

And then,

"Merlinda!" Frank said.

"Frank!"

12

What I first thought was that Frank had somehow recruited Sonia for William's seminars, which was crazy. I had only just recruited him. And Frank had never had my address, so how could he have met Sonia?

Aurelia wasn't at home yet, and Sonia – mumbling to Frank "Thank you for coming back with me" – at once ran upstairs to her room humping a bag of groceries (where from?) and leaving Frank and myself by ourselves in the hallway, totally puzzled at seeing each other. I've no idea if Sonia heard us talking together in the next five minutes as if we were well acquainted – which of course we were. And no idea what she thought if she came downstairs later and saw that we'd gone out together.

When Sonia's door closed behind her, Frank stood there looking at me, and said "I didn't know where you lived".

"Did you know Sonia lived here?" I asked him.

"Who?"

"Sonia." I was a bit sharp, and it could have sounded like a kind of jealous accusation. Frank looked perplexed hearing Sonia's name for the first time, which proved to me that they couldn't have been known to each very long. About ninety minutes as it turned out. There was a pause while he got things straight. But he said no more about it there and then.

And he suddenly wanted to know, "Have you had your dinner yet?"

"No."

I was glad that he seemed about to suggest a way out of a very peculiar coincidence.

"Would you like to find somewhere for something to eat?" he asked me. I looked at him, doubtfully I suppose.

"Yes, maybe... Where?"

"God knows!"

"Godneau's Restaurant?"

"Yes. Well we do know that one. Though you might be tired of it."

"No," I said, though I was still hesitating before agreeing. Then I thought, "Well, he is inviting me", and I added, "And we know it's quiet."

I was going along with the idea because I felt Frank obviously had something he wanted to say about Sonia. And it would do Godneau a good turn.

Frank drew some cash from a hole in the wall before we entered the underground, explaining that he'd just spent all his money on a taxi. It was becoming more and more intriguing, and he wasn't going to try to explain against all the noise of our District Line journey west.

It was not only quiet in the restaurant, which was very suitable, but Godneau himself remained deathly silent for nearly all the time we were there. He looked stricken with gloom, not smiling once when he took our orders and served us. All he said was, "Business very bad – you the first people I see in three days. No money out there." I'd got used to hearing those last two words as a term for the consuming population, which always made me think of some wild, cold, indifferent place you only ventured into at terrific risk. It didn't help Godneau that we declined the offer of his house wine on this occasion, as a serious purpose – and a mysterious one? – had brought us there.

"You've been living in the same house as that 'Sonia' for a while?" Frank asked me in a sort-of strict manner. There was a frown in the question, which he put a bit oddly, I thought; plus some bewilderment.

" Since we left uni. Two years – nearly."

"Then you're friends?" He gave me an almost suspicious look.

"Yes." I was now a friend of Frank's also, I suppose. He could ask me questions. But it was the first time we'd ever been in an unexplained situation like this, and I was afraid of him being someone who would cross-question me.

"I don't think she's very well?" he said.

That was true enough. But I didn't want to go into it. For a few minutes, though, I couldn't stop him, because it explained how he came to be at No.18 with her and taking me out for a meal.

He told me his afternoon's story, about seeing her drop a grapefruit on an escalator in a shopping Mall and how he followed her, and watched her – I couldn't understand why – and then the part about helping her when she was accused by a security person and fainted, and the taxi journey. But I had a feeling he wasn't telling me everything.

There were unexplained motives in his actions – though I wouldn't have thought he was trying to get off with her and you could say he had behaved very thoughtfully towards Sonia. All the same, I was I was glad when he finished his account and said he wanted to talk about William's class, which was why he'd been in the store that afternoon – except he didn't really elaborate on that reason over dinner in Godneau's, which was strange. That was only clear later.

When we reached coffee stage I looked over at poor Godneau, the only other person in the room, drumming his fingers on his silent cash register and sighing, the kind of sigh you do by drawing a long deep breath and then exhaling even more slowly. So when Frank gave me an intent sideways glance across our window table I felt he must be sharing my pity for Godneau and preparing to say something about him as he reached for his wallet to pay the bill. But no, he wanted to speak seriously about something else.

"I have been thinking a lot," he assured. "In recent weeks, events in life have been coming together for me in a rather strange way. There was meeting you in this restaurant originally – and hearing about what William Bridgnorth was doing, having known about him in the past and recently seen him again. And then there was meeting someone outside William's flat…"

I waited with some anxiety for whatever he was going to say next. But to my relief he didn't appear to have come to any worrying conclusions about this train of circumstances, because he stopped there, smiled, and changed the subject a little: "As for William, though, I am very eager to join the class, and do my best for him. Will you please tell him that from me?"

I'd been thinking about Sonia, and listening to Frank, and was about to promise to give William that undertaking when my attention was seized by something different. I had been noticing two quite large dogs passing and re-passing the window, sometimes hanging around for a moment or two and sniffing at the gutters, then moving away, then coming into sight again. These were strays obviously, though not mongrels – they still showed signs of their former owners' care. Their coats had not very long ago been trimmed, but now they had an abandoned look. The incredible thing was I believed I recognised one of these animals from an assignment ten days before.

A very tall, erect, black man now suddenly made his way along the pavement across the screen of our window from right to left. He was leading, or being pulled by, a heavy dog on a short, taut lead and had to half-run to keep up with this straining creature. But he didn't seem to mind, and maybe this was an evening ritual. Then his dog stopped, immediately in front of us. It stood there with its lead slackening in its owner's hand, and it barked. From our left the two earlier dogs reappeared and attacked it, all three barking and growling and leaping and the largest appearing the equal of the other two together. But two dogs are more mobile than one, and things looked bad for the black man's animal. He was vigorously but in vain tugging on its lead, shouting a name in a pointless attempt to drag it away from the melee.

"Ackerley! Ackerley!"

I had to try to help, especially as none of the three looked the sort of dog liable to savage a human being. They were more intent on injuring each other, for no clear reason except that their purpose in existing was to be aggressive dogs. So I got up too quickly for Frank to restrain me, ran to the door, pulled it open, and called "Toby, Toby!" Then, remembering what I had called him to distinguish him from his possible father, I tried, "Young Toby!" And the extra word worked.

"Young Toby, you must do as you are told", I announced in a passable pentameter.

He looked at me and barked. And stopped barking, as did his companion. The latter was not going to approach me, but Young Toby was. Out of breath and looking in a way relieved to be distracted from this obsessed attack on the other dog, he trotted over to me as a friend, for patting and praise – for obedience, not for violent behaviour. "Is he yours?" The owner of the large dog made it an accusation.

"No!" I said. Fact. But I wasn't going to explain, in case responsibility for Young Toby was planted on me.

"Off, boy. Off!" I commanded. This worked also.

"Thank you." It really meant, "That was the least you could do." To his own dog he said, "Come on, Ackerley", and they walked away in the direction from which they had arrived.

"That was well done," Frank assured me when I returned. I felt my working experience with dogs was paying off.

There were days, though, when I wondered what was happening to me. Had the pressure, the madness, of working for Hemingway and Faulkner over these intensive weeks got to me? I'd been drawn into William's verse classes as a diversion, but I absolutely could not try to describe them to Aurelia and Sonia and Rick, let alone tell them that I was in the middle of persuading Jake – and now Frank – into taking them up, for reasons of their own. I could imagine Aurelia's face. My fellow-lodgers (and friends) wouldn't believe what I thought: that my leisure pursuits were at least as sane as anything else I was doing in life, probably saner. I had followed up William's innocent little advert in a desperate attempt to find something to do in life when I dreaded finding myself unemployable in any sane capacity – that was a dread which the lunacy of the Laughter Studio and the despair of TheEndemic restaurants only increased.

Aurelia always, and Sonia sometimes and Rick occasionally, were keen to hear about my experiences at work. For a start I told them about the charter airline HandF had put me onto at my interview as a test of my "creative thinking". Air Glendower had consulted HandF about failing to get enough passengers to break even, when they thought they had the perfect recipe for a novel kind of niche travel experience. The company flew out of a remote airport in a mountainous region of central Wales to destinations – which I'd better not name – claiming to offer good inexpensive hotel and self-catering accommodation with the advantage of direct flights. With old but smartly refurbished carriers they could make the travel time alone a uniquely attractive proposition. It should have brought in lots of people who complained about the cramped discomfort, costly food and general lack of civilised facilities on most low-cost airlines. Air Glendower produced haute cuisine of "supreme" standard, everything freshly cooked onboard in their "superGalley" as they called it and served up in lush cinema-style seats in front of individual screens showing the latest film releases. On long-haul flights there was a Niteflite Club, which meant a live cabaret (Business) section at the far end, and in one aircraft they provided their proudest offer, a Multisex HyperSauna with male or female attendants, all services available. Order for vintage wines – from an amazing list – would be taken at the check-in desk, and the bottles brought up from their special "cellar" in the cargo space before take-off. I was not to receive any free trips, only given access to their online publicity and shown some hard copy material, to analyse and comment upon. One of my conclusions was that their name didn't help. I suggested "perfectAir."

"Yes, that's a brill start", said one of the two guys at HandF.

I knew from the way he said it that he meant the opposite. "But there's a problem you haven't noticed?" (Everything he said was, literally, projected like a question).

"What problem?" I asked at once, having learned to challenge these people. They expected it.

"The only places they've got the licences to fly to are crap resorts? What they want is not us. They need an agency to redesign their advertising."

"Not better destinations?" I suggested.

"The fucking destinations don't matter," came the reply. "Get the publicity right and you can forget them?"

I decided when I knew that William wanted to have us telling chunks of our life stories in verse as part of his advanced course that I would give an account of some of my experiences with Hemingway and Faulkner. Just as Jake would – as he told me over a dinner with wine one evening – reveal all about his treatment for sexual dysfunction in the foreign hospital – and Frank (I knew eventually, but not yet) would let us in on his years of kleptomania.

A few evenings after that night when Sonia turned up at the door with Frank I was on my own with no work to finish off or prepare, and cash was getting really desperate because HandF had produced no expenses at all, despite my having delivered all my receipts, and forms I'd filled in detail. I knew there was no food in the cupboard, and I couldn't see myself borrowing from Aurelia to go out and buy something when I was behind with the rent.

I closed the door of No.18 firmly, a habit of mine to make it known who has come in – I never call out anything to the others. I listened, and there was no sound of Sonia in the house, but Aurelia's voice did a pretty weary call of "Hi, Merly! Want some coffee?" She could either tell it was me by the way I closed the door or else she knew Sonia and Rick were already in. She was sitting in the kitchen turning over the pages of a sporting magazine. "Sonia's dead again", she said now. "There's coffee in the thing."

I could see it bubbling, but I didn't feel like any. I was sorry to know Sonia was unwell – or that was what I assumed. I would go up and see her. Aurelia's first cold remark delayed me telling her anything about my day, and her next words assured me I wanted to get away from her as soon as possible.

"Merly!" she said. Very neutrally. No warmth.

All right, I would have some coffee, because I sensed what was coming. It wouldn't be welcome after a day spent trying to be the smart consultant and all I wanted to do was get out of these business clothes.

"Mm?"

"It's the 13th already." She said it with that nearly horizontal smile she has, and that bright-eyed expression she always used when forcing herself to look pleasant.

"Oh I know. Look — I'm sorry. I thought I could manage something by now. I will –"

"When you can? Please. I'm having a really shitty month with the budget."

Aurelia, with everyone's agreement, conducted all the dealings with the landlord. We'd thought – to be honest – we'd been rather ingenious to let the one of us earning the highest salary – the real businesswoman – send in the monthly rent and collect it from the others. Sonia usually did it on the first day of the month but Rick often had to be reminded. I'd kept it up fairly well so far, but my small pot of savings from vacation jobs and Dad's birthday gifts was shrinking fast and I had a loan instalment to meet, debited direct and giving the bank an opportunity to charge for an overdraft.

I stood there in our (former) Happy Room, which is what we used to call our communal kitchen when we moved in, and cupped the cooling black coffee in my hands and almost gave up. What could I say?

"It ought to be all right by next week," I said. And Aurelia's straight-smiling silence was worse than if she'd gone on talking about this rent. It occurred to me yet again that there was nothing like living with friends for finding out what they were really like – except Aurelia was really a very recent acquaintance.

Rick's footsteps on the stairs were never a welcome sound at this sort of hour because he always reached the early evening full of energy, probably the result of going to bed late after working in the store and sleeping a long time. When he bounded into the kitchen now he seemed at first to be in his tiresome mood because he began to talk – whatever anyone else might be in the middle of saying – about nothing we could possibly be interested in, special offers for sporting events or something, which he chose to regard as very funny. But he provided a relief from Aurelia.

He moved in the direction of the coffee machine to pour himself some. Then he did something significant which Aurelia didn't see. He looked at me and pointed up to the ceiling and raised his eyebrows. This, not an offer of free tickets for Great Year Hockey, could have been the real reason for Rick coming down as soon as heard me come home. I understood at once and don't think Aurelia noticed me nodding at him to agree. In a few minutes' time I would knock on his door quietly and join him for a private talk, most likely about Sonia.

If Sonia was happily wanting to be by herself she would put a post-it on her bedroom door saying something like "She's asleep" or "She's pretending to work", words written in a speech bubble coming out of the mouth of a little animal. If there was nothing on her door and it was closed and she was known to be in – during the daytime, that is, because Sonia was never out after ten-thirty at night – it usually meant she wasn't well and didn't even feel like leaving a message to tell people to leave her in peace.

When I passed Sonia's closed door a couple of minutes after this there was certainly no notice. She was in, and not eating (there wasn't anything), and feeling too low to be seen at around seven on a light summer night.

Rick's door was half-open.

"Don't close it," he murmured. "It would look like we were conspiring."

To our relief we heard a small cry of "Later!" from downstairs and knew Aurelia had gone out for the evening, probably for dinner because she'd shown no concern about supplies. Therefore we could talk unheard, though I should now close the door in case Sonia was awake and realised we were in conference about her.

"Look. What I'm worried about–"

He stopped. And suddenly I knew again that I really liked Rick, not loved but liked very much despite grumbling about his tiresomeness as a friend to live with. That made it more practical if we had problems on our hands. His awkward pause showed he didn't want to talk about Sonia because she was a friend, but he felt he had to. Rick wasn't somebody to talk about nothing for the sake of it.

"What I'm worried about is – she seems disturbed about something, but wouldn't let on if we asked."

"Disturbed… In the same way as before?"

"Maybe".

"This evening? Now?"

"Earlier. I think she's asleep now."

We paused and fidgeted before I risked the next question.

"How do you know? Anything you've seen?"

"I think I heard."

Then he shrugged as if to say there was nothing we could do except to try to understand Sonia and help. And perhaps protect.

"When I came in I heard Aurelia saying to her – this thing again about – 'You're getting distant' and 'You're drifting away from me.' They were in the kitchen and I couldn't hear exactly. Suddenly Sonia's running up to her room – slamming the door. Then there's silence for a long time, so I find a reason for going past – and I hear this –" He hesitated. "I don't know. Sort of moaning." As he said that, he turned his head aside.

"You didn't go in?"

Rick shook his head impatiently, as if that were impossible and how could I have asked him? But I was suddenly aware of my hunger and getting impatient with the situation.

"We could knock and go in together now if she's awake, and see if she wants to eat."

"There is nothing," he said. We didn't knock.

With what Rick lent me I went to the corner minimarket for half-a-dozen eggs to make the inevitable omelette, and for some sliced bread. We still left Sonia alone and silent in her bedroom, perplexed about her, guilty to be eating by ourselves. As we finished, still feeling hungry, her door opened. We were silent as she came downstairs yawning and joined us in the kitchen where there had only been one egg left out of six, the remains of the loaf, and the last scrapings of margarine in a tub.

Sonia looked at the table and sighed.

"Oh, wait a minute," she said.

She went back to her room and returned with a bunch of four bananas and an unwrapped chunk of very fresh cheese. Not luxury, but it really helped. There was now no way Rick and I could talk to her about anything.

13

Merlinda was not so much reticent with Jake Coleman and Frank Winterfield about how she had found each of them for William Bridgnorth – as totally and deliberately uncommunicative. There was no reason either should want to know, and the lack of knowledge increased the respect each had for the other, whom they only met in the classes; until the day of the Fun Parade. As the regular meetings advanced towards the climax of their three individual "performances" William congratulated her so lavishly on her perception in spotting natural talent and her skill in encouraging it that she even began to wonder whether her future lay in recruitment for fields such as this more than in the consultancy profession.

His rule was that as time went by, during this sinisterly tropical season in a London of organised jubilation, all his students should speak iambic pentameters for spells of increasing length, so as to prepare for the performance of substantial personal narratives in verse. Finally, a full afternoon class devoted to each one of three autobiographical exercises in this form would be given by Frank Winterfield, Merlinda Cassell and Jake Coleman. But no one other than the last (inevitably) would know his or her scheduled date in advance, to ensure that they would be ready to deliver spontaneously. It would put them to the severest of tests, and were they prepared to submit themselves to the discipline? If they required time to think about it, William was willing for them to have it. After due consideration they could report an ultimate, understandable reluctance to continue, and withdraw with dignity. But having stayed so long and committed themselves so deeply, none of them did in fact opt to reconsider, let alone withdraw. Besides, where as late as this would a replacement have been found?

Duly they accepted from William three dates on the first of which they would draw lots for one student to begin.

* * *

It was clear that William had the highest hopes of this afternoon, the first of the three occasions on which one of us (but which?) was going to be required to take the leap and tell the others the extended story he – or she – had prepared about a personal experience. William had obviously been out earlier today to the unknown bakery somewhere up the King's Road where he purchased his cakes, because a shining clean white box was set squarely on the table in front of the white wall which displayed the iambic pentameters, and there were plates and knives beside it. It was a sign that he saw this as an extremely special occasion.

What were we three signed-up students, or guests, of William Bridgnorth thinking about each other as we sat down in his deep old armchairs on that stifling afternoon while London geared up for all the ceremonies of the latest Great Year? What would the authorities have thought of our interpretation of the philosophy of Fun which the entire population was encouraged – largely compelled – to adopt?

"I seem to think that we have all agreed," William suddenly declared, with an amiable smile that still suggested a vigorous hour or more ahead for the one who drew the lot, "that he – or she – who draws the fateful slip/ will earn the privilege of going first,/ and have the rest of this warm afternoon/ to give us an account in best blank verse/ of some intriguing aspect of their lives./ Although, you may begin with a few words/ in prose to introduce what you intend/ to offer us."

Here he produced from his pocket a tiny polished wooden box, which he shook so that we could all hear folded slips of paper rattling modestly inside it. Everything about William was ceremonious when he wanted it to be, but relaxed if he chose that. This procedure of drawing lots was utterly formal. I think each of us was by now fully prepared to speak from our prose notes, and we sat there with folders of papers on our laps – William had excluded anything involving computer technology because he thought that manipulating such devices while we spoke would interrupt the flow of our narratives. We were permitted to speak dramatically when we wished to, the iambic pentameter being, after all, the vehicle of the greatest drama in our language But he expected us also to be fluent and to sound spontaneous and relaxed, using blank verse as what it was: the natural manner of speaking which lay just below the surface of the English language as spoken daily by everyone in this third decade of the twenty-first century.

Now he rose very solemnly from his chair, raised the lid of the box, and offered it to me first! I was torn. First I really wanted to find an instruction to begin on the opened slip of paper, so as to get the challenge over. Then, when I saw it was a blank I had this tremendous rush of relief. I was so glad I wasn't starting. William was silent. His face revealing nothing, he turned to Jake. For a second I thought Jake might be losing his nerve because he looked very hesitant about taking one of the two remaining slips. He looked at William, then slowly at me and Frank in turn, as if needing encouragement to go on. But we didn't say a word. Then Jake laughed – and what an odd sound a lone nervous laugh makes in circumstances like this – and put out a trembling hand to the open box.

When he'd opened the folded scrap of paper, Jake stood there holding it in front of him gazing at William. William could see as well as Jake what was written on it, but I couldn't. There was no doubting in that second, though, that Jake had "won."

William now sat down again.

"Read it out, if you would, we'd like to hear," he pronounced. Jake obliged, but I'd never heard him utter anything so falteringly.

"'You have the privilege of starting this'", was what we heard him say. Then, "May I sit down?"

William nodded, and Jake sat, and lost his notes down the side of his chair, and uncrossed his legs and stood up again and found his papers, and shuffled them.

"I want us all to realise," he said, "that this is going to be a sketchy account of a visit I made to Northern Europe during the winter of 20– trying to get an answer to a psychological problem which has been troubling me for a long time. I need to be frank about it and I hope you won't be embarrassed or offended. I shall be exposing some weak parts of my character, and I hope it can all be kept absolutely confidential?"

Everybody consented to this. I think we were all the more eager to hear Jake now he had made this confession. I looked at William. He had composed himself in a comfortable listening position, an elbow on each arm of his armchair and hands held completely still together, face utterly impassive. I don't know that he moved an inch during what followed, which lasted something approaching two hours.

The room was silent. The block was silent. The street outside was silent. Jake Coleman began.

[Note: It would do Jake Coleman no service, given the courage he showed with his performance, to provide verbatim the several hundred iambic pentameters in which he couched his story. William Bridgnorth praised it powerfully – and not solely to encourage Jake – as "a remarkable endeavour", and was prepared to overlook the imperfections in the verse. To reproduce those here would not be appropriate. Mr Coleman's substantial blank verse narrative has therefore been "edited" into prose, and also rendered in the third person at his request – to spare him, as he maintained, "the pain of hearing the detail of my problems given in my own voice. The third person makes it sound more distant and detached, not my own misfortunes but another man's case study."]

14

REMEMBER YOUR HEALTH was the injunction on all the booklets Jake Coleman saw on the hospital rack the day before his discharge. He could "Know About" asthma, avoiding prostate problems, organising cardiac convalescence. But he looked in vain for advice about his own experience. The matter of "Remembering" itself was Jake's problem.

There was a general booklet about obsessive disorders, but it was thin and vague about Jake's. The author, a Dr Derrick Bassetlaw, featured it in only one paragraph, which amounted to a confession of ignorance. But Bassetlaw did happen usefully to mention that a little research into the more arcane psychiatric afflictions such as Chronic Associative Disorder was, he gathered, going on in a remote resort in the post-Communist far Baltic region. Nowhere in the UK.

Jake liked his consultant, Wirelny, who said that Jake's kind of abstruse condition could become a hobby of his if he had time. He certainly made extensive notes at each of their one-to-one sessions, and promised to be in touch if he heard of anything helpful to tell him. Meanwhile there was the resting, the tranquillisers, the consultations any good psychotherapist could provide. "Try the internet?" Jake wondered. Wirelny smiled. "Visit the diagnosed disorder closest to yours, and find 30,000 useless sites. It was easier when we only had to search a haystack for the needle." What about the "far Baltic" place? Jake opened Dr Bassetlaw's booklet at the relevant page. Wirelny raised his large eyebrows and nodded. "Well, I know Bassetlaw, it's true," he said. "I can probably find out where that is." Then he suddenly became discouraging. "But you should be sure you feel sufficiently recovered before you embark on an expedition. Leave it for a few months and consider it again."

Jake believed that, as it would be winter by then, Wirelny assumed he would forget the idea altogether. The doctor might feel responsible for sending him on an expensive trip that would prove useless, even harmful.

And yet Wirelny actually bothered to be very decent. When Jake went back for an outpatient's visit three week later he received from the doctor not only an e-mail address for the Baltic clinic but a reference for an article in an American medical journal, by one Dr Mikhail Erznik, an expert in just this affliction. This impressed Jake and touched him, and with the invested money from the sale of his father's business coming through – at despicably low rates of interest – he could afford to make the trip.

And he would, winter or no winter.

* * *

Gradually the snowy landscape changed. Small pinewoods became forests, and were followed by long open stretches. In the distance Jake Coleman could see eerie hills and darkening clouds from the window of this small compartment in which he sat alone. So far on this journey no disturbing intricacies of association had occurred to worry him. The weather might be very cold but the train was warm, the buttoned carriage-cloth, as he believed this old-fashioned upholstery was known, was comfortable. He congratulated himself on venturing to come.

At every small town or village stop a uniformed stationmaster or –mistress saluted them in and out again. The tall, self-possessed young woman performing this office at one township was so amazingly, imperially handsome and sexually overwhelming that Jake wrote down the name of the place in his diary: Uzjarvi. In his memory she connected in appearance and manner with no woman from his past, and it was reassuring that he felt no fears about resolving to remember her.

An ordinary tourist phrase-book might have proved more practical than this, which had ambitions of making the serious reader proficient in the language in three months; Jake's three hours with the book had given him only a few courteous but inaccurate phrases – with the exception of one helpful category of usages.

"Forgive me, you proceed the Seven Sources Hotel? It is a medical resort", he asked the taxi driver outside the station in the fallen winter darkness.

"Hotel Seven Springs? In you get, Major, five minutes at most," the man replied colloquially, in his own language, naturally. Jake grasped nothing of that except the word "hotel" and the good-humoured title, which had been accorded him for the first time since he arrived. The phrase-book had, early on, provided a list of military ranks, to help visitors with a traditional habit practised by taxi-drivers, shopkeepers, waiters and others in addressing customers and clients. They often gave you a military title out of courtesy. It somewhat resembled the affable, antiquated English "Guv'nor" or "Squire", but was employed much more frequently, almost systematically. It could, though, suggest a rapid appraisal, by the user, of the rank actually merited by the person addressed, and sometimes be used ironically.

At Reception Jake was already reduced in status from the cab-driver's "Major" by the young male clerk who looked up sharply when he made to speak to the girl beside him. He produced a very large form for him to complete, dropping a ballpoint across it with a curt snap.

"Fill in everything please, Captain," he said, fingering all available spaces.

"Mr Gentleman", said Jake, using the most archaically polite form he had learnt, "you need everything?"

"Yep. The lot I'm afraid... Captain." The pause before the repetition of the title was not polite. It implied a reluctance to use any courtesy at all. Jake saw the girl, whom he suddenly realised was hugely desirable, smile quietly and raise her eyebrows with sympathy at her colleague's curtness. He saw from her identity disc that she was "Melanita", and had unusually soft auburn hair falling over shoulders clothed in a sepia blouse – a luminous, fetching shade of sepia.

Jake believed that you know the moment you enter a hotel room whether you can put up with it for however long is necessary. 327 in the Hotel Seven Springs was almost opposite the lifts, but well soundproofed, and spacious. He was a good judge of beds. Here there was a comfortable-looking double bed with plenty of pillows reducing the cold look of a plain pine bedboard. It took up no more than a fifth of the space, which was good. The two deep armchairs had arms with useful flat surfaces on which most things could be set down without immediately falling onto the floor. The window overlooked a wide courtyard where a single lamp lit up the frost-covered plants and shrubs. He believed that he could feel private and comfortable here for the three weeks of his treatment.

"Chronic Associative Disorder", or CAD, was the term attached to Jake's illness in the recent study in the American journal printed out for him by Dr Wirelny. Four cases were provided, but unfortunately none closely resembling Jake's. As he re-read it yet again, he wondered whether he himself was not simply cursed with a wider imagination and a better memory than others. Their problems were much more like ordinary, familiar phobias. He began to fear that his journey might have been in vain; but he enjoyed foreign places and would stay.

The first necessity was to get familiar with the hotel. He found three regular ways of reaching Reception and Melanita. A right turn out of his door took him to what he privately called the Grand Staircase, a wide, crimson-carpeted descent which gave him a feeling of imperial importance. Going left gave him the Discreet Stairs, much narrower, steeper, covered in linoleum, mainly a hotel staff route. Straight ahead were the two spacious lifts and their mirrors, the words (in this language) REMEMBER YOUR HEALTH prominent on the wall in each.

Jake began to make a ritual of using each of these routes alternately on his way to the restaurant or out into the town, approaching Melanita from different sides in turn. That caused her to smile with a charming feigned surprise, which increased his hope; and he studied the phrase-book for useful social phrases. He started to leave his small room key with her each time he went out – not strictly necessary, but it was a reason for thanking her and smiling each time he came back. Also exchanging the odd word or two. She always smiled. Perhaps his English accent pleased her, one never knew.

"Pleasing you, carbonated water of the source," he said to the waiter in the restaurant on his first night. The man looked bewildered, then exclaimed, "Oh, you mean the fizzy stuff, Colonel? Right you are." In Jake's hand was something he had suddenly become very curious about, Wirelny's sealed and confidential letter to whoever here could read it in English, in an envelope only very lightly glued. Handled with care, a thin-bladed dinner knife could open it and leave enough adhesive for re-sealing.

The contents surprised him greatly. Wirelny had written a covering note to a longer, typed letter signed by Dr Derrick Bassetlaw, no less, in the language of this very country, with translator's name added under the scrawled signature. Plainly Wirelny had deferred to Bassetlaw's eminence in order to obtain a full translated account of Jake's affliction from the one English authority on it. He did not like the word "psychozomatik" – he

100

had not come all this way to be received as a hypochondriac. But he was impressed by what the National Health Service was even now capable of doing for him.

Inside the large white door in the East Courtyard corridor declaring (he assumed) "Medical Department for Specialised Diseases" was a desk where he presented himself at eight-thirty next morning. It was still dark outside. "Speak you English?" he enquired of one of the two women's faces, pale and blue in the light from their screens. She looked up myopically, as if seeing a human face was most unusual. "This is from doctor mine in England." She opened it, read it, said nothing, rose and walked away with it indifferently.

"Dr Erznik will see you right away," she said when she returned. "Second on the left." He understood nothing, so she led him impatiently through to where the doctor's name appeared in commanding letters on a door which –

But – Erznik? That was the name of the author of the article he had been sent by Wirelny. He had not realised that Erznik himself was from this country and he soon found out that he had indeed been a Visiting Professor in the United States when he wrote it.

Jake Coleman found himself looking at a very big, thickly-bearded, broadly-smiling man wearing a magenta cape round his shoulders, indicating very senior medical rank. Dr Mikhail Erznik shook his hand with painful vigour, motioned him to sit, and picked up the letter.

"I am not familiar with the name of your consultant", he said, establishing his superiority from the start, perhaps; and he spoke in fast, fluent English, perfect except in only a few common expressions. A great relief.

"But there is a letter from Dr Bass–" Jake began.

"Yes, there is. And how did you know?" Caught out. "No matter. To business – Br-rigadier!" His tone was good-humoured, jokingly parodying the eccentric national custom; he never used a title again in addressing Jake. But Jake sensed a slight reprimand for opening the letter and prying into the secret ways of doctors. "We can narrow this down. You are what we can call a C-A-D – a Cad – yes? A sufferer from Chronic Associative Disorder?" Jake nodded. "It qualifies in some respects as an Obsessive Compulsive Disorder, but in other ways it is different. It is exclusively sexual in nature?" "Yes." "And nothing compels you to repeat and complete an action. But the unforeseen repetition of an experience, or a memory of an unfortunate experience, or even the sight of some attribute of a woman that evokes an experience can produce impotence, nausea, even dizziness and loss of consciousness?"

Jake now nodded very firmly. Erznik had the right idea. "Something to which we might apply the term 'Total Sexual Recall Syndrome'. You have been treated by sedation, tranquillisation – if there is the word – and bed rest in a quiet, very plain room, no pictures, no newspapers. Temporarily you forget the associations. But of course they return. Here we shall not try conventional British methods. We propose to enumerate and confront your personal memories and associations and render them irrelevant to the attraction or the novelty – or the durability – of any fresh sexual experience."

Jake Coleman saw Melanita, her welcoming smile, the sepia blouse. Dr Erznik rang a bell on his desk.

"Behind the screen," he commanded. "Only the top for now."

"The top?"

"I am asking you to undress to your waist."

When Jake emerged, the assistant from reception had arrived to take his blood pressure and Erznik was ready with a stethoscope.

"What do you associate with this?" He was pressing the cold disc against various points on Jake's chest and back. Every question and reply would now be translated for the nurse to note it down. "Does it call up any ominous memories?"

"No. I don't understand why it –"

"I may be impolite? We are going to look into many deep corners. You never recollect you fuck a doctor or a nurse?"

"No."

"I don't like to use such words so often. It weakens them. Your great Professor Tolkien once said 'Usage burns away a word.' Hence Harry Potter never 'fucks'. Over to your right, on the wall." The disc felt even colder pressed on Jake's heart region. "There is the photograph of the High School Girls' Handball Team. Last year their achievement matched their beauty. Not usually the case. Any reaction?"

Jake looked as instructed for a few moments, and thought about it.

"Not really." The schoolgirls carrying hockey sticks in the High Street on the Wednesdays of his adolescence did not count as a disturbing memory.

"Good. My daughter is in the picture."

He opened a drawer and the nurse prepared to tick boxes on a sheet. Out of a file he took a thick stratum of photographs which he placed in front of Jake one by one.

"Tell me, please, your degree of apprehension on a scale of one to five in each case, and give me the number on the back. If you experience no fears, say nothing but still tell me the number."

There were topless film stars, banal swimwear beauties, resentful lingerie demonstrators, catwalkers who had had their muscles lightly anaesthetised to remove any danger of smiling, female martial arts demonstrators. Whenever Jake murmured "Yes" or "Possibly" and "One" or "Four", the nurse noted the numbers. At the end she handed Erznik the completed sheet and left in silence as if for a comparable duty somewhere else. The doctor looked at them thoughtfully, and said, "A very helpful start. Yes… Yes." He wrote on a pad. "I shall give you a little physio-behavioural therapy to begin with – on the bicycle in the Blank Room, given that you have no associations evoked by girl cyclists. Followed by a viewing session in our cinema. Then an hour in a comfortable room with a ceiling and a microphone. You can take your full daily schedule from Hotel Reception in –" he looked at his watch – "one hour and a half."

How to pass these ninety minutes of suspense while waiting to see what these treatments involved? He made going out for coffee in the city an excuse to descend the Discreet Stairs and pass Melanita.

"I go out now," he observed, putting his key down in front of her slowly.

"I can see that," she replied. Her smile was still coming in his direction when he turned round at the swing door.

But the coffee house visit was not a success. A brusque girl at the counter couldn't understand his simplest request, and called him Sergeant". He made his way back to the Seven Springs at least forty minutes too soon. Or so he thought, because Melanita handed him a sheet of paper with an official stamp on it; and the key to his room with the usual encouraging smile.

So now he was contemplating the prospect of the stationary bicycle in the Blank Room, a small but airy cube of plainness in which patients were encouraged to free associate while pedalling themselves into improved physical health and get any distressing thoughts into perspective.

He had never been a cyclist. He mounted the hard saddle with caution, gripped the handles determinedly, fixed his feet on the rubber pedals, pressed down so that they began to turn heavily – and suddenly, it was beyond his power to stop them. But no associations occurred to him. The empty walls suggested nothing, no after-images from the past reared up on them. When, after twenty minutes of this, the young male attendant stopped him, he had to mark on a sheet the degree of anxiety he had experienced, on a scale from 0 to 10. Happily he ticked "0.5", and where there was space for comments he wrote nothing.

For his second treatment he was sent to find what Erznik had called "the Cinema". Seated on a hard wooden chair he was shown, this time, photographic images that moved briefly on a screen. Sometimes these were sequences of action, and he was to call out "Yes" if any stirred him to connect them with personal experiences. Therefore he declared "Yes", with some degree of distress, when a shop assistant smiled, and invited a man to enter a cubicle for trying on some trousers. As he manoeuvred himself awkwardly into them and looked at himself in a mirror, the camera cut repeatedly to the woman's face smiling in approval. And this undoubtedly recalled for Jake someone called -- if he remembered correctly – Gemma, in a place in Oxford Street.

The barmaids, the waitresses, a uniformed woman ticket inspector on a swaying train, a huge-breasted discus thrower yielding to the elaborate embraces of her coach... They all passed by while Jake remained silent. Then a youngish, short-skirted blonde librarian appeared, under high shelves of leather-bound books, chatting on a cellphone. She was wearing thick spectacles. The resemblance was astonishing, and he bellowed "Yes!" with real pain. If the likes of this Jennifer ever reappeared in his sex life, especially among books in a library or shop, it would be a profoundly traumatic event. The liaison with her had taken place entirely behind enormous shelves of classical literature – Frontinus on Roman aqueducts, Columella on agriculture and so on. Jake was not by any means a reader of classical literature but because of Jennifer he remembered those names from looking over her shoulder. Jennifer had lost her job because one day a reader, unnoticed in the library before this happened, turned one of the big handles of the mobile shelves and trapped the two of them, so that an alarm had to be activated before they could be released.

The doctor had promised a "calm and simple" conclusion to each morning's treatment. Jake Coleman had to go to the Ordinary Chamber, a warmer and more comfortable place where he almost literally "sank" into a padded armchair, gaped at a bare sepia wall, and related the plot of any sexual association that occurred at random. Later Erznik would listen to recordings of what Jake told the microphone given him by a girl who sat behind a small window and ran the tapes. He stated at once that the sepia colour of the walls here did remind him of a woman in a fetching sepia blouse. He did not name Melanita; but she had changed into a dark blue sweater by that evening.

"The blonde librarian," said Erznik next morning in the course of his first brief daily check on Jake's sessions. "Is the mobile phone important? No? Good. We can narrow this down to any blonde, bespectacled librarian of, shall we say, under thirty-five – a less numerous class? Excellent. I feared for a moment that it might be any young woman using a mobile." He shrugged in mock despair. "In that case we would have been into a pathless jungle indeed."

He had now undergone a whole week of treatments, suffered a dreary week-end when Melanita was not at Reception, walked the icy, snow-covered streets and squares alone, returned to the coffee-house where he had become known and sat there longer, tried an excellent-looking restaurant where ignorance of the language and sheer confusion had delivered him a spicy stew he could not finish, arriving finally to receive Erznik's interim report on the same kind of dark Monday morning as the last.

He had no idea what the doctor would tell him, but he knew what he was telling himself. After a week here, the tall Melanita with the wonderful legs (judging from his occasional glimpses of them) was stamped irremoveably on his consciousness. Jake intended to exploit the safety of a country, a town and a hotel where no past association had returned in a really distressful form (in fact, one or two had been briefly evoked by the treatment and successfully exorcised by it: it would be unnecessary in future to be afraid of approaching blonde librarians). He was going to try his luck with Melanita, whom he had seen on his way back from breakfast.

He noticed the difference between the smiles she gave him and the unsmiling courtesy she produced for other guests. Once she did grant him another smile, a wild little expression of humorous surprise and delight, widening her eyes to take the key he was handing in as if it were a present. Then, when he returned to claim a key she would find some way of denying it to him: taking it from its hook and hiding it behind her back, concealing it in one of two closed hands and asking him to guess which, even giving him the wrong key once, which he noticed immediately.

"Judging by these data," said Erznik correctly, consulting his papers, "you are responding well. We appear to have helped you quite a lot already. But as you are a man with – if I may say so – a large variety of sexual inclinations, there are numerous other avenues to explore. We shall therefore increase the range of images we present you with."

Leaving Dr Erznik's room he made straight for Reception with a plan in mind: he would invite Melanita out to dinner. But at this moment she was not there. Outside snow was falling thickly and the sky was darkening moment by moment. The ceiling lights flashed on with enhanced brilliance as he went on a time-killing walk along various long corridors. But ten minutes later she was still not at her counter. So he sauntered with pretended casualness towards the lift, pressed the Up button and waited for the changes in the lighted panel above the door to tell him it was condescending to rise from the basement to the lower ground floor and up to this level.

When it arrived and the doors opened, Melanita was in it. She was alone, and for some reason continuing upwards. Jake pressed the button for the third floor, his own destination.

She was even taller than she appeared to be when sitting at Reception, and he confirmed that her lower half, which he had never seen completely before, more than fulfilled the promise of the rest. In this lift he stood well apart from her, there was space enough. She was reflected in all the mirrors. He looked at the real version and smiled. Melanita smiled back, though not quite so readily and mischievously as before. And yet she went on looking at him, and he searched his memory of the *Teach Yourself* for the right words in this situation. All this in about five seconds.

The lift rose very slowly. Between the first and second floors he found the time to venture a remark, and at least remembered some figures.

"My number of room is 327," he said.

"3-2-7. I need to make a careful note of that," Melanita replied, wit a quiet laugh. As if she didn't know it, after about fifty exchanges of its key!

"Tonight is when the finish hour for you?"

"As it happens it's a six-thirty night," she told him. He recognised the time she was quoting.

"At six-thirty you like dinner – my guest – in pleasant restaurant in city?"

106

Melanita didn't seem to fathom that, or pretended not to. He repeated it more slowly, even more politely.

They were standing perhaps six or seven feet apart, Jake not feeling he could move any closer, yet. He was looking at a creature of flawlessly intriguing sexual attractiveness in her new dark blue sweater, and a tight skirt of the same colour down to exactly the level of her knees. He took in all of Melanita from her unusually soft auburn hair down to the polished toes of her shoes, and she was – she was perfect, in every feature and detail, and not to be passed up.

Her silence seemed too long, ominously too long, as they waited for the lift to settle in a position that confirmed the red figure "3" in the panel above the doors. But in it there was time for Melanita to do something. She did it almost as if the lift's adjustment to the precise level at which its doors would open caused her to do it unconsciously. It was no more than this, but it awakened in Jake Coleman a completely irresistible sexual desire for her: Melanita relaxed her left hip and bent her left knee forwards towards him. He saw that knee momentarily emerge from behind the hem of her skirt, and the beauty of the long and substantial thigh above it was emphasised by this small action.

"I'll come to your room – 3-2-7 – at six-forty-five."

For a man as sexually obsessed as Jake Coleman, so experienced in the unpredictable alternation of success and letdown, in the malign or benign – interventions of sickness, weather, power cuts, trains missed or cancelled, he was wholly unprepared for the strange set of events that constituted his relationship with Melanita. Her knock on his door at six forty-five was loud, commanding and – he thought – unmistakeable. When he opened up, she entered the small hallway carrying over an arm a thick coat and a scarf, and smiled; pleasing to see, because she was not about to make some excuse for not going ahead with the evening. Or so he believed.

"Happy is me you agree this," he said. She laid the coat over the back of an armchair – not cluttering the bed, he observed.

"I'm bound to say that there are factors we need to clarify at the start," she said, incomprehensibly for Jake. Because she continued to smile, he believed there was a chance that a small, easy gesture of affection would not be out of place. And she did permit him to take her hand into his, and with his free hand motion her to sit down beside him on the bed; which she did.

"I comprehend nothing of what you say," he began. "But to me this moment is inordinately happy."

"O.K., fine", was Melanita's reply. Then she gave a gay, pealing laugh before adding, "But the first thing I need to say is that I'm not employed in this outfit as part of the therapy. Do you understand me?" She reached across the coverlet, pressed his hand firmly, then released it.

Jake's error now was to read as encouragement a gesture of consolation that was intended to put him in his place – he had recognised the word "therapy", after all. He shifted in Melanita's direction, looked directly and silently into her perfect eyes, and was attempting what he thought was a delicate yet high-powered charm.

"That's marvellous," he said, taking her retreating hand and raising it to his lips. But when he lowered it to the bed again she put it back in her lap.

"Treatment only happens behind the white door," she affirmed. He misunderstood her.

"Closed is my door here very safely," he assured her."

But then he remembered that in his haste to welcome her he had not turned the key in the lock. He jumped up now, wrongly thinking that in referring to a door she was requesting a safeguard against intruders. The look she gave when he returned was nearer the prim expression he had seen her bestow on other people at Reception.

"I am honoured to accept an invitation from you," she said. "But you need to understand that anything more is not on my agenda. In fact I would be in some degree of jeopardy already if it were known that I had called on you."

And yet she did at first allow him to take her hand again as he sat down, somewhat closer to her on the bed than before. It was when he resumed his deep, meaningful gaze into her eyes and moved his lips towards hers that she suddenly recovered all of her resolution and stood up angrily.

"No! I am not hungry, and that's final," she declared, with an unmistakeable determination to leave.

"I am sorry. I understand not. I am thinking you take dinner with me, no more," he protested.

"Well, I am afraid you can think again," she insisted.

She must have noticed that he had come back from the door without the key, and correctly assumed it was still in the lock. Because she now turned it, went out quickly into the corridor, and was pressing the button at the lift doors before he could explain and entreat any further. He knew better than to follow her.

He had got something badly wrong. No amount of practice in suffering this particular variety of humiliation, this specific injury to his pride, had ever accustomed Jake to the searing emptiness as he now closed the door again very quietly and locked it for the second time in five minutes.

On the other hand, he did not think for a moment that he should reproach himself for Melanita's waywardness. And a whole tide of hope would flood in again if some unexpected gesture of regard were once again conferred on him.

Melanita restored Jake's spirits in just that way next morning. As he passed Reception on his way to his treatments (that was strictly unnecessary, but he would try it) she smiled at him as if nothing had happened, giving him the cue to speak the words he had rehearsed.

"I am sorry for our problem to-night – last night."

"There is no need to apologise," she said, something he fully understood from her expression and tone of voice. "I shall telephone you."

At this moment her young male colleague appeared, looked at Jake and murmured suspiciously, "Good morning, lieutenant," but disappeared again.

"At what hour?" Jake asked eagerly.

"Before lunch time."

To his immense satisfaction, and with some excitement, he understood her. It could only be in the hour of the morning that remained after his therapy ended.

He knew about the agony of waiting in a situation like this; a lot of his life had been passed in such tracts of blighted time. He pedalled harder than before on the bicycle, ignored the associations presented to him in the cinema, allowed nothing new to occur to him as he sat, microphone in hand, in the deep armchair. He did not divulge this to the microphone, but this was turning into something frighteningly like love.

The phone rang almost as soon as he closed the door behind him just after noon.

"Good day, this is Melanita from Reception," she said, very officially. "This is in fact my afternoon off. Listen carefully, please. Can you come in half-an-hour – thirty minutes – *thirty* – to my home? I will have a little lunch for us." She was being slow and clear now, and he understood everything. "I live in Arcania Street – Ar – ca – ni- a – near the cathedral. Block Number 2 on the left. Staircase A, second floor, apartment 22. Do you understand that? Is it clear?"

Yes, it was. And it was an astonishing thought. Why should she be doing this? He had seen the street, it was close to the coffee house, he could picture the block itself, he was eagerly writing all this down.

"Come here now. You understand? Repeat for me, what is the street? What is the block?"

He repeated all of these details and had them right.

It was his first, and as it turned out his only, visit to a private home Jake made in this country, in a high tower of workers' flats, one of six blocks along Arcania Street going north. Melanita's impeccable smartness and desirable beauty had not prepared him for this modest location; but then she was certainly a worker and not necessarily well paid by the privatised Hotel Seven Springs.

The daily snow had started, and he was glad to be out of it and into the comparative warmth of the entry hall. When he emerged from the dim glow of the tiny lift onto the landing he could not see a bell at No. 22, and she was some time answering his tentative knocking with one knuckle on the plain wooden door. He could hear footsteps inside, perhaps Melanita chasing round to have things tidy before she let him in. When she did open the door her smile was wide, radiant and reassuring.

She took his hat, coat and scarf and hung them briskly on a stand. She had changed out of her hotel dress and wore a sleek black skirt and sweater.

"Will you drink a little of our brandy?"

He understood this from her gesture at the bottle on the low table set in front of the sofa in this unusually large lounge. This was different…

You do not decline such an offer He sat down on the long sofa, negotiated his way among several large cushions, stretched his legs in the warmth of the room, sipped at the powerful drink, watched Melanita with lusting fascination as she brought small dishes of savouries, salads, butter and bread from the kitchen, with plates, forks and knives. Then she took her place, next to him.

"I am exceedingly proud of this!"

He allowed her to spoon out some of the aubergine salad onto his plate, nodding with approval even before tasting it. Then Melanita began, unpropitiously soon, he thought later, to come to the point.

"I wish to tell you something – of which I am as sure as the fact that it is snowing outside," she began. "I am sure there is no future for me in this country. But your England has hotels and it needs workers."

"England"and "hotels" he heard. "Workers" he grasped when Melanita pointed at herself and ran her fingers over an invisible keyboard.

"Yes, we have in England hotels – and workers from many countries." Now he was beginning to understand.

"Do you have workers from this country?"

He hesitated.

"No. Perhaps. I not know."

They ate their way through further pauses and confusions. Some of the time she seemed to Jake to be telling him about her childhood in this city, the loss of her parents, her underpaid work in the hotel – all this said with melancholy laughter and light touches on his forearm and hand. But finally, and this was a considerable surprise (perhaps she had been learning some in preparation) she spoke to him in primitive English.

"Me is sorry last night – because I think we is friends?" But then she broke off into several sentences in her own tongue before she resumed in English to say, "Please you find me job – in good hotel in London, yes? I learn speak good English for good job in hotel in London."

She took his left hand with her right and her own left hand went to his right knee. It means she had to turn the upper half of her body tantalisingly towards him.

Jake Coleman's first reaction was to fear any kind of inhibiting memory this action might stir. But it didn't. He put out a hand to Melanita's nearer shoulder as she extended her left knee over his lap, and crossed it over his right leg, and pressed him down into the cushions. It gave him, so far, the fullest happiness and the most passionate, unblemished hope he had felt for many months.

"Please – you know in London the Hotel Ritz, the Hotels Hiltons, the two or three of Hiltons. They have many people work at Reception?"

All this was impossible, but the idea that he might somehow organise access to Melanita in London delayed his denial of any hope.

She went on fast, dejectedly in her own language as if he would understand all this, which he did not: "We believed the end of Communism would change my country – and it hasn't. The Communists are still secretly in charge and they have all the money and they make sure everything gets worse. The only answer is to get out."

When she began to sob Jake felt he could put an arm round her back and hug her consolingly. And suddenly she was kissing him on his lips, a short series of hard, insistent little pressures that he wanted to prolong if he could only manage to take her lovely head and the smooth auburn hair into his hands. Should he go farther here, on the sofa, he wondered, or perhaps with these cushions on the floor? Or risk breaking it off and leading her to her bedroom?

There was a knock, or a sort of odd thud, at the window, the weird impact of something. A bird flying into the glass? But no birds were flying anywhere in this snow. It happened again. And again. And Jake realised he was hearing – and, as he turned that way, seeing – a series of snowballs, well aimed at the window from below.

With a growl Melanita pulled herself free from Jake, leaving him trembling and aching on the sofa, and ran to the window exclaiming in English, "You must go!" Then she ran out to the hallway, seized his hat, scarf and coat for him to take, and repeated it: "Go – you go." She put an ear to the lift door. "You no wait! Down the stairs."

He was outside into a blizzard before he could button up his coat, adjust his scarf, pull his hat down over his eyes, walking away in the snowing and blowing air, lifting his feet above drifts which reached well above his ankles.

Jake ate dinner alone in the hotel restaurant – that is, apart from two men he had never seen before who were content with two beers and regular glances in his direction, for no discernible reason. He was striving to analyse what had happened throughout the meal and well on into the small hours. Melanita's coming to London, if not to somewhere as grand as the Ritz, might be contrived because people were increasingly looking to employ foreigners at below the going rate for Britain. But if there was a rival for her affections important enough – even dangerous enough? – to cause him to propel him out of her apartment and down the back stairs, he might be taking a risk, in a foreign country at that, with a culture he did not understand and laws with which he was not familiar.

Nothing at all, no qualm or fear of any kind rooted in unhappy memories of other experiences, had inhibited him. Perhaps Erznik's comprehensive remedies were working? As Jake and Melanita embraced in her warm flat above the snow-blocked city no disabling association had occurred to him, and had there not been someone announcing their presence by snowballing her window…

But next morning Reception was empty, both when he passed it on his way to Dr Erznik's white door and when he returned to it after his morning therapeutic sessions – in which he took care not to mention anything happening the day before. He tried re-approaching it from other directions, as he had been doing so often, but for some reason it appeared to be unstaffed. Other patients he saw waiting there briefly, then giving up with a shrug when no one came out of the inner office.

So after his usual small restaurant lunch what was there to do but tug his galoshes onto his shoes and go out onto the icy pavements for further exercise, perhaps ending up at what had become his habitual coffee house.

Twice he slipped, staggered forward for several paces before he recovered his balance. If he trod in the deep mounds of snow piled up in the gutters he sank in it almost up to his knees, but at least he didn't lose his footing. The hard flurries of snow blinded him as he trudged on, only able to see two yards ahead of him at a time. There were few other people in the streets, so there was space for them to walk without the danger of sliding or cannoning into each other. Then why was this tall, blackly-muffled figure making deliberately towards him in the hill of snow at the side of the carriageway? And why was he stopping Jake Coleman abruptly, rudely with a flat gloved hand on his chest?

"I'm inclined to think we might have a word or two? Agreed?" he exclaimed in his own language.

The interrogative sounds at the end of his phrases, and something similar about his gestures led Jake to think he was being asked for directions.

"It fears me I cannot help with information," he said, with a shivering smile and a wide, amiable shrug. But this was not taken well. The man's face was all but hidden entirely behind the thick scarf and fur hat, but there was a vaguely recognisable look about the eyes, and he was without doubt showing hostility. Over his shoulder Jake could now see standing in a doorway the two beer-drinkers from the hotel restaurant last night.

"On the contrary, corporal, you can help me," he said.

The title seemed icier than the snow which collected on the two of them where they stood. The stranger lifted a hand and brushed some

113

away from his shoulder, and the action was menacing. As he did that the scarf dropped from across his mouth and Jake saw that he was Melanita's young male colleague from Reception.

"You have been diverting yourself with a close friend of mine – even entertaining her in your room. Melanita. And I suspect hanging out in her apartment? Do you understand me? My name is Ferronok, in our language 'will of iron.'" And he said the last three words in English. "I am instructing you now to leave. Not to leave to-night because you would not have time to make the train. But to leave to-morrow, there is a train at 9.47."

Jake understood the words 'to-morrow" and "train" and the time he was being offered. But he had eight or nine days' more treatment with Dr Erznik scheduled. A very few shivering people hurried past, bent against the driving snow. In less than a minute it had thickened again on Ferronok's shoulders, so that when he vigorously brushed away more of it one passing individual noticed the emphatic gesture and stared hard at both of them, obviously suspecting trouble. Then he dipped his head again and walked on.

Jake decided to misinterpret the command as a suggestion, or even a question.

"I end my treatment on 28 this month. I leave end of week the next."

"You leave to-fucking-morrow," Ferronok said in English, with a shocking command of the latest form of football abuse – inserting obscenities not just between words but between syllables. And this time he left no question of his meaning in Jake Coleman's mind by actually hitting him in the chest. Although the blow was softened by his glove and the several layers Jake wore against the cold, it was hard enough to have him staggering to regain his balance.

* * *

The 9.47 moved even more slowly than the afternoon train which had brought him to this winter city and to his curtailed stay in the Hotel Seven Springs. As it advanced with diminishing speed – or increasing caution? – over a snow-hidden landscape from which only low hills, woods, and the occasional silent and abject village would emerge, Jake had plenty of time in which to reflect on his retreat from the only place and doctor in the world apparently addressing his problem. Put very plainly it was, of course, a variety of impotence.

Almost every time Jake Coleman attempted to initiate a process of seduction they would come flooding into his head: the visual, aural, tactile associations with past encounters, usually unsuccessful, which had converted his gallantries into ashes. The brunette in the computer room would ruin his approach to any brunette in a confined space, the tall quiet Norwegian in the long green trousers would recur to haunt a meeting with any tall girl of Scandinavian appearance, especially if she kept her mobile in a small black pouch. The wholly logical and rational man Erznik – who must by now have read Jake's long letter of apology for deserting him after an emergency message from London – was to identify as many specific associations as possible, and eliminate them in a kind of psychotherapeutic exorcism. He argued that it was just not necessary to be inhibited by thoughts of the flat-breasted volleyball player with the unusually elegant thighs if he was with another sportswoman who even faintly resembled her. In the course of just a few full, intensive, odd, revealing and beneficial days Jake had been well on the way, he thought, to a commonsense cure. And now...

He cursed himself in his dejection as the landscape slowly edged past. Then suddenly the train stopped altogether with a heavy shudder on a stretch of flat land where there must have been open roads before the snowfall, but now you could only see poles, signs, and the occasional roof of an abandoned car. Again he was alone in an eight-seat compartment with its decorative embellishment, the faded card in a glass frame above his head, the slogan advising in this foreign language that you REMEMBER YOUR HEALTH, displayed because its destination was a notable health resort. Had he really needed to take Ferronok's threat seriously? He concluded that where you were unsure of the code governing sexual relations, discretion was more advisable than courage; and Ferronok's behaviour had been threatening indeed.

The train shifted forward again with a jerk, uncertainly, after a long sorrowing wail from the engine at the front. Then there came the curiously dismaying sound of footsteps clattering nearer down the corridor. They were those of the ticket inspector, opening the sliding doors of compartments, shouting out something, slamming them again. Now he was at Jake's door.

"Sorry-to-be-bringing-you-this-feedback. Due to heavy snowfalls this service will terminate at Uzjarvi and the next train onwards from Uzjarvi will be at 15.48 to-morrow. Voyagers will be provided with accommodation at the Uzjarvi Station Hotel. We apologise for the inconvenience." Jake understood "terminate", heard "to-morrow" and "hotel", and realised what he had to face before he took his melancholy and frustration back to London.

At Uzjarvi there was no uniformed stationmaster to greet them. Except – wasn't this where the official in question was a tall, finely-proportioned official saluting them? He had resolved to remember her and he had. But where was she? She was not standing to greet the large group of disconsolate persons descending to the ice-coated open air platform and filing through the brief warmth of a waiting room towards an empty lamplit yard. On the other side of which was the entrance to the large Station Hotel.

It seemed built for a bigger town in better times. It was scented with decay but maintained its pretensions with thick, obscurely-patterned curtains reaching down to the floor of every ground floor room facing the yard.

The group of people at Reception blocked Jake's view of the official dealing with these perplexed and impatient travellers, but he could hear a commanding female voice doing its best with strained patience in response to self-righteous anger and intense questioning. Gradually this cluster broke up, people making off with luggage, and keys in their hands, to the lifts. Jake was the last to step up to the receptionist, whom he now saw to be, unmistakeably, the Stationmistress seen from the train ten days before.

Everything suggested by that brief view of Claudina (as her badge named her) was immediately confirmed. She was probably in her late twenties, no older, with large, open features and glossy black hair. She wore the railway uniform but clearly carried the two jobs because she had complete control of the routines of Reception.

"You are from the train also, General?"

He grasped enough of that to nod and take the expected form pushed across to him.

"The State Railway will pay for your night here," she said.

When Jake Coleman had provided all the required details and signed at the end he dared a small but lingering smile at Claudina.

"So – from England?" was her reaction to that. With this enquiry she returned a vigorous, almost a laughing smile he had not seen her give to the last few of her compatriots in the queue. And she held up his key between a flirtatious forefinger and thumb with its ring and its room number dangling under it.

"4-4-4," she pronounced very slowly in English. And as he made, suitcases in hand, to the lifts, he looked back and saw her eyes following him intently.

Scarlet curtains down to the floor in 444, as Jake rather expected. He locked the door on his impossible world and fell into a chair, feeling unexpectedly hungry. When he looked at his watch it surprised him to see it was still only four-thirty. Deep darkness had fallen and the lights had gone out in the station buildings opposite. There would be no more railway activity today. From what he could see of it Uzjarvi seemed dismal and not worth exploring, but without any alternative he prepared himself to endure it for a free night. And then there was Claudina, who might justify a visit to Reception, perhaps to enquire about dinner here –– yes, he was becoming hungry now, and where else? Melanita still commanded his imagination, but she had probably left his life for ever. It must be three months since he had known sexual contact of any kind. Claudina had been coping alone at Reception, no colleague male or female helping her. Yes, he needed to go and ask her about dinner.

He had not noticed where the telephone was because everything in the room, including that, was of the same scarlet colour. When it rang, loudly, it took him several seconds to see it. After several repetitions of a long, jarring note he made out where it came from, ran across, stumbled as he reached it and dropped the receiver when he lifted it. That must have cut him off because no one answered his "Hullo? Hullo?" He replaced it on its stand and there was no second call, even though he gave it time.

He lifted his smaller suitcase onto the one large bed and clicked open its plastic catches. Then he unzipped it, and was throwing back the lid to look for his toilet goods when the knock came. He had heard no footsteps in the corridor. "What on earth –?" he exclaimed with loud irritation. Why on earth should someone – or so he assumed – be bothering him about some hotel bureaucracy already? He wanted nothing beyond being left alone to pity himself for proving a coward and letting himself be ejected from Dr Erznik's haven of hope.

But when he unlocked and opened the door Claudina was standing there, completely still, with one hand on an ample hip. Between the thumb and forefinger of the other hand she held an unlighted cigarette.

"Do you possess a light please, General?"

"Well – well no – I don't smoke any more."

117

"In that case, do you like sex, with a condom?" All this she was saying in English.

"I – well, I –"

He was saying to himself that of course he did, but he was temporarily without words to reply with. Disconcertingly, almost threateningly, Claudina had entered, closed the door behind her, and set her back against it as if forbidding him to leave. "I phone three minutes ago," she said, "to be sure you definitely in your room." It disturbed him to think of Melanita's phone call to his room to invite him to lunch.

"I come now to ask for something you can give me – love yes, but more than only love."

Something he could give her? This was utterly confusing. Sex? Love? That was clear enough, he supposed. Except, how –? Could his confessed fascination with women have travelled back along this railway line and stirred a woman of exceptional sexual allure? And something *more* to give Claudina?

"In our country we need exchange," she said.

"Well, yes, I am ready to help", he murmured.

She crossed suddenly to the bed, removed the half-opened suitcase and sat down, bouncing approvingly, on the scarlet coverlet.

"Oh this is comfortable!" she exclaimed, as if she knew nothing before now about the hotel where she worked when she was not saluting trains. She patted the space beside her, inviting Jake to sit down; which he did, receiving an arm round his shoulder.

"It is cold with the snow," she said. "But really in my country all life now is cold. Except we are warm in our hearts."

With this encouragement he turned his head and kissed her, quickly and not very accurately. With her two hands cupping his cheeks, she moved him from the corner of her mouth to the centre, though only opening her lips a very little. Finally she ended this stage of the proceedings with a final application of her lips to his, something between a dry affirmation of passion and a small admonitory smack on the mouth. Then she stood up and took two steps backwards away from him, far enough for Jake to take in her entire firm, straight and very lovely figure.

Claudina was incomparably beautiful. He would not resist any impulse at all to subject her to his desires – And yet that need to affirm such a feeling did betray some kind of reluctance requiring to be overcome, didn't it? What was wrong? He could see all of her, and every action she performed, and he wanted her. And yet...

She released the top button of her scarlet blouse (this colour was not one that either Melanita or any preceding woman or girl had favoured; so that was all right, there were no dismaying associations there). She undid a second button and opened a small area of skin just above her bra; and paused, and looked across at him attentively with her knees pressed firmly back as if she wanted to increase her imposing height even further.

It was not the anticipated hardness of the next statement that brought these moments to their terrible conclusion, but something else altogether.

"We must settle the terms," she said in English.

He would have expected that, or an equivalent sentiment. Nothing in that was likely to disturb or deter him. No. It was something Claudina did, something completely unconscious, a very small physical action that cancelled all his desire just when...

As she stood still and erect and gazed at him waiting for an answer to her last words, her fingers waiting by a third blouse button, Claudina relaxed her left hip by letting her knee drop forward in Jake's direction and uncover itself for him from under her scarlet skirt. The smooth fullness of her skirted thigh she advanced for him, the vertical stillness of the other leg, the way her mouth opened with the smallest of smiles. All of it.

Instantly he could see again the wonderful, profoundly desirable Melanita in the lift between the second and third floors of the Hotel Seven Springs. Melanita the same distance away, standing and smiling and bending towards him the knee exposed by that action. Smiling. It was all exactly the same.

Desire, hope, action, progress, reverse, humiliation, defeat. Melanita meant merely that familiar sequence of events. If, the next time Jake had seen a woman he loved – yes, he loved Melanita – stand as closely to him as that, and smile, and bend her knee towards him in that way, and it had been a shorter woman, or even a tall smiling woman who was not dark-haired, or was all of these things but not in this kind of snow-stricken place, it might have been different. But now there was an immediate connection with Melanita, an inevitable association with Melanita and the defeat he had experienced – and she too, after all, had sought his company for help of a kind he could not give.

The entire laborious, infinitely meticulous and detailed, process of investigation, elucidation and elimination that Erznik had slowly been bringing into action had been ruined by the fateful nature of this coincidence with something comparable and equally distressing. And if his treatment could not provide the answer in this instance, then – it seemed to Jake – every other nullification or "cure" of a traumatic, disabling association was jeopardised. All of Erznik's psychotherapy aimed at ridding his patient of an agonising, obsessive habit of connecting one sexual moment with something in a hyperactive sexual past was simply invalid.

Which explains why when he looked up from the bed at Claudina's pausing fingers and challenging smile, he was weeping. Shuddering, scratching at and gripping the scarlet counterpane, pulling it up in huge folds, throwing them down and shouting, "No – it can't be!" Then he turned over on his side and pulled a pillow over his face.

But Claudina proved that a genuine, decent concern was not outside her determined nature, and ruled out by her stratagems, by leaning over Jake where he lay sobbing. She could not see his face, but she could feel the convulsive movements of his shoulders. So she rested a hand on one of them and said all that she could say in these perplexing circumstances:

"Are you all right? Field-Marshal – are you well?"

15

Three days later they all received an e-mail from William Bridgnorth:

> I may have made it only too rudely clear
> That I dislike this medium. My eyes
> Are painful after ten minutes with a screen,
> Since much of what I am compelled to see
> Flashed up in front of me makes little sense.
> I haven't asked for most of it, and when
> Some "friend" who has discovered my "address"
> Ventures to contact me, I find he slips
> Too often into "nerdspeak",that technical
> Vocabulary one cannot use to say
> Anything calm and sensible, let alone
> Discerning and profound. If I write now
> To each of you by such means it's because
> It might prove quicker to convey to you
> – All of you – some proposals which I have
> For a particular day which falls within
> The culmination of this Year's "Great Year
> Festivities" (I think that is the word).
> E-mailing won't be a habit; to transform
> Computer language into civilised
> Discourse would be a task for another year...

William went on to express further praise for what he described in a rather plain way on the afternoon as Jake's "forthright and unusual narrative" – as if playing down a sense of shock at the content – and confirmed the dates agreed for hearing Merlinda's and Frank's contributions. But he mainly wanted to interest not only them but other current students in taking part in the Fun Parade. This was to take place in central London on the final Saturday of the Great Year Events. It was to be open to all to join, and William believed, despite his reservations about the nature of such events, or perhaps *because* of his reservations, that anyone with something to celebrate that was relevant to an occasion of national celebration would be entitled – indeed welcome – to participate. He was convinced that his own cause could only benefit from the publicity it would receive by so doing. Some current students from another part of England had volunteered to design a banner, and everyone was urged to be there at 12 noon on the Embankment on the day, for a march along the riverside, across Westminster Bridge and up Whitehall to Trafalgar Square, Piccadilly and eventually Hyde Park.

Frank Winterfield received William's e-mail in a curious way. It was not the first time he had been located by Trackdown, but he hadn't been found so frequently by this method that he was familiar with it, and still found it sinister. He was seated in the Underground on the Jubilee Line between Baker Street and St John's Wood, one of the longer stretches in the system, so there was time for him to be sought out and for all of this to happen while he was still on the train.

The passenger next to him was an elderly woman gazing at her own phone and tapping it, and Frank could not see what sort of images or message she might be studying or sending. When it rang – an occurrence ordinary enough on a sophisticated instrument since calls had become possible to receive in Underground tunnels – she did not answer it herself. She turned to Frank.

"This is for you," she said, altogether matter-of-factly; as if this could happen at any time and she was used to that. "Someone called Anna," she told him, courteously putting the smartphone into his incredulous hand.

"Anna? How did you find me on someone else's number?" There was obvious shock of every kind in his voice, at being contacted in this way, and by her of all people, when he was seeing her in a few minutes and –

This she ignored, probably aware that Trackdown was expensive, and wanting to keep the conversation brief.

"Will you join William on this Fun Parade?" she demanded. "Saturday week? Or is it *Saturday*?"

Because he had not opened his e-mail inbox today he was perplexed by this, though much more bewildered to be traced in this way and take a phone call in these circumstances. It was also difficult to hear her.

"He sent us all an e-mail with regard – to going on the Fun Parade. *Please look!*"

He realised that Anna's sentences had been ten syllables long. He thought he should reply as William had taught and encouraged them but she was not giving him much opportunity.

"And there's a thing I've absolutely got – to hear from you about. I'll let you know."

There was a silence into which Frank began to speak, only to be interrupted by a loud droning. Anna had either finished her call, leaving him wholly bewildered as to how and why she had made it; or they had been disconnected.

"How did you know it was me she was calling", he asked the stranger as he returned her phone.

"Your picture came up. Was she ringing from London?"

"Yes – I suppose so –"

"It's still a bit tricky from outside the 020 area. Do you have your phone with you?"

"Well yes – it's switched off."

"It doesn't have to be switched on, there's no problem about tracing you for a call if you've used your phone in the last few hours – and if you're on camera of course. And they've found me in the same way. You're Mr Winterfield, yes?"

"Yes".

"All I had to do was respond to the URGENT flash, read your name – and your caller's name – check you with the photo they provided. And you have your call. Isn't it absolutely *wonderful?* To think that at one time my husband couldn't be traced if he'd switched his mobile off. Now I can find where he is and speak to him on other people's phones even if he's left his phone at home. Wonderful!"

Almost trembling, Frank found his mobile in his trouser pocket and read William's e-mail. He couldn't decide whether learning that Anna would be there was an incentive or a deterrent if he was having to decide about the Fun Parade, but he knew he would attend.

Jake Coleman came to it as the last of five messages in his inbox on a screen in the Oak Lounge at the Orthopaedic clinic he was attending for his outpatient appointment. As the chance was there to catch up with his e-mails during his long wait, he took it.

All the waiting areas, long converted into "lounges", had been given names suggesting positive attitudes to the afflictions the different clinics were treating. If you were there on account of COPD (Chronic Obstructive Pulmonary Disease) you relaxed in the Seabreeze area. For Neurology the Halcyon space, with its carpeted seclusion, implied a serious commitment to peace of mind. Jake supposed that "Oak Lounge" was intended to hint that this was where tree-like strength would be given to weak limbs or restored to broken ones. The background music here was the Fun theme tune, "A great, great unforgettable year", which it seemed impossible to escape, but softened and speeded up in a jaunty wordless version. Prominently on the wall above the reception desk was a certificate announcing that the hospital had recently received the annual award for "the most improved customer waiting areas in south-east England".

Jake also assumed that the odd comfort of these spaces represented a deliberate dedication to making up for the dreary length of time you had to spend in them. The further provision of free wi-fi and a row of computers for people to use without charge was another device compensating for the hours of their lives consumed by hospital appointments. It distracted attention from the fact that doctors and nurses were dwindling in number year by year.

Forty minutes after registering his arrival on time, Jake took a vacant seat and pulled his chair up to the screen. These were state-of-the-art desktops, donated to the hospital for good advertising reasons, and Jake's details came up quickly. Since his medical trip to northern Europe and his romantic interest in certain of its inhabitants, the commercial appeals by travel and dating agencies connected with the region had been incessant. Here was a company calling itself Neverlite, telling him to "Ignore All The Global Warnings" (the 'n' pushing out the 'm' in the second word) and 'Come where it's pitch dark all day for a Yuletide you'll never forget'. And another beginning "Why languish alone for yet another festive season?" followed that with "We have the ideal Snow Queen just for you!" After that came a series of faces, names – and bodies, some sparsely clad for cold weather – calculated to draw lonely men like Jake to the north in the depths of winter.

The third of these five messages kept him longer. The address came at him out of a far-away past, the years of his early twenties when he was not yet bored and dismayed by the prospect of succeeding father in the firm: it was tray.thorobone@beanfeast.com. *"Hi Jake!"* the message began, *"thought you might like to be reminded of me. How **R** things 4 U right now?"* The capital R in her message was done in a bold typeface as a reminder of a custom followed when most of her e-mails would start with phrases like *"Hi Jake, how **R** U?"* or *"Hi Jake, thought I'd find out how things **R** 4 U 4 Saturday?"*

Tray – Tracy – worked in a neighbouring sportswear concern, originally "Thorobone and Daughter". It was through business connections that they met and how she imagined them to have fallen in love after a dozen or so datings– or wished Jake to believe they had. Tray was not unattractive, but Jake appeared to have no rivals for her affections. Which left him first curious and then suspicious. Then he began to sense an attempt to draw him in by involving him in discussions about changing the name of her father's shops. "Thorobone and Daughter" was just too peculiar in an age when even "Thorobone and Son" would sound out-of-date for places selling smart sports clothing, keeping up with the least whim of the newest celebrities. It was around this time that Jake started to lose faith in his own father's business, so that taking Tray out dancing and ending up talking alternative names for her Dad's enterprise when he hoped that at last something she did or said might raise some extra sexual desire for her slowed down and eventually ended the relationship.

All the same, he sat at the screen today and couldn't decide whether to be more irritated or pleased by the sudden arrival of this news from the past. But then he was aware that a single name being repeatedly called out across the room was intended for him: "Bernard... He had long abandoned that in favour of Jake but he supposed they had found it in some computer record, and the policy of putting everyone at their ease had meant that surnames had long been abandoned.

He had to respond to the summons and follow the Sunshine Volunteer down the corridor to a room where his weight and height were measured and his blood pressure and temperature taken. No one in this outpatients department, so far, seemed to be employed by the hospital itself, or by anyone at all; they were all from voluntary organisations helping out. His own Volunteer today was delighted to be of assistance in a crisis, if that was what brought her here, full of concern for this patient should he need help from his seat in front of the computer and back again, and reassurance that the blood pressure test was nothing to worry about. Jake declined her offer to escort him back.

When he resumed his seat at the computer the screen was dark, and he had to summon up his inbox a second time. With his curiosity about Tray's e-mail satisfied, he went on to the fourth waiting message, from his "Special Financial Advisers", employed at no little expense since he came into the money from the sale of his father's store, and consulted spasmodically for *Your Week With Us*.

Jake could not believe the unconcealed uncertainty of the predictions his expensive financial advisers were making. It seemed safest to assume that storm clouds were gathering, although when a storm would break it was impossible for the experts to agree. They only concurred in the fact that they been grievously wrong so often in the past that they were obliged to be cautious now. Hardly anything was a guaranteed safe investment. Land and property were continuing to be a shaky proposition. When a bank keeps declaring itself to be as safe as a cliff, one said, take a look at the waves. Maybe one little thing you can do to provide for your children's birthdays is draw some cash from a few safe currencies and put it in your pocket for the few weeks ahead. But which currencies?

Jake saw that the last e-mail was from William, and addressed to everyone in the group. He opened it eagerly and resolved there and then to support the cause. Perhaps he would draw some extra cash to be sure of enjoying himself on the day of the Parade.

Merlinda was making her third and last visit, alone, as a pretended member of the audience in the Laughter Studio without the knowledge of the company, and preparing in her mind the report which she hoped HandF would approve – with her advice on the improvement of the restaurants and the rounding up of dogs – so as to launch her into a salaried job. But what was there to say? If anything, the audience today– for a different and even worse comedy series going out in the New Year – was the most pitiable and least promising she had seen: ill-fed, shabby and lethargic. Did they hate themselves for having to be here? Champagne on arrival instead of tea and plain biscuits at the end would be agreeable in itself and might make some difference to the spirit of the laughter. But that would be too expensive and she dare not recommend it. She sensed an increasing despair about Clive Sangley's presentation today. Ever more elaborate apologies for recycling jokes members of his audience might have heard before didn't make them funnier. Merlinda began to feel that the only work she could ever hope to obtain – but had she been listening to Rick? – would imprison her for life in a world of exploitative rubbish.

Sitting there with thirty minutes to go before the end, she thought of Sonia, and Frank, and then she naturally worried about her own oration to William's group. Once again she fought boredom by checking her diary dates, including the afternoon fixed for that – or for Frank's performance, according to how the lot fell. With the day clear in her mind she was tempted to leave early today – again –because she had had enough. But suddenly someone sat down in the vacant seat between Merlinda and the aisle, and blocked her exit. So she kept her phone on, went to her inbox, and discovered William's command to represent his cause in the Great Year Fun Parade.

She really wondered whether they would, as an "unofficial" exhibit, be entitled – more to the point allowed – to take part. The e-mail she read in the darkness amid the raucous babble from the entertainment and the deathly laughter, was full of an innocent conviction that their small tableau would naturally be a welcome feature in the event. Merlinda was sure that there would be less deserving entries in the procession, but she was also convinced that William would not have observed the time limit and all the other conditions for offering his exhibit. Or paid a fee. There was a danger that they would arrive on the day only to be excluded by the parade officials and the police. She would have to make him aware of this; yet already it might be too late.

One of the occasional beams of light that circled and picked out laughing faces showed Merlinda who it was sitting next to her – a familiar figure now sound asleep despite all the false mirth going on around him; until something instinctive, or professional even now, caused him to wake and realise that he was supposed to be working.

Clive Sangley was conscious enough to take in that her attention was on her smartphone, not the action on the screen.

"D'you have the time?"

She could not believe she had either recognised or heard him correctly. "Excuse me?"

"Will your phone tell me the time of day?" he was asking.

"Yes. I didn't – I'm sorry –"

"Well I'm *incredibly* sorry, Merlinda darling. For me mostly, but you as well, and everyone in this crew of crap-crunchers – though they at least won't have me for a minute after twelve-thirty today – to which hour I am contracted by those corporate bastards at TVB – and I have to be seen to stay on the premises, or I don't get my redundancy money. But not one fucking second more. I know your name? Yes, they thought it would be fun to tell me someone was coming from a 'consultant's' to 'inspect' me, and it wasn't much trouble to find out the name and the details – that you were an intern, with no more power than the dead wood she might be employed to clear out. You were easy to spot. Everyone else in the audience was nearly as old as me."

She looked at Clive – with the tired eyes under the make-up very visible to her, close up, with the shirt open at the neck to a few very grey hairs, and the jeans quite like those he wore in his young children's shows in the first decade of the millenium. Perhaps those items caused Merlinda to think of the sympathetic remark she came up with:

"I used to watch you with my Mum," she said, instantly wishing she hadn't.

"Let me know who you're watching with her these days," Clive said.

16

As the Underground train went on from station to station farther out into suburban north-west London and the carriage almost emptied, the remaining passengers were all talking into very ordinary mobiles, those older cellphones for which even now there was no signal in the tunnel. Frank began using his own as soon as the obliging elderly neighbour with Trackdown had gone.

She had stayed sitting next to him, a bit uncomfortably, although most seats beyond her or opposite became vacant. It would have seemed not very friendly to move away at the first opportunity, but eventually, at Eastcote, she stood up, went to the opening doors, turned back towards him with a small smile, and stepped out onto the platform. The train resumed its journey and she did not look back as Frank passed in the window. For her, the call from Anna had seemed an everyday incident. For Frank it had been most curious. It was not the wish or the ability of Anna to reach him that was strange, but her need to do so when they were due to meet in about half-an-hour.

Then he realised. Probably she had called because she wanted to establish she was telephoning someone still a fair distance away from where she and Frank had actually arranged to see each other. Her message conveyed a perfectly legitimate piece of information to a person not identifiable to Jeffrey, and it could be deliberately intended to suggest that there was no meeting going on between her and a man. It might calm Jeffrey's suspicious nature if he had tracked down on a state-of-the-art computer the fact of a call and its innocent content. The technology of the ever more sophisticated social media tempted some people into paranoid investigations of this sort. Anna had to hope that a London Underground train in a tunnel did not yet have a camera which would link into the system and provide a picture of the person responding to your telephone call – revealing Frank – as was possible on the High Speed rail lines.

They had set up today's meeting – in a remote suburban art cinema – by getting in touch through letters, now becoming a far safer means of communication again than anything electronic. Anna's opening note in planning today's meeting, a considerable surprise to Frank when it arrived, had been very brief, but it conveyed a deal of tension and distress. Things had been going so badly for her lately. Frank was one of the few men she felt – on the basis of their lovely weeks together – she could still really trust. Seeing him outside William's flat had been a stunning coincidence, and surely they were meant to resume this romance? The idea took a grip on Frank during this old-fashioned correspondence. He had begun to desire her again.

Dates and places had been discussed by mail and Anna had suggested they meet in distant north-west London in the middle of the afternoon. It would not be anywhere out-of-doors. It had to be inside an anonymous public place where they were unlikely to be spotted. They should arrive separately, Frank after Anna, at a small picture house which she had seen close to a particular tube station but had never actually patronised: the "nMAH", short for New Metroland Art House.

Frank's eagerness to observe the secret details of their plan drove any thought of what film they might be seeing out of his mind. He simply paid at the little counter, his twenty pound note being taken by an assistant looking up without interest from the smartphone she was staring at. Once inside the auditorium's darkness, with no one to direct him to a seat, he had to set himself to discover where Anna might be sitting, which was difficult. He had no sense of the size of the hall, or where she might choose to go. Besides, the shrieking trailer on the screen for an adult vampire movie was itself very dark, all black and grey and breasts and bloodied fangs. He had to wait for something brighter to come up, and fortunately a new Great Year short soon illuminated the place with sunshine, happy faces, the high praise of Security – and publicity for the imminent Fun Parade. For several seconds he could quite clearly see Anna sitting alone by the far wall. Carefully he reached her row and fumbled his way along it in the newly-resumed blackness.

"Good! So you've had no problem finding it", she whispered. And for over two hours their talk was going to be entirely in whispers, in case they could be recorded if or when they were audible above the soundtrack. "Look – please – I had to see you somewhere soon", she went on. He appreciated that these were blank verse lines.

But he was not proposing to conduct this encounter in iambic pentameters himself. "Why did you leave me in the first place?" he demanded. Anna at first replied in the same way. "I dreaded Jeffrey would find out. After all, he lived in the rooms upstairs from where I'd just come down. Can't you see that?"

"Yes, I can see that. But couldn't you have told me you were going?" Frank was aware that something he didn't expect was entering his voice: a pleading protest at Anna's behaviour that would be interpreted as a hope of re-starting their affair.

He looked at her with his eyes now more used to the dark, and thought she looked pale; so he listened more intently. The name of the film came and went – he supposed, because he didn't take it in – before he could register it. All he did think was, "Ah, it's in black-and-white. The colours will be better." He owed this maxim to his father, who had grown up in a pre-colour age.

Anna started, as a kind of excuse, on the story of how she met Jeffrey in the first place. She had been looking for a job like everybody else, but in her case one of her dozens of letters, by post and e-mail, had actually produced a response and an interview. It had not been for one of the jobs she thought she had a chance of, no. She went through a list of those as Frank's attention was suddenly won by the images on the screen. Anna was not looking at those at all, and did not expect Frank to be doing so. They hadn't met here for that purpose. When he looked away from her she moved his chin round to face her again, and the first time he missed something important happening was when a man apparently on his death-bed in a dark gothic chamber dropped an object which smashed on the floor while murmuring a word Frank failed to catch.

Anna seemed to think that pentameters would enable Frank to concentrate: "You had to call up people who'd called up/ call centres, to check up to see if they/ were practising their training. Anyone/ who failed to use exactly the right words/ talking to someone… Or somebody who/got into any kind of pointless chat/ with members of the public had to go," she spelt out in the dark. So it transpired that Anna's hoped-for job was as a checker of checkers – so far as Frank could follow it – three stages away from the consumers themselves, and Jeffrey, responsible for making the appointment, was seeing five applicants for it, one of whom was Anna, and he was all charm and reassurance at first.

But now, on the screen here – was this another short feature film he was seeing, out of the corner of his eye? A "newsreel" of the sort he had seen in his very early childhood had seemingly replaced the main film. No, not true. It was part of the main film, because an important celebrity had died and the question was, What was the secret of his life that nobody had uncovered? The character appeared to be an enigma in himself.

In real life, in Anna's narrative, each of Jeffrey's job interviewees were seen one by one by a board consisting of two other persons and Jeffrey himself, whose main duty was to collect them from a waiting room where they sat together nervously. Jeffrey said he would come back at the finish and give them the answer that day. Meanwhile, a woman in the film had become rich because of a lodger where she lived leaving her the deed to an abandoned mineshaft. This was, Frank couldn't help thinking, the only kind of totally unlikely luck which would save anyone here in the third decade of the twenty-first century. Frank's inadvertent glances at the film meant that he was hardly listening to Anna at all. A committee of the Congress of the United States was receiving a statement to the effect that the dead man at the beginning had been a Communist, although a big crowd at an open air meeting of workers was told he was a Fascist. The moment of decision on Anna's application came, she was trying to make Frank understand, but when Jeffrey returned to the candidates in the waiting room all semblance of hope and charm had vanished from his appearance.

> "Jeffrey – I couldn't even start to think
> How this had happened – had himself been sacked
> During the interviewing. He'd been forced
> To apologise to us for having called
> Five people when there wasn't even one
> Bloody vacancy…"

Frank took this in with as much surprise and disbelief as he could manage when the film was distracting him with considerable success. A group of heavily smoking journalists was arguing about the merits of the newsreel they had apparently all been watching. One believed it lacked an essential element which was needed in order to characterise the rich and powerful newspaper magnate who had died, and perhaps there was a clue to that in – but here Anna became very sure that Frank wasn't giving her his full attention. Frank denied that, gripped her hand tightly, turned away from the film, and missed the key final word the tycoon uttered as he died. He did understand that one young investigator was going to be dispatched to find out what this word signified.

One by one Anna's fellow interviewees had got over this crushing disappointment and made their farewells. Anna lingered, feeling a bit sorry for Jeffrey. All the hardness she had detected in him as a possible employer dropped away. In a few seconds Jeffrey had become one of them, the huge legion of the unemployed, to be pitied and not feared.

"Do you get notice –and some compensation?" Anna had asked him. She told Frank Jeffrey's answer now in verse: "No none at all, you wouldn't think it but

> "No none at all, you wouldn't think it but
> The shit falls fast in places of this kind."

Meanwhile the journalist in the film was given no help or sympathy at all by the dead tycoon's wife. She turned out to be a faded beauty, a nightclub singer on the bottle who shouted at him to "Get out!" when he tried to interview her about her husband, the subject of the newsreel, a Mr Kane. When he tipped the head waiter for any light he might throw on Mr Kane's mystery word, the man replied, "When the papers were full of it I asked her. She never heard of –" But once again Frank failed to catch the important word because Anna was demanding all his attention.

"Why don't you listen to me, for fuck's sake?" she complained. "We haven't got all day – at least I haven't."

"I am listening. It's just that –" He was going to say that the film was winning the competition, but he knew that there was no way he could coax Anna outside so as to go on talking. It all had to be done in secret in here, and only here. But in truth he was beginning to be more interested in the picture, though he didn't dare tell her that. It also occurred to him that if they left the cinema might stop the screening, because when he looked round he could see that they were alone in the auditorium.

The investigative journalist, Mr Thompson, had entered a vast library hall lighted by columns of dusty sunshine falling through high windows. A severe woman librarian was giving him a large register full of unpublished memoirs to look at for his researches – "pages 83 to 142 regarding Mr

Kane", with no permission to quote from them. An account began of an incident in the hero's childhood. Anna was telling Frank some things Jeffrey had told her about his own childhood. How had this come up? It seemed that Anna and Jeffrey had exchanged a disconcerting profusion of details about objects and sensations that had attracted both of them – but mainly Jeffrey – at an early age. (Frank had to assume they had become intimate friends very rapidly as a result of Jeffrey's sacking: "I couldn't stop feeling sad for him," she declared). Jeffrey apparently enjoyed his boyhood memories of bathroom equipment: the shower, the rubber mats, the loofahs of a well-heeled Surrey infancy. For Frank, most distracting of all at around this stage of Anna's account – it became increasingly alarming – was a mixture of concern and severity in the mother of the young boy Charlie Kane, now appearing in the film. Her unsmiling features contrasted so much for Frank with the kind, tolerant behaviour of his own mother. But unfortunately he had never come into an immense fortune like the boy in this film – who was now a smart, ambitious young man thinking "it would be fun to run a newspaper." Anna had made a discovery, that she and Jeffrey had something in common. They had each separated from a long-term partner, a frequent revelation for people in their late thirties. Jeffrey was perfectly free to invite Anna to share his flat. It would be her decision whether to stay after, say, a month – or three months? – or six? Come to think of it Frank, who had lived in his own flat for the last eight years of his marriage, had begun to notice Anna on the stairs about seven months before, just after Sara had left.

"So you moved in around January?"

"I moved in on January the first,"Anna was saying.

"And left – on some day in the seventh month. To stay with me the following three weeks?"

In the dark, but Frank didn't see Anna was smiling at the thought that those were the first lines of verse she had coaxed out of him by speaking in iambic pentameters herself for three-quarters of an hour. Life had been moving fast and strangely for him in these recent weeks: Anna's coming, going and now returning, Merlinda introducing him to William's classes, her flatmate Sonia turning up when he was seeking to research a few memories of his years of kleptomania. On the screen a very important employee of the tycoon's company who had ended up as its chairman was reminiscing in his old age about the youthful progress of the great dead man as a newspaper editor and recalling the power of momentary romantic attraction.

Yes, Anna had settled in to Jeffrey's flat very quickly, although two things worried her greatly about him and caused her to think theirs would only be a temporary arrangement, wouldn't it? If a chance came of finding somewhere else to live, she would go. The first problem was that she could never speak without Jeffrey interrupting her, contradicting her. He was a repetitive, bullying talker, determined to get his message across. She supposed it went with his employment in the call centre profession. "'People in Shakespeare's plays', I said to him, 'leave time for other people to reply. You need to learn to do that. Have a read of what somebody shoved into my hand this afternoon'."

That had been some time in March. William had begun to spread news of his classes in the first week of his forced retirement. He had prepared the way during his final year in the Environment Department with a quite elementary website on which his programme was set out in blank verse lines. When only two people had responded to it in two months, each of them believing he was offering a course in dramatic speaking, he woke up one morning to a moment of revelation. "One of my rare Of course! epiphanies", as he put it. "Of course, of course! They need to hear me speak!" Presenting himself as oral evidence of the success of his own teaching, he recruited Anna with a leaflet one spring afternoon in the King's Road. Anna in turn recruited Jeffrey for the cause in an attempt to get him to think before he spoke – or she would give up talking to him altogether. Then she accepted a few pounds from William (ill afforded from his pension) to hand out copies of his manifesto in Oxford Street (where she much later realised she was competing with a distributor of leaflets for the Laughter Studio who had stirred Jake Coleman's curiosity). In the film now, the dead "hero" was watching the dawn come up in his newspaper office with his own manifesto, a "Declaration of Principles: …a daily paper that will tell all the news honestly." His friend and main colleague vowed he would keep the original document, which might turn out to be "pretty important… like the Declaration of Independence, or the Constitution". Frank heard enough of the film dialogue at this point to come close to one of his own much rarer moments of revelation. Was the film being satirical? Were these principles on that piece of paper really as sacred and enduring as that? Was the Constitution as sacred as that? Through many minutes of the action from now onwards Frank lost the sequence of its events – except for realising that Mr Kane's newspaper was flourishing; his colleagues and employees basked in its success. There was a riotous party with dancing girls prancing his praises and the young Charlie Kane cavorting with them. He was travelling abroad and searching out priceless works of art such as classical statues and collecting diamonds for the niece of the President of the United States, whom he was marrying. And yet his closest associates had doubts about him. "Maybe I wasn't his friend," one was saying, but if I wasn't he never had one."

So Anna had managed to stem the flow of Jeffrey's lecturing, which was the first thing she found difficult and worrying about him. Jeffrey took surprisingly well to William Bridgnorth's disciplines, which made a difference because after a few sessions with William he and Anna were able to conduct their bitter rows in verse. It slowed things up somewhat, and lowered the fever of their exchanges. But the second problem about Jeffrey was not to be solved so easily. Frank had listened to Jake Coleman's verse narrative with incredulity. Sure, people had a variety of sexual hang-ups. But Frank had never heard somebody speak about such complexities at first hand. And, on top of that, Anna was now, on the hottest day of the summer so far, in the darkness of a suburban art-house cinema, reciting Jeffrey's fetishes and phobias while Charles Kane's marriage was falling to pieces at the breakfast table. Jeffrey, completely Jake's opposite in this regard, could only achieve satisfaction in bright artificial light and through objects to which he could attach sexual associations. Frank recalled the loofah Anna had mentioned. She had spoken about it on the day she moved into his flat. He had not heard about shower gels and their canisters, heated towel rails, heavily-scented angular bars of soap, toothbrushes. A young woman on the screen shouted at a mud-bespattered Mr Kane, angrily telling him she had "a toothache!" The film reference to teeth caused Anna to look up at what was happening on the screen for a moment, and she even stopped speaking while the girl with the toothache displayed her vocal talents to the visitor she had invited in for some hot water to clean his filthy trousers.

She was soon back to a story which Frank assumed must have a purpose – why otherwise should she have wanted to meet, and conduct their meeting in such secrecy? When she had made a decision Anna acted upon it fast: to live with him and then not to live with him, for example. What had she decided now? To restart their relationship?

Would he welcome that? On the way to meet her this afternoon he would have said, Yes. But now?

"He made me… He made me… Then he threatened me with it."

Threatened her with what? Frank wasn't following. Anna, in furious whispers, was reciting endless examples of Jeffrey's demands, so that Frank wondered whether she hadn't been infected with Jeffrey's habit of assertive repetition. He could hardly credit any of this, even in someone completely unknown to him apart from the voice that resounded upstairs in firm, slow pentameters. "I had to smear myself with shaving foam," she complained. "Was that in bed or in the bath?" Frank asked in a cynical and not very respectful tone. She hadn't taken that in, so she didn't say.

Suddenly Mr Kane was abandoning his political ambitions. Or they were abandoning him, because his connection with the young woman with toothache had developed into a scandal which in turn developed into a second marriage and a determination to turn his hostess of that evening into a great opera star. Except, when the curtain rises on her premiere performance in Chicago, Frank thinks she is singing "Oh cruel one! You have heard me for too long." And this is possibly true, because her voice was excruciating, a sad parody of what an opera singer's should be. Besides, the light in which Jeffrey expected Anna to make love with him could be crucial. Bright sunshine might be fine, but low energy bulbs, now the only legal kind, turned Jeffrey off altogether. Hence the arrival of Anna at Frank's door on that afternoon of black clouds and failing light all those long weeks ago. Had Frank been able to find a full-strength bulb for Anna in his kitchen drawer? He couldn't actually recall, but he did remember that she stayed with him and she had not made any contact with Jeffrey at all (so far as he knew) while she and Frank were together.

Only at this point did Anna come to the matter of her movements after she left Frank. She had gone straight from him to take up life again with Duncan, the Plumstead boyfriend who had supported her before she took up with Jeffrey. Slowly it became clear to Frank that his function had only been to provide temporary comfort. This would have seemed a ludicrous, or a deplorable, injury to his pride if he had not, in the last hour, been driven to re-cast Anna as a woman in a state of desperation. She required sympathy and help, and there in that darkness with only the film for company, he realised that he could not necessarily provide much of either.

Were not all the main characters in this film tangled up in their own desperations? Despite the virtual impossibility of following the plot, Frank could sympathise with each of them in his own plight; even the singing teacher "tasked" with preparing the new wife for her first night on the opera stage and dreading the damage to his reputation; and the toothache sufferer who would end up as a night club singer on the bottle; and the close friend and colleague of the rich, yet pitiable and vulnerable, Charles Kane, who sent back his Declaration of Principles and tore up the cheque for $25,000 sent as compensation for firing him after he wrote the truth about Mrs Kane's performance in the newspaper – this last character cynical at the end in his old people's home. Frank thought he really must find out what this picture was called. Anna's whispering was becoming faster and fiercer. "Will you? Can you do it for me?" In her urgency she was dropping any attempt to say it in verse, and he realised he had not been listening. "I'll have to see," he promised, unsure why they should both be whispering at all. "I don't think you understand what I am asking you," she insisted. "I don't know anyone else who could help me."

"Yes, O.K. Tell me again – I missed it because I was watching something in the film."

"Get it away from him!"

"Yes, all right. But get what?"

Anna slumped against the wall in despair and irritation.

"The gun."

The word came off the roof of her mouth like the click of a trigger.

"Get that *gun* away from Jeffrey."

"Gun?" was Frank's softer, disbelieving response. So all Anna's talk about what she had endured with Jeffrey had been leading up to this?

He had to meet her here in this secret way because of – a gun?

"You didn't understand he had a gun?"

"I never knew anything about a gun." He was now so alarmed he was forgetting to be astonished.

"It's not an up-to-date weapon. It's an antique. But –"

"Then why should I have to help you – get it away from him, you say?"

"Because he's worked on it – and it can *fire*."

"It can *fire*?"

He couldn't believe it, but she convinced him as the film moved towards a haunting conclusion. About a century ago Jeffrey's grandfather had dug up in his back garden what he called "buried gold". This was a revolver from possibly the Boer War, or the First World War. To be rid of it, to be sure. But why should that have been necessary? Was it kept illegally after army service? Surely the authorities would have checked on all weapons issued? So could it have been stolen? Worse, had some dreadful use been made of it that its possession should be denied? Whatever the reason, the gun had not functioned until Jeffrey inherited it, cleaned it up and restored it as a kind of hobby in the months between the departure of his wife and Anna's arrival. Somehow, through an illicit dealer in such things, he had acquired a full complement of antique bullets and a supply of gunpowder. She believed it was now fully primed and useable. It had to be got away from Jeffrey before he maimed or killed himself or someone else. He had once brandished it, loaded as it was, at Anna.

On the screen poor Susan, the failed singer, was adjusting to life after her release from the ordeal of audience mockery in opera houses all over the United States. Frank noticed the subtlety with which make-up created the impression of her having matured and hardened since that humiliation. The end of her operatic career – which only her egotistic husband had ever wanted; her success would have rescued him from his own humiliations – had exposed Susan's pitiful dearth of resources as a human being. All that remained for her was doing vast jigsaws – putting a life together somehow? – in the huge palace her husband had built for her to be a famous hostess and entertain her friends. Charles Foster Kane's visible ageing showed just how much time had passed in this stretch of their sad, incompatible existences. "Forty-nine thousand acres of scenery and statues. I'm lonesome," was how she put it.

"I kept a key and it will let you in," Anna assured Frank in terse and practical single syllables. She was taking it as already fixed that he would enter Jeffrey's flat at a convenient time, go to the drawer under the divan where the gun was kept in the soft folds of spare duvets and remove it without in any way disturbing the premises. He would leave no evidence of a break-in.

"If I did this, though," Frank asked himself, "*why* would I be doing it? Yes, I would be doing it for Anna. But why? We aren't lovers any more. As a good turn, then? To prevent some horrific harm happening? Wouldn't telling the police be the safer resort? What am I letting myself in for?"

Charles and Susan Kane travelled to a picnic in the Everglades in a slow-moving flotilla of cars with scores of invited guests. Every moment and every image advanced the plot to what could only be an unhappy, even a tragic, ending with some bearing on what we knew from the start: the death of one and the deterioration of the other. Susan was once again the girl in the muddy street where she and Charles first met, shouting at him (though not "Toothache!" these days). At this point in their marriage, every second passing with them pressed together in the claustrophobic back seat of the limousine showed his irreversible vanity and her uncontrollable temper. What could have been more ironically appropriate, and in this atmosphere more sinister, than the lyric projected to a scarcely seen company of guests by the huge black jazz singer? –

> It can't be love
> For there is no true love
> I know I've played at the game
> Like a moth in a blue flame
> Lost in the end just the same

The power of the disillusion was underlined by every movement of the camera now, from the singer to the dancers, to the barbecue pit, back to the faces of Susan goading Charles and Charles vainly attempting to bully her into gratitude. Which she had to express as love for him, didn't she, and he couldn't bear to be told that and he slapped her across the face in the only moment of physical violence in a film almost unique in its understanding of what mental control – whether on the individual or on the mass level – does to both perpetrator and victim.

The silence outside the tent – as if all the guests could see what was happening, though they can't – was broken by a woman distantly screaming. These alarming frames of the film, the images and the sounds, left Anna and Frank wordless for some seconds. From here onwards they saw the film through to its end: Susan's departure from her monstrous palace, the journalist's eventual interview with her in the nightclub, Charles Kane's insane wrecking of his wife's room, the butler's vow that he could explain the mystery word in Kane's life for a thousand dollars. Only at this point in the film was Frank clear as to what it was: Rosebud. But he failed to see its explanation in the concluding moments because Anna was resolved to have his undertaking confirmed before they had to leave the cinema.

"You will for me, won't you! Make that a promise now."

A fact that Frank Winterfield was intrigued to note was that Charles Kane had not only tried to soothe his fired friend (the one who was writing such a damning review of his wife in one of Charles's own newspapers) with a cheque for $25,000 – he had also paid $25,000 for a classical statue of "a dame without a head" (noticed by one of the removal men clearing away his collection). It could well be said, Frank thought, that Susan had been another "dame without a head." At least, Frank thought, I do not have 50,000 of any currency to spend on dames without heads.

Anna absolutely insisted they leave the cinema separately. By then she had sworn Frank to the firm undertaking that he would let himself into Jeffrey's flat and collect the gun at a time when Jeffrey would assume he was marching somewhere in the Fun Parade with William Bridgnorth and his party. She left the little auditorium without waiting for the extended credits introducing all the principal actors. A few minutes later Frank, too, stood up and followed. She was not in the foyer when he stood blinking in the late afternoon light.

"What's this, young lady?" he asked the box office assistant when she tried to give him a flyer for the next film.

"To enjoy more of our classic film series," she said; without commitment in her voice.

He took the flyer; but wanted to find out the title of this afternoon's film. Any posters telling him that had been replaced by information about next week's vampire presentation.

It was as if she was uninterested in the enquiry and in her job – when she was lucky to have one – because she confused today's picture with the one showing in the first half of the week.

"Excuse me – what have I just seen?" he asked her.

"Oh – er, *Brief Encounter*", she told him.

17

I wanted them all to promise before I set about preparing and delivering my contribution to William's seminar that they would treat everything as confidential. This was not only for personal reasons but also because a lot of it would be confidential.

I've never really understood what keeping something commercially confidential is about. But the phrase has been impressed on me very rigorously while I've been working for Hemingway and Faulkner, so it has become a habit to use it and impose it on other people. There is hardly any transaction that doesn't involve commercial confidentiality and there are legal restrictions on how you divulge the data – though if I say something like that to Rick he bursts out laughing..

I'd been frantic to get any work at all, and I'd been searching on the internet for most of most days, or it felt like that. I'd done the newspapers of course, and even the boards outside newsagents and in libraries. (And if you're wondering about it, yes, I'd done some cleaning and child-minding). You soon develop a thick skin to get you past the websites that are really wanting not to reward you for what you will do for them but to get something out of you for no payment. You recognise ads that week by week never change, on the internet or in the little Classified columns in the newspapers, like nets perpetually waiting in waters where few fish ever swim. A lot of those that are out to exploit you suggest terrific training now and great salaries later – you're like interns that are never going to be paid. Unless of course you end up as the boss's latest.

What made me go back and click again on "Hemingway and Faulkner", or "H and F", or finally just "HandF" (later they told me that unpronounceability was the point; it was a struggle to say it, so you wouldn't forget it) was the fact that it was fairly new on the internet and you only got something fresh about once a fortnight. Also, their approach was unusual. Their website said, "What do we want? To consult you about working for us. When do we want that? Within one hour." I liked the sound of that, they'd heard the chants that go up on demonstrations. I hadn't realised then that commerce pretending to be revolution was common. Rick knew all about that.

That day too, a supplement about "'fulfilling' companies to work for" dropped out of one of the newspapers I went to read in the Library – and a high percentage were consultancies, which "HandF" was. They spoke of selecting people to work for them who "looked like achievers of happiness." They mentioned training, but they emphasised that in doing any given job you were automatically training by doing it, from the beginning, and there was a good feeling about training yourself rather than having somebody instruct you in routines. Besides, HandF guaranteed a salary from the start – which I didn't realise was ambiguous because they didn't specify what they took "the start" to be and I have now been working for about four weeks without reaching it.

As they pressed you to do, I e-mailed them for their Introductory Data. And while waiting for their response I went on questing through page after page of "Opportunities" and "Advantages", moving from file 1 to 3, right along the row of digits at the bottom of the page until about 8 or 9 and the chances were looking more and more vague and unpromising, or plain irrelevant. And eventually I gave up, left the laptop on, and tried the *Guardian* I'd picked up on the way home. I wanted to browse the Classified columns in case they could give me any ideas. In a few moments I had forgotten I was waiting for HandF to pitch their Data at me and I found – as it turned out – William Bridgnorth.

The ad was under "Offers", and sometimes even "Offers" got me thinking of things I might do. "Are you interested," it asked very modestly, "in speaking English normally and easily in verse, with rhythms and cadences possibly familiar to you from Shakespeare, or Pope, or Wordsworth? I can train you to use blank verse as your natural and preferred mode of expression. Small charges for very small classes in my London home. Contact Mr William Bridgnorth at –" This was so different from what I had been flicking through that I suddenly felt like trying it. I believe a lot of graduates like me get this fright in case they're never going to use or go back to the subject they've studied at uni. They blame themselves for letting ignorance creep up on them, it's a real guilt. Some people go in for another degree, but I had to get a bit of work behind me and earn a little money. I hardly ever had more than enough to pay the rent and eat, and get around London looking for jobs.

But this Mr Bridgnorth spoke of charges.

Oh I could at least find out what he was offering.

When I rang William that first time, I think he understood my problems perfectly because he invited me to come to one session for free. I could join a couple who were in the early stages of a course with him and made up two-thirds of a normal class of three people. I would see what he provided, perhaps make a few first attempts myself, then decide in my own time whether I would like to take it up. All of this he told me in such courteous blank verse that I was immediately charmed and agreed to turn up and meet these two, who were called Anna and Jeffrey.

How Anna and Jeffrey came to be taking up William's offer I didn't see at first. But I came to believe they were making a peculiar attempt to fill a gap in their own lives. William had been recommended to them by a counsellor who specialised in relationships that had begun promisingly but looked as if they were about to founder. Rick – he knows about things like this – quoted a jazz lyric to me:

You wouldn't be angry with me, would you –
And if I perhaps misunderstood you?
Why have a falling-out just as we're falling in love?

William appeared to be suggesting they needed a mode of civilised discourse that would assist them in calming down and clarifying the nature of their relationship. A bit unexpectedly, they had both taken immediately to the discipline of conducting all their dialogue in blank verse – or, as he put it, "recovering their traditional language." I only had the one meeting with Anna and Jeffrey, and didn't make friends with them. William told me later that they were still attending – but separately.

None of us – Jake, Frank or myself – would, I guess, qualify as nervous people, or we couldn't have submitted ourselves to the test of speaking in verse at all, let alone the task of uttering long addresses in it. But I was pretty frightened about giving what I had chosen to – an account in verse of my work experiences representing Hemingway and Faulkner. For one thing, there seemed to be far too much to relate, and for another, Jake had seen the Laughter Studio for himself. O.K., leaving that out would reduce the length a little… But my first absurd encounter with HandF might be enough…

[Merlinda's narrative, like Jake Coleman's, is rendered here in a prose version as she was modestly reluctant to have the blank verse version published. In places, a sentence will nevertheless reveal a regular rhythm, and Merlinda is naturally very happy to let those stand].

You could say I had problems finding them.

It was my first chance of a job in eighteen months and I was not going to mess things up. I did an online location of the premises in Regent Street, quite near Piccadilly Circus, very central and impressive. I left myself, I thought, all the time in the world to get there, and I made sure I was completely smart without looking as if I was straining for style. Aurelia said I should make them feel it would be a privilege to engage me, but without implying that I was superior to them. I should certainly not give the impression that I knew all about the job already.

But I left so much time to reach Piccadilly Circus on the Underground that I was in danger of being much too early. A little early is fine, say five minutes or so. Twenty minutes looks like over-eagerness (Aurelia said), or a mistake. A very bad thing about being very early is that you could throw them by turning up before your interviewers arrived, if it was early in the morning, or any time before about three-fifteen after lunch. People want to get their breath back before they call you in, or cool down if the weather is hot. Which it was. My appointment – curious in itself – was for 10.07 a.m.

There's a special panic I get if I've left so much time to reach somewhere that I squander it, then end up terrified of actually being late. The numbering of the shops and offices in Regent's Street – like anywhere else in commercial Inner London, I suppose – is incredibly confusing. Most shops don't show a number at all. You need to find somewhere that does, and work out the place you want from that. I passed the entrance to HandF twice, even crossed over to the other side – a blunder which meant I was almost late. Then I realised there was this side door in a narrow passage between two large and pricey clothes shops, and beside it a collection of company names alongside a series of bells.

After the bright sun in the morning street I couldn't see to read the names in the semi-darkness of the passage. When I could, I realised I wanted the last in the list, which meant I might have to get to the top floor. But how many floors would there be? I hadn't worked that out. There was more than one company on each floor and probably a lot of bewildering entrances and front offices.

I gathered you had to speak into an intercom. I pressed the final button and waited. I looked at my watch and it was 10.04. There was no reply from the little black panel at which I assumed I had to announce myself. So I rang again. Again a silence, again several seconds long. I was just about to try a third time when a female voice answered. Not with "Yes?" or a "Hullo!" but with a laugh that was nothing to do with me, I imagined, because I heard a remark being made to someone else. Finally, "Your name, please?"

"Oh – Merlinda Cassell. I have an appointment with Hemingway and Faulkner."

No reply to this, only a short buzz.

The door was heavy but it opened when I pushed on it hard; and a light came on. I was in a lobby with the blank aluminium door of a lift in front of me. This opened before I did anything to cause it to, and once I was inside it closed so quickly that I thought it wanted to trap me.

None of this felt pleasant or natural. There was nothing on the wall of the lift to help you find the floor you actually needed. Only buttons with numbers. I made to press "4", the highest, but before my finger could touch it the lift began to work. When a red "4" shone above the door it opened at once and I was into a lobby opposite an office entrance with HandF Consultancy on it, printed on a small card in a frame.

I knocked. Whatever confidence I had attempted was gone. I was all nerves and bewilderment. Most places you go to in search of employment will put you off at first sight and make you think, "Do I – like – really want to work here for any reason except the money?" HandF was worse. It utterly terrified me. Then the door opened of its own accord onto a small room with a secretary at a table, trimly got up with very fashionable hexagonal spectacles and giving me a hostile look over the top of her screen. All she said was, "Go in, Merlinda."

But I hadn't seen a door to go in through. There was just a wall-sized photograph of the City of London in the direction she nodded me to.

"Please, where –?" I said, after several seconds looking for a door, both in that and in the other walls. They were all obstructed by furniture.

"Touch the dome of St Paul's," she said.

When I did that, a neat door which included the cathedral opened at once. I went through it into the next room.

146

This was larger, much larger than I'd expected. Mostly because it was narrow and unexpectedly long. Also windowless and dimly lit. At a table about, I don't know, as much as thirty feet from the door sat these two guys and a young woman of around my age. She had a sheet of paper in front of her, but she said and did nothing at all during my "interview".

Halfway down the room was a wooden chair. Like a kind of dining chair but with solid arms, and placed in the middle of the floor. It faced those three people but it was not quite straight…

[At this point William Bridgnorth, with elaborate apologies, asked Merlinda to pause for a moment.

"You may not realise" [he said] "and I bitterly
Regret having to tell you this, but in
Your excellent desire to tell this tale
In full elaborate detail you have lapsed
Into a steady prose, the which is not
The medium we are resolved to use.
But your last words, if I remember them
– 'It faced those three but it was not quite straight' –
Were as they should be, so – try to keep that up.
Please accept my apologies. Go on!"

Merlinda experienced some moments of surprised embarrassment, but the gentleness and courtesy William brought to his chiding allowed her to recover quickly and continue.

"A lapse", she soon replied, "I feel ashamed of, and admit
That things will sound suitably peculiar
In blank verse, and the dreadful creepiness
Is what I most of all want to convey."]

To paraphrase in prose how she went on: The chair was at this sort-of oblique angle, so I would have to straighten it to sit on it, and face them properly. It didn't look as if they wanted me to pick it up and carry it to nearer the table. But before I could touch it, one of the two men settled matters by barking out very abruptly, "Do take a seat!"

"Thank you – Mr Faulkner?" I said. A bit boldly, hoping to get him to introduce himself. And naturally I went to correct the angle of the chair before I sat down. But that brought a shock. The fact was, I couldn't move it at all. It wouldn't shift. Was it screwed or glued into the floor?

"I'm Will Green," he called out across the space between them and me. "The tall one with the charismatic haircut, t-shirt and jeans. And this is Ashley Henbrook – short and rigorous, wears a suit some days, not today, and a tie with it. We are Hemingway and Faulkner. Bring the chair closer if you like."

"I'm sorry. But I –" I said. I said it like that while trying to see if I could lift it or something. I couldn't.

"Oh, excuse me?" Will said, as if he was asking me a question. I saw his hand move forward across the table and probably press a button or something, because the chair suddenly shifted in my hand.

When I carried it to a position in front of their table, maybe two feet away from them, I could take in more of what I'd seen and heard behind them when I entered. Most of the wall was a big glass panel showing an inner office which went on into an unbelievable distance. It was a deep perspective of row after row of people, mainly young but with a few older, harassed-looking individuals at desks, all gazing at computers. There was a very distant sound of light and rapid tapping on keys, and snatches of talk; and occasionally someone would lean back in their chair and stretch their arms up, perhaps yawning, then drop them and lean forward again and go on gazing. A girl younger than me, expensively fitted out, very Fashion Week in clothes you couldn't think anyone ever actually wore, came down the aisle between the desks. It was a very long aisle, because the room looked even longer from where I was sitting now and she came to have a quick word with someone near the front, who laughed. It encouraged me to see such a young person working here, it gave me hope even though she seemed too junior to be a graduate, and I'd got to wondering lately if my degree wasn't a disadvantage.

Not until about twenty minutes later, when I was well into the interview, did I understand what I was seeing. I realised it when the very same young girl came down to the front, just inside the glass panel, a second time. I was not looking at a real office but watching a film of an office going round in a loop, everything being repeated. I was hearing a sound track of bored people typing away, mesmerising themselves with the technology so as to keep their jobs. For the second time I began to think that I might not enjoy working in this set-up. But both Aurelia and Sonia had come back home with weird accounts of their first days at work, and they had soon got used to their own routines.

Ashley Henbrook spoke next. Sharply.

"You left home pretty early to get here. About 8.37."

"Yes"

"Are you thinking, how did he know?"

"Yes – but–"

"You realise you can see anyone wherever they are in the modern world. Yes?"

"Er – yes. I realise it's possible."

"It was possible for us at 8.40 today. We were able to 'go and ogle' the front door of where you live, and see you leaving."

Of course I knew that was technologically possible. But I didn't really expect anyone to do it. You could feel alarmed about a thing like that. And yet once you got over the first amazement, and the first fear at the thought of 24/7 micro-surveillance, you forgot. You end up unaware of it until it's brought home to you.

"We are the consultants," Ashley went on, "but I'd first like to consult *you* on something. You could consult us on how to improve your employment prospects, but you wouldn't have the fee we would require. If we consult you on something, your fee for that could indicate the kind of salary you have in mind for this job."

"Therefore" – and Ashley spoke now – "we want you tell us how to improve our Reception."

I opened my mouth but I couldn't say anything until I forced out the only words that came into my head: "Well– the receptionist greeted me very efficiently, but –" slightly desperate and absurd ideas were coming to me now, with a feeling that I had nothing to lose by quoting them – "I wasn't made to feel at home."

I surely couldn't say anything about the difficulty of finding their office, the dark alley outside, the puzzling intercom, the eerie elevator – could I?

"That's good!" Ashley exclaimed. Suddenly I felt pleased. "That's quite frank and to the point. Most people would ramble on politely about putting a brass plate next to the outer door, or installing a better light in the lift, or having some flowers on Magdalena's desk. Obvious stuff. But Magdalena suffers from hay fever. Now go on – and be very honest."

I really was getting to think I wouldn't want to work here.

"Maybe you could put clients at their ease more quickly."

Now they both laughed.

"But you're not a client, are you!" Will said. "We never greet clients like this. We want to see how adaptable you are. Whether you would appreciate the needs and demands of clients when you are out in the field."

"And so far you are appreciating us rather well," Ashley told me.

"You're taking in what we are teaching you."

"By the way," Will put in, "have you noticed that we are flattering you? I hope you are. One of the first laws of consultancy is Flatter the Client. Make him or her believe that their inside knowledge and innate wisdom have been about to come up with the radical solutions we propose, and it only needed a little nudging from us for them to see it. Brilliantly formulated nudging."

"So what is your fee so far?" Ashley asked.

I stuttered at that. It came too suddenly. But I think I smiled. Perhaps I had to be seeing the joke in all this, none of it could be serious.

"Seventeen hundred and fifty pounds," I replied. And then – could it be that this was the turning point? – "plus VAT?"

This time I thought they laughed naturally, not as an act.

"Good enough. Good enough," Ashley said. "But seriously, then – your knowledge of what it is you are about to undertake. What *is* consultancy? When did the word first come into use to denote a profession?"

I'd gone to the internet about this, so I could answer confidently.

"1955," I said. "The same year as 'due diligence' came into commercial use – although you will find that expression in Shakespeare."

This was an item learnt from my tutor at Yarmouth.

"Yes," Ashley replied, not admitting any knowledge he had himself of its occurrence in Gower's introduction to Act III of *Pericles, Prince of Tyre,* but eager to continue a prepared recital of his own. "And yet the consultancy profession existed centuries before that, wouldn't you agree? Don't you think Hitler, and Napoleon, and Peter the Great – and, well, Nero, Caesar, Genghis Khan would sometimes say 'I need to consult' about some big decision? And they employed for that purpose people who wouldn't tell them the old stuff their ministers would?"

"And a cave man" – Will put in; so that it sounded like a rehearsed double act was being performed, because Ashley knew how to continue:

"A cave man might say, 'Old Boris in the next cave knows better than me how to sharpen flints, I'll go and ask him.'"

"And Boris would expect some favour in return," Will added. "By the way, do you have any qualifications or experience that might help in this work?"

"No."

"Excellent! It's far better that you haven't," Ashley came in. "It might have fogged your mind when what you need is a clear and cool head and a skill in looking convincing."

"Yes, above all *convincing*." Will.

"Don't go and read up on business management, or accountancy or taxation laws." Ashley. "Just go and convince them that you know it all. Of course pick up the language for convincing them, and use it with a ring of confidence, a clarity of purpose."

"Do you know anything about engineering? Or graphic design? Or waste management and recycling?" Ashley still.

"No, I'm afraid –"

"Then we are very relieved." Will.

"You don't need to know anything at all about the work the client does, the processes, the outcomes," Ashley declared. "You just have to tell them convincingly how to do it all better. With a different kind of management structure, naturally."

"You heard Ashley speak about 'clarity of purpose'?" Will asked me now.

"Yes."

"Define what that means."

I thought, I've really got to play this game hard, it must be what it's all about. I've got to convince these two that I could do what they might employ me for. Where I got the cheek from I don't know, perhaps doing school and university drama. And maybe listening to Aurelia, so I did owe her something – that is, if this was going to be my life.

"Clarity of purpose means – it means – sort of – appearing 'purposeful' and 'clear' in your approach."

Will Green and Ashley Henbrook seemed enchanted with this reply. And their silent woman assistant, who seemed to have no role whatsoever in these proceedings, smiled with them.

"Exactly. *Exactly.* In other words it means fuck-all. What you have to do above all in this profession is give fuck-all an air of meaning and purpose. And a semblance of clarity. Note the emptiness of the terms – never go *concrete* on us!" Ashley.

"Human resources? Strategy? Process management? Performance measurement? Psychodynamics? None of them mean anything. But get the *words!*"

"They mean what clients can be persuaded to feel they mean," I suggested. They were so pleased with this that I began to feel kind-of ashamed at succeeding with them.

Then there was a moment of silence among us. The girl in the film loop came down to the front of the office yet again. Ashley drummed the fingers of his right hand on the table, softly. Suddenly he swung his head round abruptly to look Will in the eyes.

"Shall we?" he asked.

"I think we can," Will agreed.

"We propose to employ you on three initial missions," he went on.

It was the word 'employ' that almost stopped me listening to the details that followed. But I think he said something like, "We have a client that produces the laughter for television comedy shows that aren't in the least amusing. And another client is a film company that requires to know how to obtain intelligent dogs without crippling expense. For a film they are making involving a great many dogs. And for the third – I have to ask you, do you go to a lot of restaurants?"

I hadn't been to any restaurant for, I suppose, about two years. It was a rare and special experience. To tell the truth I'd only ever been to one when taken by my parents, or when there was a student deal in a local place when I was at uni, or when I had a boyfriend who could afford it (that had been three times in my life).

"No – I can't say I do really –"

"Well, you should be able to now, because one of your tasks involves it, and your expenses will be met."

As soon as Will finished this speech Ashley picked up the remote, and the room was suddenly flooded with plain bright light. And it was a lot smaller than I thought. The film images on the wall behind the three people at the table vanished, and I saw that wall too included a door, the outline of which hadn't been visible when the film was showing.

Ashley Henbrook opened a drawer, took out some document files and signalled to me to bring my chair up close and look at them. Without any mention of salary so far, or any sight of a contract, and quite without any chance for me to ask questions, we were into a schedule for my first fortnight's work. I must have looked a bit bewildered maybe, because at one point Will said, "And you will be receiving a letter to confirm what we have agreed –" (but had I agreed anything?) – "and give you everything in hard copy."

I took out a notepad I had brought and began to take down a lot of detail. I would first go down to the Laughter Studio in New Cross three times as a member of an audience for a show, and write a full report for them on what was wrong with the venue, the welcome, the handling of the occasion. HandF would approve it before it was passed on to the directors with an invoice.

"Wherever you go in the next few days, be studying the Street Dog," Ashley said. "Have you noticed the Street Dog?"

"I've seen packs of dogs in the streets," I told him.

"Some of them very respectable dogs?"

"Sometimes, yes."

"The film company we mentioned can't afford to hire dogs from devoted owners who will charge, and interfere, and hope their pet becomes a money-earning star."

"We believe the dog parts in the film can all be taken by strays roaming the streets at the moment," Will said. We haven't told them that. We want you to tell them that, and show them they can easily collect, feed and train their own animals. Do you drive?"

"I have a licence, but I don't have a car."

"No matter. You wouldn't have the kind of vehicle you'll require. We'll tell Amberwood Films to provide a van for you."

I went on listening.

"And a driver with it who can help with rounding them up." Will.

"We understand –" Ashley again – "they will need at least three or four dogs of different breeds for the principal parts, plus understudies, and about thirty for supporting roles and as extras."

"And they are all to be found among packs of strays in the street?" I asked them.

"How else?" Will.

"Understand that Amberwood can't afford lots of duplicates," Ashley said. "No more than three or four as the lead actors."

"Duplicates?" I didn't know what he meant.

"Have you never realised that when a Hollywood company makes a dog film – a Lassie or a Rin Tin Tin – they don't shoot with one animal all the time."

I hadn't, but I said nothing.

"Go to the studio gate very early one day and you'll see a truck going in full of barking dogs – they're all Lassies."

"Do I receive a contract?" I had the courage to ask them this now because Aurelia said they would expect me to and would consider me very naive if I didn't. There was just the shortest of silences, a tiny pause but long enough to be noticeable before Ashley spoke. He was looking at my face, but not my eyes. His gaze landed, I'd guess, on my right cheek. Will was looking down at some papers in front of him.

"It will come with our letter of confirmation," Ashley said slowly. "And I think you will be very happy with what we are giving you."

"Because we are happy with you. Good luck."

Those two words I had long realised meant "Good-bye and good riddance."

I took my leave and went out through Magdalena's reception lobby to the lift. Outside in Regent Street I felt dazed, a bit frightened, and above all confused. I needed to sit somewhere, quite alone – I would be telling Sonia and Aurelia about the whole thing later – and try to get things straight.

I went into a very posh coffee shop and bought an espresso and a single chocolate cookie, waiting for change from a fiver which didn't come (and they all kept saying there was still no inflation). I looked at the other people in this place and wondered how they could afford what they were having, the big slices from cakes which would never be finished, the tall glasses of herbal tea with underwater leaves they agitated with long spoons.

Then I saw through the window – and, happening in Regent Street, it was really a sign of the times – a pack, or club, of street dogs which would have been suitable for my work if it had been anywhere but here.

Nobody was taking any notice of them, that was the first conclusion I came to. Why? Mainly because they were they were nothing new, not even in superior streets in inner London. If you left them alone dogs didn't bother you, they weren't predatory or aggressive. Domesticated dogs abandoned by their owners seemed to be capable of finding their way to clubs of this kind, sensing at once that they would be accepted in roving animal communities that had become a natural feature of urban life. There was a roughness about this club's behaviour, suggesting the dogs hadn't been owned and instructed and restrained for some time. But they looked as if they had come from good homes. There was an air of pedigree about them, well some at least, which got me thinking they had been chosen for what they were, no ordinary creatures. Maybe they'd needed too much expensive care. It would make them easier to round up. But I might not find this kind of dog everywhere. Maybe there were dog class differences between Regent Street strays and similar packs in, say, Kilburn.

* * *

And so the van.

It turned up at home next day at ten thirty in the morning, as HandF had promised, and the driver was Max. He agreed to take us first to the butcher from whom I had arranged to pick up a large, cheap parcel of raw scraps and bones of all sizes.

When I saw Max was around my age and I found out from his abrupt answers to my questions that he was a graduate of Bodmin University I thought we might have things in common. Did he feel what I felt sometimes, that we were from a student generation fated to reach forty with nothing made available to us to achieve? And that this was because there was very little that was worthwhile to go for, and no chance even of achieving something worthless?

No response came from him to my questions except raised eyebrows and shrugs. Max was not a conversationalist. He wasn't motivated to talk at all, about anything. He appeared to want to do nothing except get through the day. Nothing drove him. Nothing excited him. I thought he seemed the sort of person – of whom there were increasing numbers – who made Rick angry because he accepted this situation and took no action; and Aurelia angry because he was not being punished for it.

I had to put on all the confidence and strength I could find to keep Max happy – we had nothing to say to each other for the first hour of slow traffic. He left it to me to decide where to go and work out which groups of dogs were a good prospect. He hadn't thought of doing the basic internet research I had done on the temperaments of the various breeds. Somewhere in Streatham I broke the silence and asked him if he preferred cats. He said "No." By now it was midday and we had only once stopped and got out, packets of dry dog food in our hands, to try to tempt one of the various collections of nondescript wanderers we had passed. These particular hounds seemed to have been sufficiently fed. One or two mongrels came and sniffed at what we held out to them but immediately ran away as if they had better things to do. Max moved slowly all the time and looked completely indifferent.

"Have you ever had a dog?" I asked him

"Plenty."

"Do you know how to talk to dogs?"

Again a shrug, as if that was irrelevant to our mission. Silently he drove on, looking for places not only where there might be dogs but also a chance of parking.

Maybe it was Wandsworth Common – I didn't recognise it – but Max eventually pulled up when I told him to, beside a wide stretch of grass with trees on a section of the road where he could park free for a limit of one hour (not to return within another hour, but we certainly wouldn't do that!) And here, sitting or wandering around in a close group, was easily the most varied collection of strays I had ever seen. One really imposing animal was, I suppose, a labrador – but there had been a bit of crossbreeding somewhere in his ancestry. He looked like the leader of the group, a dog that would have the best ideas about where to find food, or places to hide and survive and avoid danger. As we approached the pack, several dogs looked at us and barked, and then turned their heads briefly towards him. Seeing that we held something in our hands he – assuming it was a he, we couldn't make out yet! – trotted towards us in an amiable way, apparently giving a signal to the others that we were not hostile, even though he couldn't guarantee that we were friendly. If we could make friends with this one and lead him to the van, the others might follow…

Just behind him, the next to rise from sitting positions in the grass, were two more large animals I thought might be father and son. Both were mongrels, cross-bred over many generations but I guessed that a recent forebear might have been a German Shepherd Dog, except that the length of their light brown coats and the manes of hair drooped over their long melancholy faces suggested the involvement of an Afghan Hound. Both animals had a formidable air; it might be advisable to make friends of them, not enemies. Yet they had an amiable look and had probably been cast out by a family which had once been proud of them.

"Go and get the real food to show them. Open the door," I said to Max, "and I'll talk to them and see what happens."

I went towards the labrador and these two with a big bone-shaped biscuit in each hand – and then saw Max emerging from the van bringing with him the parcel of raw dog-meat, unwrapping it and apparently about to drop it on the ground.

"No!" I shouted, and grabbed it from him. "Open the back and put the ramp down!" Already I had almost every dog in the pack jumping and barking and whining around me. With a rougher and hungrier crowd it might have been dangerous, but it was noisy enough for me to tell myself that I shouldn't show any fear.

"Good boys! Come on then," I called out, wishing I had a few fashionable dog names I could try. It was really hard to get through them to go back to the van, but I was managing it, gradually. "Bonzo!" I said to the father mongrel. And *that* had no effect!

"Go round behind them and get them in – all of them – when I tell you," I instructed Max, who had opened the back door and was standing beside it aimlessly. I wanted to be sure this opportunity wouldn't go for nothing. Somehow I got up the ramp through that barking mob into the interior of the van, unwrapped the bloody flesh and bones and dropped everything on the floor, then tried to escape from the bellowing mob. Which wasn't easy.

"Good Fido", I said to one, daring to heave its shuddering body away by hand, and scramble past it back to the door. "Toby!" I shouted at another, the mongrel son of the father – and both dogs forgot the food for a second and came over to me while I was struggling to slam the doors on about sixteen animals we had succeeded in tempting into the van. "Toby!" I said again. "Old Toby – *Young* Toby".

Was I the nearest to a mistress and owner they had encountered possibly for months? I got the doors closed, but before I could do that the younger one had run back down the ramp and was free. I had separated Young Toby from his father… But there was no question of trying to force him back into the van with the bedraggled collie, the basset hound, the foxhound and the array of smaller dogs (the whippet, the spaniel, the Melanesian micro-terrier, most fashionable of choices because tinier than the average cat.)

I reckoned – and how had it taken this long? – we had only about five minutes' parking time left when I crammed myself, sweating and miserable, back into the passenger seat beside Max. He started the engine eagerly, only too glad to get away. But when he put the gear into reverse in order to back up a little and achieve space to move away he naturally saw the two uniformed police in his mirror before I did.

They lumbered round to the front of the van and stood in front of us. One of them signalled to Max by doing a small manual imitation of a car key being turned to cut the engine. It meant also that the driver should emerge and answer some enquiries.

I owed it to Max to get out also to support him, and part of me thought that I might be able to handle whatever happened now with more efficiency. I turned out to be wrong about that. Behind us, making the first minutes of our dialogue with the Law inaudible, our gang of captured strays yelped and howled and scratched and thudded against the walls of the van.

"Are these your dogs you've just collected, sir?" was the first question, useless in itself because nothing was less likely, and nothing less likely to be believed if we'd tried to make out we owned them.

"No," said Max. With emphasis, and a very slight shaking of his head. And with complete assurance. And the trace of a smile, to convince the copper that his question was utterly unnecessary..

"Then where are you taking them, sir?"

"Kentish," Max said.

This was a brilliant reply – amounting to a very skilful abbreviation – and surely Max had thought up a story before we set out. My estimation of him was rising with every moment. To say "Kentish Town", the full name of the locality where the main North London dog pound had been set up, would have been right, of course. But saying "Kentish" made it sound he was so familiar with it he needn't use the full title.

"Not Southfields?" Southfields, south of the river where we were at the moment, was definitely the nearest "houndpound". But the film studios were out to the north and "Kentish" was on the way there.

"All we know is that's what they told us at TEDORLO." Max blended a look of stubborn innocence with pleading courtesy.

After a short pause of disbelief the copper went on to another tack.

"You're not wearing the uniform. Are you, sir."

It was a statement, not a question. And to split the sentence into two halves made it an accusation.

Max sank a hand into the pocket of his jeans and took out a badge, a small round bright object with black lettering round an emoticon-type grinning little face. The letters were TEDORLO, "Team Dog Rehabilitation London". It was amazing that he had provided for such a demand.

"TEDORLO said we'd get uniforms to-morrow," Max said. "We're GYVOLS."

At this the second police officer, who seemed junior to the one doing all the talking, looked slightly bewildered, and turned to the first for an explanation of the term. To his credit this man didn't patronise him by spelling it out, but turned to us again.

"You're really saying you're Great Year Volunteers?" He gave me a rather nasty look as he said that – I didn't fit in to any scenario of petty crime he could imagine.

For some reason there was a great barrage of barking behind us in the van at this moment. Perhaps the dogs had finished all the food and wanted their freedom back.

"You must like animals," the copper suggested unpleasantly. "You'd better get on your way. And wear that badge where I can see it."

"Thank you for understanding, Sergeant," Max said. The man wasn't a sergeant, and Max certainly knew that. The words could have sounded sarcastic, and prolonged our difficulties. But he let us go nevertheless, probably thinking that detaining two persons and preparing a charge of kidnapping a vanload of stray dogs would have required even more paperwork than he was capable of handling.

18

Rick came home at eight fifteen one evening, letting himself in quietly as he did from habit when he'd finished stacking and left the store at eleven-thirty.

There was nobody else in the house – or so he thought – or out in the garden when he looked through the window. In the kitchen breakfast plates still cluttered the sink. That morning Merlinda had called out, "Won't be in at all this ev-en-ing!" and Aurelia had held back her croissant from her lips to say, "That mean you're out overnight?" She put the question with an eager, teasing grin which Rick noticed. "No – eleven or a little later," Merlinda replied. She had a last restaurant to visit, one of theEndemics but not Godneau's. "You're in, Sonia?" Aurelia asked casually across the table. Sonia gave her a low "Yes", and nodded. These questions spurred Rick to inform her, as if he was required to do so by regulation, that he wouldn't be in until approaching twelve. He was not pleased by this necessity, imposed on him for today by his manager without apology only the previous afternoon. But it had turned out that had been released from this late shift an hour ago.

Rick was "starving", as he liked to say, and angry to see that no one had thrown out the frozen joint of pork dated last December, which he didn't propose to roast. He knew that the sliced wholemeal bread in the bin was also old, as were the last two croissants. Well, an egg would have to be fine. But when he looked in the box in the fridge only the one remained, the usual story. So this was everything left for four people to feed on if they all came in hungry… The wrapper on the sliced bread had not been folded very neatly; odd, because Merlinda was a precise and tidy person in the kitchen and she had been the final one to leave this morning. But then he realised that the top two plates in the sink were cleaner than those underneath, and had been used. Some light eating had been going on some time since breakfast. Strange.

Oh, he would have the egg. He could afford to go out later before the others returned, and he had just enough cash to buy a few more. Soon, the omelette with its flavouring of herbs spread out agreeably in frilled folds in the pan and for the time being, with two slices of toasted wholemeal, it looked absolutely enough.

Eating it slowly allowed Rick to think more clearly and calmly. But he jumped when he heard sounds of movement from somewhere in the building, yes definitely inside the house and not outside in the falling shadows of the evening street, or in the garden, or next door. And it was not anybody letting herself in. The noises came from above, and he had been sure no one else was at home when he came back, although he hadn't looked or listened. Wouldn't someone else have come down to the kitchen by now?

Was Aurelia in? In her room under the gable at the top? "O.K.", he murmured, softly. He said it in the way people say it to acknowledge an unwelcome fact or remark, meaning in this case, "I don't like the idea of her being in and not letting me know, and starting my suspicions of an intruder, but I'll accept it." He couldn't help connecting this with other small, inexplicable moments that had aroused his suspicions about Aurelia. And some of them he connected with Sonia. Why? Any problems Sonia had were her own, nothing to do with Aurelia, were they? He and Merlinda had spoken about Sonia on that previous occasion… Whatever she was unhappy about – she was alone with that, wasn't she?

Aurelia's treatment of Sonia… It troubled him. There was an element about it of someone – someone giving orders, expecting to be obeyed? Schoolmistressly? Not exactly. But commanding, if you like. A tone of voice Aurelia did not use to Merlinda, who would have given her dismissive glances and sharp replies. And never to him; he would have ignored her. He believed Merlinda also ignored problems like Aurelia's bossy demands for the rent when the others were a few days late (she collected it from them and paid the landlords the whole sum herself).

As for the two recent plates in the sink, the users not wanting to leave them on the table – or, heaven knows, wash them – but stacking them with the ones left from breakfast. Could they mean that Aurelia and Sonia were both in the house, upstairs? But now Merlinda came in, also much earlier than she thought, Rick having finished the omelette and started thinking of an instant coffee from the almost empty jar on the shelf.

"Hi! Have you eaten?" He asked guiltily. He would definitely go out and get Merlinda something.

"Sort of eaten. Don't worry." She smiled ruefully and sat down, dropping a bag, not making to go up to her room. He guessed she had something to talk about, the same as he did.

"I couldn't wait," she told him, and laughed, beginning to explain what had happened to cut short her evening's work. Finally she asked, "Anyone in?"

"Don't know. Could be."

But they didn't go to that subject at once because she wanted to describe her disappointment first. This evening she had had to take a miserable meal at her own expense in a pizza place, because theEndemic restaurant she was supposed to dine at appeared to have shut down. The white plastic card with black lettering in the glass door was turned to CLOSED, and through the window she could see signs of the place having been abandoned in haste. Chairs were not straightened at the tables, at some of which used dishes and cutlery had not been cleared away. The phone number she dialled on her mobile gave only a standard message of welcome with information about how to reserve a table, including of course online booking arrangements for which you could obtain a ten per cent reduction –except for Valentine's Day, Armed Forces' Day, Financial New Year's Eve, Remembrance Week, and New Year's Eve. Merlinda decided she would have to visit another restaurant in the chain for information, but that was for to-morrow. Thus the pizza and her early return home.

But what was that Rick said about their friends being, or not being, in the house? Merlinda listened now and couldn't hear any sound beyond themselves in the kitchen.

"You say no one's in?"

Rick pushed away his plate with an odd gesture of impatience.

"What's the matter?"

These four people didn't often ask questions like that. They might say, "You hungry?" or "You tired?" or even "Did it go well?" But none of them had a relationship of concern with another, Rick thought. He looked up at Merlinda.

"Nothing. Aurelia and Sonia might be at home."

Merlinda's instinct was to smile at this as if a notion of that kind might be suspicious. Why so? Was that what Rick intended?

"I was home early and I don't know why I haven't seen them," he went on.

"Neither of them?"

He shook his head.

"You're sure they're both in?"

"No."

"You think they might be?"

"Yes – they might be."

"Would you think they'd both be up in their rooms?" he wondered.

"They're not downstairs, are they."

"Should we go and see? I mean – to be sure it's not anybody else?"

Neither Rick nor Merlinda knew what they were proposing or why it should matter. Were they puzzled and frustrated at not knowing about such an unimportant concern? The day had not ended well in other respects for either. Were they inventing a redress for that at the expense of their friends?

In the pause they looked at each other uneasily. This was stupid, what on earth were they worrying themselves about?

"I think," Merlinda said, "we could both go and check."

They had made a pact, an alliance. They were in cahoots.

A faintly comic clause of the agreement was to go upstairs to pry on their fellow-tenants very quietly indeed, turning curiosity – anxiety even – into a joke. On the first floor landing with bare feet, Merlinda grinned and pointed at Sonia's bedroom door with a silent question. Rick nodded, so she went along to it on tiptoe and listened. They were like children. She tapped softly at the door, but didn't speak. She opened it, looked in, looked back at Rick and shook her head. He pointed to the narrow, newish pine steps up to the loft conversion.

Merlinda went first. It had been her idea, Rick decided later when asking himself if either of them should take particular blame for the outcome of this adventure. When they arrived at the top she pointed at the peculiar phenomenon of a light shining under Aurelia's door. It was as if she had drawn the curtains and gone to bed to read by the bedside lamp. Then Merlinda and Rick turned one to the other simultaneously to ask what the next sensation meant. It was a smell, only noticeable at this level, faint and yet quite definite, the smell of a scented candle. Or candles. Scents. When he looked again, Rick thought that the illumination under Aurelia's door came with the occasional flicker.

Did they catch low voices?

The loft under the not-very-high gables must have been converted not long before the present tenants had taken over from a previous quartet of young professional housemates. It might have been only two or three years old, so it looked new and bright. It was only about the size of one-and-a-half of the first floor rooms altogether, but wider and larger than people expected, and gave a spacious impression. When Aurelia, Merlinda and Sonia were first shown it, Aurelia was quick to say, "Ah, this would do very nicely for me". From that second the two other women assumed they had lost any right to it. Aurelia made her way up automatically on the day of their "occupation". Rick and Merlinda had hardly ever been in here before this; it was more convenient and, well, more natural for Aurelia to come downstairs to them. It had become Aurelia's special, secluded, out-of-bounds domain.

"Knock first," Merlinda said to Rick, who was closer to the door than her, mouthing the words, not speaking them aloud, motioning to him with one hand and miming the action with the other. There was a small cry from inside the room. Of surprise or hurt? There was no time to wonder, because it was almost simultaneous with Rick following Merlinda's instruction.

He knocked fairly sharply and turned the handle. He – they – should not have done any of this. It was an act of mischief which was only unconsciously taking what was imagined to be a minor revenge on Aurelia for the discomforts her personality provided. And come on, these were friends living together, it was a joke, and because it was a joke Rick didn't wait for an answer to his knock but quickly pushed open the door, calling out "Hi, Aurelia!" – and both he and Merlinda walked in.

They only expected, perhaps, to see Aurelia sitting in a chair and reading, or arranging her hair in the mirror on the chest. But their action was wrong since in this community no one normally went, whatever the intention or the mood, into another's room without permission. To do so without any more warning than a greeting called out as you did it, was even worse.

The black curtains were drawn on this hot summer night on a room lighted by four small candles of different colours in glass or transparent plastic holders. They were arranged on the carpet, in space on its right hand side and at its foot. The scent they gave out varied, Merlinda thought – lime, lily, cherry? – parsnip? – and the smoke winding up delicately from small sweet flames was also, in each case, of a different colour.

Aurelia sat astride Sonia; as if she had forced her down, but there were no signs of any struggle or contest having happened before this position was achieved. The bedclothes were in no way disturbed. Both of them were naked. It looked like the performance of a ritual. Merlinda and Rick had arrived so suddenly that Aurelia did not even manage to turn her head and face them until they were fully into the room, where very long seconds passed as they stood halted by shock and incomprehension. Thus they saw the back of Aurelia's head with her long hair down, then a hand going up to pull aside the long black strands displaced by her sudden movement. The hand doing this held a yellow plastic clip of the kind used to hold together, for example, a collection of hard copy A4 office documents, such aids not being a by-product of computers. Rick only later revealed, as he felt he should, the next thing he observed, which Merlinda missed: standing a foot or two closer to the bed than her he could see that a second yellow clip was attached to the nipple of one of Sonia's bare breasts.

"Out, please!"

Aurelia. An angry, impatient, feral growl, and they had never heard anything like it from her before.

Because they had pictured Aurelia and Sonia sitting together and talking, and that the two of them would be merely surprised and only liable to reprimand them gently for bursting in like that, neither Rick nor Merlinda moved at once. The shock of the inexplicable held them there. For seconds they stood and looked. But for long seconds only. And then they turned. Rick pulled the door towards him as he followed Merlinda out again, but it refused to close neatly the first time; after all, it was an unfamiliar door. So after failing to close it at all he and Merlinda went in silence down the narrow pine steps to the silent rest of the house, which knew or understood nothing of what was happening in the loft conversion. As they reached the first floor landing, Aurelia's door was definitively closed with a loud abruptness which told them they had committed a dreadful mistake.

They went down to the kitchen again and sat at the table. Merlinda searched in her memory for comparable human episodes of unbelievable embarrassment to which she had had to face up. Or actions like theirs she had had to apologise for. There were none.

"I think," Rick eventually said, softly and slowly and not looking at Merlinda, "that we are going to have to ignore it. All of us are".

"As if it never took place?"

"Yes… Except that it did."

A pause, in which they still did not look at each other, only stared down at the table while they shared an acute sense of alarm and quandary. Could they ever look at their friends again with the same innocence?

"Should we go for a walk?" Rick's tame but useful idea. Neither wanted to have to face Aurelia or Sonia if or when they came downstairs.

He made sure they closed first the kitchen door, firmly, unnecessary in this heat but he was making a point. And then the front door, with an emphasis that would surely he heard upstairs, and anywhere else in this soundless house. He wanted Aurelia and Sonia to know they were free to emerge.

It was dusk now. Rick looked at the houses, and the neat, or neglected, or plain wild front gardens, and the parked cars; and recalled a phrase from a poem set for exams: "a common greyness silvers everything." It seemed suitable for the atmosphere and the view of the street after yet another radiant day. So he quoted it, and Merlinda turned towards him.

"Poetry," she said.

"Yes."

They went on silently past window after window decorated with symbols of the latest Great Year and posters for the Fun Parade. Merlinda had appreciated his quoting a line of poetry in response to the evening light, though "a common brightness" might have been more appropriate. It left Rick sad to see how easily, as he put it to another underemployed graduate stacking shelves at the store, people were "pulled into the swim". Staying out of it was made to feel uncomfortable. You were treated as eccentric, even anti-social, if you had never in your life been to a Great Year event and took no interest in them. "Didn't your parents ever take you? Mine did," friends would say. It was as if such institutions were established thirty years ago, not just a mere seven or eight; the incessant public relations campaigning gave the impression that the festivities were an historical phenomenon – England, and all the United Kingdom, had always been merry.

At the end of the street where it met the Upper High Road they turned right, and realised they had for ten minutes been talking about nothing in particular and certainly not Aurelia and Sonia, because the twilight traffic was too noisy for them to have any conversation at all. They were, by instinctive agreement, going round a long block, and as they entered a quieter street on the ten-minute walk back Merlinda did speak about what had brought them out. By now she felt far enough removed from Aurelia by what she had seen to refer to her sharply, without any preliminaries.

"I wondered – the first day she moved in with us."

"Just about *her?*"

"Yes. Not both. Something in her attitude to me, first."

"God!" He said it with almost a laugh, which Merlinda corrected

"She can be whatever she likes," she maintained. "Just that it doesn't have to involve my friend…" Rick and Merlinda were finding a gradual way to get into a discussion about what they had seen.

"Did you think that was Sonia's side of the street?"he asked.

"No – never." There was not only the emphasis in the way she said this. There was also an angry and protective tone and Rick caught the note of real concern. He paused a long time before he said anything else.

"But did you see any sign of anything – I mean before today"

A singular moment in both of their lives had arrived and changed a great deal.

"No. That's to say, yes I did. But only in the way she *treated* Sonia. Nothing going on."

"Nothing mutual?"

Merlinda shook her head in saying "No". But then she added, "Unless it was kept discreet."

Did she believe that to have been possible? She suddenly felt ashamed at being able to speak so shamelessly about Sonia in particular, turning her into a stranger. Both she and Aurelia were now really distant people. She was miserable as well as shocked to be talking like this, so when Rick casually remarked, "Nothing to be done," she came back abruptly. "Why should there be?" This recovered the subject from Rick to leave it with the two women, and it might have closed it altogether as far as relations between her and Rick were concerned had they not – without a syllable about this passing between them – agreed to follow the route back to their own street provided by a short and narrow footpath between two tracts of back gardens.

It was not possible to walk two abreast along this with any ease, and Rick stood aside to let Merlinda go first. The path lasted for no more than thirty yards and they were almost at the end when Sonia and Aurelia turned into it from the other direction. It was nearly dark, so Merlinda stood aside to let two young female strangers pass before she saw who they were. A lamppost lit the entrance to the path, but the light did not adequately illuminate the place where they stood. All Merlinda could say, awkwardly, when she recognised Aurelia (first) and then Sonia was, "Oh – Hullo, then."

They all paused, and of course had come closely together in this narrow space, blocking the way along the short cut. But no strangers arrived to disturb or interrupt them, and since they all knew there was going to have to be a conversation as the four tenants of No.18 they started to have it now.

Sonia had been in front of Aurelia and she returned Merlinda's greeting with a tiny, muffled "Hi!" Then Aurelia said, "Rick, we're thinking we'll move out."

Rick began to speak as he was spoken to. But Merlinda came in before he could say anything, conscious of being ignored – and why should she be?

"Sorry – who is moving out?"

"We are."

"Who are *we*?"

Merlinda put this to her almost fiercely.

"Sonia and me."

"Sonia's not."

Merlinda stood closer to Sonia than anybody else. She touched Sonia's arm. It was a slight gesture only, but it still signified a protective intention. And what she had said was a challenge to Sonia.

"I think Sonia will decide," Aurelia claimed. Not very surely. And suddenly Sonia was not prepared to have her movements settled by others as if she was a child.

"I will decide," she murmured.

"And you'll stay, yes?" Merlinda made it a fact, not a proposition, but only because she thought it was becoming Sonia's intention. Rick couldn't see that she had anywhere else to go unless Aurelia –. Aurelia was the only one with sufficient resources to consider moving elsewhere and paying more; so perhaps she had enough to imagine subsidising Sonia? Would it honestly go that far?

"I was *thinking* of leaving," Aurelia said plainly.

Merlinda, who found she was trembling with a physical fear of Aurelia which had reached a climax now after many months of brisk words and edgy movements around the house, was surprised at how quickly she had given way. But Aurelia's tone held a note of superior impatience with the others, and implied a relief that she had the option of going somewhere else if they no longer wanted her. Her posture and expression left them in no doubt that she still considered herself the leader of the group – and how would they manage without her? Her leaving would serve them right.

The space behind Aurelia on the path would have allowed her to turn and walk away in the direction from which she and Sonia had come. She did not do that. She guided Sonia aside with an extended arm so as to walk round her, flattening herself against the wire screen which held back the bushes at this point, and did the same thing with Merlinda and Rick. No one looked at her face.

Merlinda found Sonia's hand as the three left the footpath and walked the rest of the way back to No.18 without saying anything more. She did think later that Sonia might have felt like a rescued victim of an accident who needed to be calmed or consoled. But she never said as much. It was best to let time pass and everyone's emotions settle down; then it would be possible to discuss what had happened with Aurelia gone and perhaps even forgotten. But time in fact quite quickly reduced any desire on Merlinda's and Rick's part to understand exactly what had occurred.

The rent was due three days later. Merlinda wondered whether, or how, Aurelia would arrange to pay her share and who should be responsible for paying the landlords now Aurelia was gone. During that seventy-two hours her presence in the house was scarcely noticeable. There had probably been in the daytimes more carting away of belongings than they had heard in the evenings; no one was to know whether she had help from friends or took taxis.

On the last day of their rent month Merlinda came in first in the evening and found an envelope with "Merlinda/Rick" on it on the kitchen table. It was not sealed. Inside was Aurelia's larger share of the rent in bright twenty-pound notes and some words on a post-it: "Mine. Enjoy. Bye. Aurelia Dolbey-Rodgers." Rick said it was the first time he'd ever known her surname. Merlinda had learnt it when she moved in but forgotten it until now. Upstairs the loft conversion was airy and empty.

19

Jake asked himself, Is William correct to think that he and his students will actually be permitted to join the Fun Parade?

He spread out the plan of the procession that fell from a Sunday newspaper. At the front, as well as the armed forces, naturally, there would be the grand official display featuring members of the government and some foreign figures of topical importance, representatives of the churches, and other notables. Behind them would appear the large contingent called the Approved Participants, groups and individuals who had applied to mount their own tableaux and exhibits as a contribution to the event. To join in, they had all needed to apply many months before the day, and be rigorously interviewed. After them would follow the "spontaneous" contributors. In theory anyone could participate, and much was made of the "fun" of simply turning up and doing something; although it was imagined that these as well would be very strictly vetted and any doubtful elements excluded. It would be harder to check the people – probably not a large number – who would arrive and just tag on to the very end for the joke, but the overall police and security presence was likely to be large and oppressive. William had vaguely mentioned putting in his application to appear as an Approved Participant, a status to which he assumed he had a right that would be recognised. But he never mentioned any document or sign of official sanction arriving.

If they did make it into the procession Jake was anxious for a different reason about the proposed centre-piece of their appearance: a large fruitcake, artistically iced and topped with effigies of poets and poetry locations, mounted on a broad trolley pushed by one of their number all the way from the starting point on the Embankment to the end in Hyde Park. He feared that as a younger man than Frank he would be required by William to do the pushing. But what if it rained? How would they shelter the cake? What was to be done with it when the Parade ended? Jake admired the idea but worried about the impracticality of the notion.

Jake had various frailties but was capable of altruism and a helpful spirit that had him wondering how to assist William Bridgnorth in anything apart from propelling the cake trolley from the Embankment Undergound station to Hyde Park. Somewhere he read, or saw on a poster, an encouragement to "Volunteer", or "Play Your Local Part", and gathered that information would be available in "your nearest Public Library". It was no longer near, but he drove one morning to the last surviving library in his borough, the larger premises to which he had been directed by the notice in the glass door of the one which had closed a few weeks earlier.

He had been here once or twice, not more than that, in his teens, when it still purposefully presented some of the dignity and authority intended by its Victorian founders. In the spaces open to everyone there then remained a few high shelves offering editions of French and German classics, comprehensive fiction and biography sections, broad spaces where up-to-date works on economics, politics and the sciences could be found and borrowed. Perhaps the awe and respect he felt on these visits had stayed with him to resurface when he became eager to succeed in William Bridgnorth's classes and even now improve himself; besides, a tendency to respect libraries had never left him since the affair with the blonde Jennifer had trapped both of them between the high shelves of her university classical collection. But the interior of this place as he found it today surprised him. There had been a transformation he could not understand, because it was so much less like a library than twenty-five years before. Outside it looked the same. It was a two-storey redbrick building with a stern frontage and high narrow windows which – or so he remembered – let in strong shafts of light on sunny mornings but meant that the entire premises relied on artificial illumination in dull days and in the winter. Which didn't matter. It was a library. You came there to consult or borrow books, or work at the study desks in the Reference Room ("the Ref" to the librarians), not gaze out at the scenery. When Jake walked in today he entered a strip-lit interior. The spaces occupied before by tall banks of books were wide open. He could not grasp why, when so many books were published, there weren't more bursting shelves of them, more crowded corners, not fewer. For a second he wondered whether it was still a library at all.

171

Set prominently in front, so that visitors would see it first, was a table where the book issue counter had once been (where did they issue books to borrowers these days?) with a smart young woman assistant arranging display items connected with the Fun Parade; although an eye-catching permanent card at one end just announced ATTRACTIONS.

Was she – a PR person? A saleswoman? She was eyeing up anyone showing an interest in what she was offering.

"Could I attract you to volunteer for the Fun Parade?" she asked. He said nothing, just heard her out. "Saturday week, 12 noon at Embankment if you want to be there. Or help it along yourself? By the river to Westminster and the Houses of Parliament, up Whitehall to Trafalgar Square, on to Piccadilly Circus? One day out. Half a day training?"

There she stopped deliberately because she had been doing her comedy act. She never recited the whole route of the Parade, all the way to Hyde Park, but did a self-deprecating imitation of a commercial routine so as to seem human and natural. Jake could see she was experienced in this performance for customers, and thought she perhaps needed a small crowd in a shopping mall to bring it off properly. What was that about "helping it along"? He looked down at the various materials on her table and saw a small pile of flyers: "Be a Great-hearted Fun Volunteer."

He was trying to read the title under her name on the disc pinned to her blue Fun Parade blouse.

"Agatha," she declared.

"Sorry?"

"You are –? I'm Agatha."

"Oh. I'm with you. I'm Jake."

"Agatha Tenby."

"Jake Coleman."

He stopped, and gave a short laugh like hers. "Is Agatha your real name?"

He expected to learn it was a joke or a nickname. Apparently her name was truly Agatha.

"Didn't you notice 'Agatha' has come back? 'Merlinda' came in after that film about the girl wizard. 'Gertrude' came in because of the Gertrudes – the rock group? We all know a Gertrude, don't we!"

"Yes." He didn't.

"Agatha had to come back. My mother is Emma and she says no one was called Emma for about a hundred years before she was given it. Now everybody's Emma or Charlotte."

172

"But do you know many more Agathas?"

"I've worked with three others."

But she was looking at him, considering something. Her disc told him that she was a GYVORG Grade 2.

"But really – you could make a good Volunteer."

"How do you know?" He laughed again.

"I'm a Great Year Volunteer Organiser – but have you ever thought about it?"

"No – but I'm coming on the Parade."

"Whereabouts?"

Did he see her looking at him closely, her eyes narrowing a little? Having started, he felt obliged to substantiate his confession and go on in an offhand way about a little group of friends led by a well-known teacher called William Bridgnorth – had she heard of him? No – who wanted to display their talents in the line of Approved Participants, and they would be bringing along an exhibit – but Agatha now became very official indeed, stern in fact, all hope of enlisting Jake as a Volunteer forgotten.

"Has he got approval from the Parade Office?"

"Oh – yes. Yes – he put in an application months ago." Jake hoped this was true. "Was there anything else we should have done?"

"Well no," she replied uncertainly. But she needed to know more about William's contribution in case she was able to remember anything about an application – which she couldn't as yet. Jake couldn't say how big a feature William proposed to present.

"I see," Agatha said. "The office may have all the details – but I haven't heard about it… There might have been things they wouldn't consider suitable – but I wouldn't know. I mean, he might be fine – as long as they've approved it and it's gone through."

He looked at her disc again, this time with impatience.

"Grade 2. Are you quite high up in the hierarchy?" he dared to ask, with one of his charming smiles; though with no effort to be pleasant and make an impression.

"Yes – high for a Volunteer."

"You're still a Volunteer – not a professional?"

"I'm high as a volunteer Organiser."

"And they give you a local Library to work in?"

"I like it," she assured him, relaxing a little. "It's what they call 'being at the Funface'. I like being with people – which they call getting to be 'Demography Literate'. You look at people all the time and assess them to find out who's going to make a good Volunteer to help keep the country on its feet."

"And people are pressed to volunteer? They don't just do it for themselves?"

"We're bringing them in every day – the country relies on them."

"And you think I could be one of those? A good Volunteer?"

"You're the right age."

20

Living quite close to people in the same house or flat you adjust to them over the months, and you're not the same for a while when someone goes. Aurelia's going changed us. First of all Rick and I had to think what to do about renting out her room. I didn't see how I, or he, or the two of us together could discuss it yet with Sonia. Sonia might, of course, come and talk about it with us herself if she was staying, because the last month's rent – and the next month's – was going to have to be paid. It was complicated. The management company would have to know Aurelia was no longer in occupation and be told who was replacing her as the person responsible for the rent, also any new tenant's name.

And the last thing I wanted was to have to think about all this while finishing my tasks for Hemingway and Faulkner. But that was a problem too. Each time I e-mailed HandF to reassure them about my progress – and hint that they could be in touch with me about my contract and salary – they sent unsigned acknowledgments which had an encouraging tone but in the end were simply thanking me for my work and looking forward to further reports. I tried phoning, but never got past that receptionist with the hay fever. She was pleasant in her chilly way, but invariably said something like "They'll be very happy you've called. I'll ask Mr Henbrook or Mr Green to get back to you." They never did. It was a bit depressing that also the website stayed the same as it had been when I first found it. No upgrading, nothing fresh.

Rick kept on giving me strong advice about going there to see them. Perhaps, he said, I should turn up and walk into their office with a wide smile and expect to talk to them assuming they'd want to catch up with what I was achieving on their behalf. "I'll come with you," he said. "I'm free in the daytime." That was true, apart from the days when he was with "a study group of semi-employed friends". He was cagey about these people, but as the days went by he seemed to be seeing them more often and I got the impression they were hatching some kind of plan. And now the Saturday of the Fun Parade was approaching rapidly and William was full of our contribution to it. The afternoon when we were due to hear Frank's address would be our last meeting before that Event.

What had Frank prepared for us? Would it be as candid as Jake's revelations? They in themselves had not been a complete shock to me because from the start I could see he was a likely womaniser, but his readiness to spell out his troubles came as a real surprise. I couldn't think Frank would do anything similar. Frank and I had spent evenings talking together at Godneau's, but we never got into confessions. I knew next-to-nothing about Frank's personal life or his background. He had been married, but wasn't any more. He never mentioned any children. He talked sometimes about his town hall work before his job had gone, and he had heard something about William's reputation for eccentricity in his similar post in another department. That was about it. I did more talking about myself on those evenings.

On Frank's great day I left double the time you'd think you needed for the journey over to William's, as you have to do to cover any distance at all in London these days. When I left Sloane Square underground station I started walking, as usual overtaking solid blocks of motionless traffic. Sloane Square itself, and the King's Road, were not on the route of the procession, but large streamers had gone up everywhere. BE PART OF THE FUN was the principal slogan (or instruction) this time – but it hardly changed from one year to the next. The celebrities featured in the publicity seemed exactly the same. There was always the little string of popular politicians, the individual rock stars and the perennial boy and girl bands (the Gertrudes inevitably among those). Quite a few had been marketed as rebellious and "culture changing", but I could see what Rick meant when he talked about them "fitting the most unadventurous of tastes." Then, on smaller posters on walls and in shop windows, came some names from the arts, or from intellectual programmes shows on tv, or their high-profile controversial blogs. I couldn't see many of those actually taking part in the Parade, but their smiling faces followed us on all the advertising sites. And not a few of the fashion followers I was dodging and side-stepping down the long King's Road had bought the t-shirts!

Here I was, then, rounding the corner at the World's End and hurrying so as not to be late, and turning into William's street – and there was Jake turning the corner just as I did and gliding up to back into a parking space which he was very lucky to find.

* * *

Jake Coleman had been driving well ahead of Merlinda in that very tailback for about fifty minutes. His thoughts had been: Was it any less miserable to be in a car of your own you were proud to possess than in a taxi or – God forbid! – a bus for a journey like this? The cost of travelling in London was not a factor for Jake in considering such a question; he only needed to weigh up the effect on his spirits.

He came to the conclusion that anything raising his morale was better than other options. The Mercedes enhanced his impression of his own worth far more than a taxi, because getting stuck in a cab in a traffic jam made him feel a fool. Pedestrians and bus passengers would be looking at him and thinking, "Stupid bugger spending fifty quid on a taxi and hoping he'd get there before the rest of us. Serve him right"

In a traffic jam Jake would sometimes switch off the engine for the little pleasure of restarting it and gliding on into the space that had suddenly opened up; though he had to be careful lest the gratifying rapidity of its acceleration should send him into the rear of the vehicle in front, in only one or two seconds. No, he felt larger and more important and infinitely more in control inside Aphrodite, as he called her, than on foot or in the No.22. Every small button or switch obeyed and pleased him, which was more than he could say of women.

The first time ever he had that thought, he smiled at himself, though only briefly because he was immediately sure he was not the first man to have had it, and his envy of people who had profound or funny notions remained very strong. Jake's personal confidence had improved greatly with the rigours of William Bridgnorth's course, but the banal old wound was unhealed as yet.

* * *

That I should (possibly) be doing it – if I go ahead – for love, Frank Winterfield was thinking.

Frank's consent to Anna's demand about Jeffrey's antique firearm left him worried for both his sanity and his safety; and this in the days leading up to his special afternoon at William's. The film he had been watching with Anna had battled for his attention all too successfully. Why else should he have been so distracted and foolish and vain as to agree to the plan and pocket there and then her spare set of keys?

Was it that he feared for Anna's safety? And because no one else was going to undertake what she asked? Was he in fact besotted with her? And willing to test his old proficiency by breaking the law because of it? It would be the first time ever he had committed one of his crimes of theft for love.

What if he was apprehended in the course of what would be regarded as illegal entry, a break-in, a burglary? He could think of no story that would convince either the police or Anna's neighbours on that floor. Suppose he was found trying to leave with an ancient but useable revolver on his person? Almost any story he tried would be bound also to incriminate Anna. If, on the other hand, he made his escape successfully with the gun and joined the others on the Fun Parade, what on earth would he do with it then? Anna wanted to see it, to be sure it was safely out of Jeffrey's hands. But he was certainly not going to render it up to her.

His thinking went round in circles of bewilderment but he had to make a decision and he arrived at this one: He would make sure he achieved the perfect burglary, doing everything he could to manage a smooth escape, after which he would leave the weapon plainly and securely wrapped in a recycling bin somewhere on his way back to the Fun Parade.

With the ample time he gave himself, he took the slow No.22 bus along the King's Road the three of four stops from home this afternoon, so as to give himself a last few moments to revise his notes and to practise, under his breath, his opening lines. So much depended on a confident beginning that would get him into his stride. That first afternoon when he had spotted William Bridgnorth from this same bus came back to him. He was going to the place where William must have broken his journey to leave his cakes at home and reappear empty-handed – causing Frank to wonder if he was mad, and seeing things. Could it have been such a short time ago? His life had moved on so far since that sighting that he could scarcely remember what everything was like before Anna arrived at his door during the thunderstorm, and he was introduced to Merlinda by Godneau, and he had allowed himself to be persuaded to take up William's class –

where Anna had been a student already – and he had met Sonia in the Mall and escorted her back to the home she shared with – Merlinda. As much had happened in that small span of time as in the twenty years before it. And, in the usual manner of turbulent periods in one's life, even more curious – and now very alarming – possibilities seemed about to occur.

Heavens, he was already at the stop where he must alight and his notes had gone unread. Entering William's street he looked at his watch, and he was not late. In fact he was early – and arriving at exactly the same time as the others. Merlinda, twenty yards or so ahead of him, was pausing a moment beside a large car edging its way into a small space – and greeting Jake as he opened the driver's door, stepped out, and fumbled in his pocket for some change for a parking meter or a mobile phone with which to pay by sending a message.

* * *

William Bridgnorth surveyed the trio on his doorstep with an undeniable glow of pride and triumph in his eyes.

> "Well, I feel this is truly wonderful", he said,
> "That you should all arrive for this great day
> Together, and exactly at the time
> Agreed when we last met. Now, Frank, come in
> And Jake, and dear Merlinda. Take your seats.
> There is no need to draw a slip of paper
> Out of a hat. We know Frank's has to be
> Our final spell of noble oratory
> Before we all adjourn to the Fun Parade
> On Saturday at twelve. I shall myself
> Be at Embankment Station before then,
> To greet our friends the bakers when they bring
> Our Cake of Celebration, to be placed
> On a trolley the Westminster Hospital
> Has hired out to me. Mr Jeffrey Shanks,
> Student of mine, friend of Miss Armitage,
> Has now agreed to pull it all the way
> To the scheduled end of the long procession
> At three o'clock in Hyde Park, where we all

Shall cut it with the splendid silver knife
My great-grandfather left my grandfather,
Who left it to my Dad, and he to me,
In their Last Wills and Testaments. Till now,
It has not left its ceremonial case
Other than to be polished for this event.
But – If you're ready, Frank – May we begin?

Frank had taken in hardly any of these details, thinking he could ask Jake or Merlinda about them later. One word alone in William's speech, the name of the trolley-pusher, had been enough to drive away for several seconds all thought of the narrative he was due to commence: Mr. Jeffrey Shanks. Frank heard it with a mixture of astonishment and fear – and then a rush of relief.

He was astonished to know that Anna's Jeffrey had retained a connection with William strong enough for him to be entrusted with pulling the cake on the trolley; unless he was the only student of William's with enough physical stamina to accomplish that task. Then, his earlier apprehension at the thought of what he had pledged himself to do while Jeffrey was marching in the Parade was lessened when he heard about the role Jeffrey was to perform. Jeffrey's important place in William's party surely guaranteed that he would be absent from his flat for the entire duration of the Parade. Frank envisaged Anna indicating to him which person Jeffrey was (somebody he would now recognise from encounters on the stairs in the block), and he himself unobtrusively leaving the group before they moved away, returning home by Underground and/or taxi, letting himself silently into Jeffrey's flat, finding the gun in the drawer under the double bed, hidden between two spare duvets, stowing it in a prepared plastic bag, and – Meanwhile Jeffrey and the trolley would probably be reaching Piccadilly Circus.

William, receiving no response from Frank, repeated his command:

Frank, we await your wisdoms. You may start!

The words broke in on Frank's thoughts, in effect waking him up. You could say he had been dreaming. He had almost forgotten where he was, and what he had to do. Perhaps that even helped him to sound spontaneous when he started. It was a quality that William and the others praised later.

"I have to go back to the age of six", he said, in the first of a series of short sentences that caught the moment-to-moment tension of the experiences he was describing. He had not been able to compile his narrative in his mind in any way other than to see it as a long succession of images which summoned up his childhood and teens with an accompanying recollection of the fear and guilt he felt with almost every instance he cited.

The Liberty School in Camberwell had been compelled to change its name from Marshland Street Infant and Junior, in keeping with the fashion of suggesting aspiration rather than locality. Yet "liberty" was not cultivated by what some parents spoke of first as Mrs Goodborough's Academy and then as Goodborough PLC, as the little institution came increasingly to resemble a commercial company. The Reception, which children approached across a small yard where local business advertising – very valuable to keep it going – filled every wall, resembled a shop foyer. Indeed, the windows featured not only the school's achievements and the superior facilities which had produced them; school uniforms were on display for sale, as were books and computers required for the children's "studies", and other Aids to Learning. Mrs Goodborough and her staff made a well-dressed, happy photograph, enlarged to provide a renewed backdrop to those features at the beginning of each Michaelmas Term. Frank had resisted the temptation to provide a full description of these features of the school. But here a state-of-the-art digital camera valued at several hundred pounds had come into service decades later. He had stolen it from a specialist store on the final morning of a family holiday in the south of France when he was nine, and today in William Bridgnorth's lounge he was able to pass round his pictures of Mrs Goodborough's academy in support of his narrative. Today, of course, Liberty School had long been closed and the building demolished.

At first sight the classrooms in Frank's pictures were bright and well-equipped. But a visitor with any knowledge of schools and teaching – a well-informed parent, or a teacher in a better establishment – would quickly see that it was all a gloss over cheap and inferior equipment and practices. The teachers were not well paid. The bargain computers repeatedly broke down, requiring to repair them expensive consultants recommended by the Borough Education Department.

The thought of the shining red colour of Gemma Sexton's fountain pen on a spring day when Frank was six-and-a-half years old was still attractive to him, decades on from that moment. All boys had to wear school caps from their sixth birthdays onwards, and that day Frank left his behind in the classroom. He had done this before, and his mother had taken him back inside from the school gate to collect it – Cleopatra, his teacher, had smiled and called him "a scatterbrain". The difference this time was that he remembered the bright red pen and saw that Gemma had left it there at her place at the end of their table. Cleopatra turned her back in conversation with his mother at the door, he was momentarily alone in the emptied and silent room, and he slipped the pen into his trouser pocket. Already I was capable of guilt [said Frank of himself]. I was aware that I could not explain, if asked, how I acquired this fountain pen. "My Dad has a Ferrari, so have I", Gemma said once [referring to the brand name of this pen].

"You should take care of it," Cleopatra advised her.

Gemma had not done that, and Frank went home with it. But – to take up the matter of guilt – he knew that he had done something definitely wrong and that he dare not reveal his action. Also, there was a chance of being found out as long as he kept the pen. There was nowhere safe to hide it, so next day while shopping with his mother he wandered off and when he could be certain no one was watching him, he dropped it down a drain.

Some while after that – "It could have been that I was eight years old", recited Frank to the group – he was out with his father throwing a ball around for (his Dad's) exercise in the park. He could usually expect an ice cream at the end of these summer Sunday afternoons, always from the same corner shop where the lady smiled at him and his father held her in conversation much longer than his mother would – the lady could be rather cool towards his Mum. While his father slid back the glass lid of the cold compartment to get at the jumble of wrapped ices and lollies, Frank established their place in the "queue", which consisted of only another father and a small girl. As the assistant went to the safe at the end of her counter to obtain a plain packet of cigarettes with its ominous X-ray motif, this girl put out a hand and transferred a chocolate bar from a rack to the plastic bag she was carrying for her Dad. But then the father took it out of the bag again, returned it to the counter – and slipped in a larger one. Both of them carried out this exercise with expressionless faces, looking as if they had often done it before.

When his father joined him bringing two mint choc-ices on sticks, Frank tried whispering to him, "Dad, did you see what that girl and the man were doing?" Instantly, "Shsh!" his father ordered. Outside, he told Frank, "Whatever they were doing wasn't our business. Never get involved." Frank had the feeling Dad wasn't interested in anything that might interrupt the little chat he would have with the lady.

Frank began a habit of waiting innocently outside shops for likely cigarette purchasers to enter – generally, older and poorer-looking men who coughed – then following them and quietly picking up something from a display and leaving with it while the assistant took a packet out of a cupboard or from a hidden shelf. An episode in the large convenience branch of the BeauCo chain not far from his new school when he was eleven gave him his best ever opportunity up to that moment. The branch sold not only groceries but Health and Beauty goods and a small range of very ordinary clothes. Using the pretence of looking for some sweets he went in and wandered round the shelves taking a close look at other customers. If anyone should ask him at he was doing he had a reply ready: "My Mum wants to know if you sell cornflour." On this occasion he couldn't at first see any chance of getting away with something, although the uniformed security man was giving all his attention to a tall man in jeans who was standing with his bag near the shelves of bottles of alcoholic drinks.

Then a bell went. Like a doorbell, but much louder and longer. In fact it didn't stop until someone turned it off. Not only the security man but all three assistants at the check-outs and several of the customers – who all appeared to have a security role also – surrounded the man, who went red in the face and declared – in a strangely deep voice – "I got this at Carney's" (a nearby liquor store). But in no time at all two of these "customers", one male and one female, each in old trousers and sweaters, had marched the individual out to the back office of the shop. One of them called back to a check-out assistant who had resumed her place, "I know this cunt. I got him twice in the time he was a lesbian."

A week later Frank asked his mother what a "lesbian" was. "Oh. Not a nice thing at all," she replied. During this puzzling incident Frank had left the shop unnoticed (while the bell was still ringing) with two anoraks, one suited to his father and the other the right size for himself. These prizes were not to be lost like Gemma's fountain pen or consumed like the chocolate. Simply to leave them anywhere would have been an awful waste (his father's conclusion, not Frank's). They were worn by both of them in the following winter. The Winterfields were glad of them in the December of the Triple Dip.

As a teenager Frank learned to test shops, large and small, for the accusing bell which would warn assistants that someone was leaving with an item for which he or she had not paid. Once, but only ever once, did he have to give apologies (which were sympathetically accepted) for mistakenly smuggling goods into his bag before the assistant could get the bar code bleeped by the computer. It was easy to do they concluded, when he was carrying a wire tray and a couple of things in his other hand, and he looked so clean and innocent, this decent teenager coming to the shop for his disabled mother. Mrs Winterfield herself had become complicit in these forays into danger, accepting each and every prize as it arrived, not altogether realising the seriousness of receiving stolen goods. But his father was sufficiently aware of the gravity of the offence to be prepared to swear on oath that his wife and his son had kept Frank's activities secret from him. Mr Winterfield had despaired of correcting any of his wife's other deplorable habits, so was prepared to protect himself from any of the consequences of Irene's and Frank's crimes.

Irene did sometimes think that Frank was going too far, and that he should stop before he was caught and needed to ask for other offences to be taken into consideration. But she was devoted to him as an only child and he always had the better of her when she gave him a serious talking-to. He listened to his mother during that hard period after he left school and had no job for several months, because he knew she was quite right to say that a conviction for shoplifting would be noticed by any potential employer. Nothing in anyone's life was secret any more from persons who wanted to find everything out. Moreover, in his job in the Borough Environmental Section he was scrupulous from the beginning about never committing any offence of any kind at work. You would be dismissed much faster than you were taken on. But away from the office, on holiday for example, he continued to indulge his addiction, becoming more sophisticated and skilful in extracting items from quiet corners in small shops and stores and feeling considerable pride at evading the cameras and detectives. Mrs Winterfield's warnings still failed to stop him. Frank knew how to start his mother giggling at almost any time. On the afternoon when he picked up someone else's paid-for butchery purchase, and unwrapped three excellent lamb chops on returning home, and mother's mouth opened in horror, his own giggle set her going within seconds. "You just shouldn't, Frank," she protested. "You really do have to give this up." As her husband was unable to correct her, so she was unable to correct her son – but didn't really want to. The family trio developed and lived with this delicate structure of indifference to what the youngest member was doing.

One day in his early twenties he told himself he would have to leave the habit behind because he was no longer a child or teenager. A responsible, and rising, local government officer would have everything to lose. The blame would fall on him faster and harder because so many people rejoiced to see a respectable individual brought down. The longer Frank went on stealing the huger the risk. The reasons accumulated. He had the opportunity to stop while no one except his parents knew about it. He began to spend more time away from home, to make more friends – including girls – and brought fewer prizes from supermarket and specialist retail outlets, keeping all of those to himself. These days Mum and Dad never explored his room because it was so much more orderly, and smelt so much better, than in his teenage years. The stolen goods filled cupboards but did not overflow – or at least not appear to do that because several large purloined articles served as excellent furnishings.

On holiday with friends he found an unexpected pleasure in exercise, most of all in rambles in hill country, where he impressed himself with what he could do when used to it. Back in London he equipped himself for the next holiday, or for a few energetic week-ends, with better shoes and sweaters, or good all-weather garments that would keep him dry and warm without being too heavy to wear at other times and too unwieldy to pack away when he had no immediate need of them. Everything he acquired at this stage was bought, nothing stolen. It was with pride and without any frisson of fear that he walked one day into a shop in the High Road that sold all kinds of strenuous gear.

The denim coat he purchased had numerous wide or deep pockets, inside and out, some with flaps, many with zips, all of these accessible with ease. At once – and he shocked himself by so doing – Frank thought that if he filled several of these recesses with thick or bulky articles – and people today carried immense quantities of stuff on their persons or in their backpacks – then something new pushed into an available pocket might pass unnoticed. He brought up on a mental screen all the shops and emporia, and in fact premises and institutions of every sort, where in the recent past he had gone without apprehension of alarms or bells or over-vigilant assistants, and where there were shelves and whole enclaves free of other customers – and where small, even sometimes large, goods had been rapidly whipped into his not-very-capacious mackintosh or overcoat pockets.. This new coat answered all the problems of space, ease of access and provision for adequate concealment which Frank's conventional clothing lacked. As for his new garment resembling something more likely to be worn on Helvellyn or Ben Nevis than in the Fulham Road… Look around you – people are garbed in absolutely anything, there is no conventional clothing any more, in business or out of it, even in the Civil Service, even in government. In recent years it's the wearer of the conventional suit who attracts attention, even in the most previously formal of settings. All Frank needed to appear natural and not be noticed was to create a worn, roughened look about his new possession.

He did not make the mistake of turning up everywhere in that same coat, or for that matter restricting himself to the same territory. In a characteristic week he might wait until Wednesday (because Monday and Tuesday were evenings of light "footfall" in most of the shops and a lone figure would be more noticeable on camera) and make a couple of visits in the rush hour, sometimes going home first to change. Late opening on Thursdays and Fridays and of course at the week-ends enabled him to mix with more fellow-customers, never in the same district two weeks running and contriving never to be recognised as a regular. He hardly ever spoke to any assistant, never smiled, never made the same legitimate purchases or went to the same check-out. He practised no typical style of placing his goods on the moving surface for the assistant to register each price – never either scrupulously neat or heedlessly untidy, he played dull and ordinary. In one place he had a bad scare which reminded him of the episode in his childhood when the alleged former lesbian had been intercepted: a loud alarm went off for someone else reaching the automatic doors, warning him that the existing surveillance system must have been recently enhanced by the addition of such a facility. Frank had not begun to unload his small, shallow trolley and stopped immediately. "Ah – forgotten something!" he muttered to the assistant, and doubled back to the row of glass-fronted shelves from which he had taken three packs of overpriced smoked salmon. These he was able to extract from a large wallet pocket in the coat when no one was looking, and he was (he trusted) beyond the stare of the ceiling camera – and put them back, as if he was simply changing his mind. It was a warm spring day and he was sad to be without the chill of the refrigerated plastic packets against his chest. This shop he struck off his list, which was shortening with the exclusion, month by month around the turn of the millennium, of numerous other places where Security had been improved at a greater cost than that involved in the loss of goods to impoverished shoplifters.

With some success he cultivated swiftness – and innocence – of movement in transferring items from the displays to his ample pockets. Not many people who wore coats or jackets of any kind walked round stores with them buttoned up, even when it was raining hard outside, and keeping his own new coat informally open naturally permitted him to secrete stolen objects faster. Mostly he would patrol the aisles with just a wire basket, putting into it as a cover things he feared he would be seen stealing because of their awkward size or bulk. He also became accomplished at achieving brief and businesslike visits, not exactly running from shelf to shelf but doing everything in a quick, efficient way, not lingering indecisively or gazing at displays as if wondering what he really needed and whether he could afford it.

When he thought about his life of larceny he came to four conclusions. The first: It was not his only life, because he had a job that was probably secure in an insecure time and he was able to save a little money; and he had friends (who knew nothing about it), including young women. Secondly, he could justify it as a small revenge for the commercial overcharging and other capitalist deceptions frequently inflicted on him, as described by his Marxist colleague; the shops he robbed deserved to be. Third, it was a secret that gave him pleasure and excitement – he was sure he knew people, at work and in his rambling club, who practised equivalent hidden pleasures, connected with sex or illegal substances. Fourthly, it was something he could give up at any time. It was not a compulsive addiction.

Frank's wardrobe, chest of drawers and cupboard in his bedroom filled up with all the objects that could not be eaten or otherwise consumed. Various items went as discreet gifts to friends at appropriate times, Christmas in particular, thus didn't remain in the house for very long. But so much did remain: technological devices, unwearable articles of clothing, household goods pilfered from ironmongers', floor mats, stools, table lamps and other small items of furniture. Gradually he was leaving himself with little space to move, and this dilemma proved a very important factor in his getting married.

His parents happened to like Sara, and were pleased for Frank (now in his mid-thirties), as well as looking forward in their sixties to a life on their own once more when Frank had gone. They did not fancy a prosecution in their old age for having all those unexplained goods on the premises. Sara had been one of the most vigorous of the ramblers, and her energy was quickly transferred to the equipping of the strangely spacious flat in the block near the World's End. [This detail did not feature in Frank's verse narrative, but both Frank Winterfield and Jeffrey Shanks had acquired leases at less than the market rate because the entire area was scheduled for demolition on account of a "planned transport development". They were safe at least until the scheme was put into action, which Frank's colleague in Planning said was unlikely to be before 2050].

Frank was reticent with Sara concerning the large quantity of smaller but very useful goods he was able to present as contributions to their marital home. He transported them cautiously to the flat one or two at a time, and they fitted in very conveniently with the much bigger objects that came from Sara's place, including the sofa, the bed, two armchairs and many kitchen items. All these were what an unmarried woman on a professional salary might acquire for living by herself (for who knows how long? For ever?) but Sara was puzzled as to why Frank had been buying so many things for his own bedroom at home. Men didn't usually do that. All the men she knew who had married after she met them had accumulated enough savings to buy a few home furnishings when that happened, none of them stocked up beforehand with modern equipment as Frank had apparently done. It seemed a bit eccentric to have done that. But Sara forgot about it as the months passed, and came to think of this cutlery, and that sideboard runner, and those vases, as her own; which of course they legally were.

"Did anyone give you any of these things?" she asked once; thinking, could have they have come from a past relationship? No. That would have been so out of character for Frank… She dismissed the idea immediately. But it continued to puzzle her. She sometimes summed up the balance between what she and her husband had provided for their home. The best pieces of furniture – well, almost all the pieces – had been hers. Yet some very up-to-date things, like the coffee grinder and the electronic kettle, had been his. The Ultra Digital TV, which you could switch on from anywhere above or below ground in London within five kilometres of home, had also been Frank's. She had met the solicitor's fees for conveyancing, but Frank had put down the deposit on the mortgage they required for the cost of a 99-year lease – and had, after all, found the flat in the first place.

[Merlinda waited in vain for Frank to say more about Sara and how they had eventually parted. The most he did was confess that fairly recently they had ceased to cohabit after various misunderstandings about the running of the household, and Sara had removed from the flat all the personal chattels she had originally brought into it. He considered by this point that he had said enough about the detail of his activities. He would now consider the moral issues involved as he saw them in the present, and make reference to an outstanding dilemma that was confronting him even as he spoke.]

Theft of any kind was wrong, Frank proposed. It had been maintained by his rather radical colleague in the Environment Department (who knew nothing at all about Frank's secret life) that property was theft in itself. Frank could not agree with that. He was prepared to tax extreme wealth, but not arbitrarily dispossess people of their land or property or wealth by revolution, or even by legislation. In leaving a supermarket one day pushing a wheeled basket he was pretending he had pushed in, he argued that he was *taxing* for his own social benefit a huge corporation which evaded its fiscal responsibilities by basing itself in an offshore haven. His socialist colleague might – wrongly, though – have applauded such a theft as a creditable act of revenge on BeauCo (or whichever rapacious monster it happened to be). But he was going to explore such questions by citing this entirely personal problem, which provided him with an extraordinary quantity of relevant material.

"I've pledged myself – this week – to undertake
A minor robbery, which might involve
Saving a life, or at the very least
Preventing injury. In short, I must
Remove the instrument with which such harms

189

Might be committed. – And, I must confess,
All this is complicated by the fact
That I have been the lover of one likely
Victim of such enormities…

The man with whom Frank's lover had formerly lived had been given to domestic violence, and among his possessions was a revolver presumably taken home illegally from the armed services. This gun had been out of service for some time but its owner had cleaned and refurbished it and purchased the ammunition to use in it from secret dealers. Clearly the woman was in danger – as Frank also might be – and had appealed to him for help. He seemed to her to qualify himself for the task of stealing the revolver by his confessed track record in larceny.

He had promised the woman [Anna, but Frank could not reveal her name] that he would enter the flat [Jeffrey's, but he did not give that name either] in a few days' time with the aid of a key she had retained from the period of her living there, and find the revolver in the secret place where she knew for certain her former lover kept it.

He justified this act, if he was to carry it out, in the following way. Entering someone's home without permission was indeed wrong and you could only attempt to defend such an entry if the resident was a close friend or relation and the intention was benevolent. None of these circumstances applied in this case. But Frank would not be "breaking and entering" (although, what was "breaking" in the eyes of the law?) He would admit himself silently, and once inside conduct himself quietly and do no damage, being assured that the gun was not locked in a desk or cupboard he would have to open by force.

Naturally he would take precautions. He would carry, in an opaque plastic bag without any identifying brand name on it, a pair of new shoes, and once outside with the gun would drop the very old shoes he had been wearing (for the first time in years) into a recycling bin in case they had left behind footprints or particles of dust which might be traceable to their owner. He assumed that very little of his DNA would be left in these shoes if he wore a pair of surgical socks. But he was straying from the moral question he had promised to address. Frank argued to himself that he would not be committing a serious burglary. He would only be "collecting" an illegal weapon from a potentially dangerous owner and doing that in the interest of the law. He would drop it somewhere – drain, or river, or landfill? – out of harm's way. Without it, the ammunition, which had apparently been distributed around the flat, would be useless and Frank could not believe that [Jeffrey] would go to the trouble of hunting for another antique revolver of this kind which would take the same bullets. No one except [Anna] need ever know of his deed, which would render a palpable service to the community and be altogether defensible on moral grounds if Frank should be obliged to justify it in a court of law.

He said at this point that he was strongly tempted to leave the resolution of the moral issue to the other members of the class. But it would be only appropriate to muster one or two arguments against his going ahead. The least important reasons were in the "Could it not be that –?" category. Could it not be that my attraction to the woman in question was setting me off on the wrong track? Could it not be that I was wanting to prove I had not lost my old kleptomaniac skill? No. Much wider moral considerations needed to be brought up and rejected. A theft of anyone's personal property, on any grounds, was wrong; he had held to that position ever since he had dropped Gemma's fountain pen down the drain. And in psychological terms stealing was bad for your character and in social terms bad for the community because it loosened the bonds of mutual respect which held society together. These were strong practical arguments which derived their power from the fact that the stability of everyday life depended on the honesty of individuals. But Frank believed that the courage invoked in an important cause, or in a readiness to use exceptional means to achieve a noble end, was a vastly grander proposition that defeated any attempt to justify the retention of a lethal weapon by a dangerous individual on the grounds that his property was "sacrosanct" because it was, well, "property".

"And 'sacrosanct' [Frank concluded] – how strange a word that is,

> Presumably intended to define,
> At the beginning, anything we should
> Hold seriously sacred, not to be
> Soiled, slandered or abused – not even touched
> By unworthy hands. Sheer hypocrisy
> Invented "sacrosanct" to save itself,
> And so the only use we have for it
> Is to deplore some holy boundary

Drawn round an undeserving false idea
– I rest my case for doing what I should.

All William Bridgnorth did at the moment when Frank finished was give a long weighty nod, as if reserving his reaction until he had digested the implications of this narrative. But then he appeared to see that he ought to preserve the custom of encouragement, which should not be given too slowly, or in a perfunctory or insincere manner.

He rose to his feet and went out to his kitchen with these words –

And what more fitting – after such a speech –
Than that we should anticipate our role
In the forthcoming Fun Parade with *this* –

He was gone long enough for Merlinda to look around in the quiet that followed his departure and reflect on what they had just heard and how the others had reacted to it.

She now knew Frank socially better than either Jake or William himself. But she was utterly astonished at the sense of drama he had deployed to bring his narrative to a conclusion, with an effort that left him looking tired and pale. She thought he would ramble towards a genial, reassuring ending, which would arrive when his stamina for spinning out iambic pentameters had expired. Instead, he had halted suddenly, leaving them all very surprised at what his tale had revealed, and pondering the questions raised by his final passages. Jake said nothing, but raised his eyebrows, tightened his lips, and stared into space for a second, making clear a kind of bewilderment about what they had heard. Merlinda wondered if she saw a disapproving expression waiting to show itself more clearly? Frank had given a small awkward smile of relief at the end of his performance. His eyes followed William to the door and remained focussed there until he came in again carrying a cake, the very finest example so far.

21

Jake Coleman had been enough of a rebel against his father to reject the option of taking over the furniture store business should he die. And he did die. And Jake didn't take it over. All the same, Frank's implicit pride in his skill – as a mere shoplifter, when it came to it – offended something Jake had retained from his upbringing: a pride, despite everything, in Dad's achievement in keeping the business on its feet through hard times. Jake had never stolen anything in his life, not even someone else's girlfriend. He had at first been conscious, in Dr. Erznik's clinic, that Melanita was attached to her young male colleague at Reception, but he had left immediately when he was made aware of that. The idea of lifting articles from commercial premises reminded him too much of his father's accounts of the losses incurred in his own store, and the dire experiences of many colleagues in retail. The expense of installing security systems of the most up-to-date kind was well worth it for Mr. Coleman Sr. Even if chests of drawers, beds, and armchairs were not likely to vanish into the households of Frank and his like, Mr. Coleman had certainly lost pillows, and pouffes and standing lamps, and several leaves from expanding dining tables.

And then there was Frank's confession, even stranger perhaps than the revelation of his kleptomania, of his intention to steal an antique revolver which was in working order and filled with bullets for maiming and killing. It said something else about Frank, that he should know a woman mixed up with a man who possessed such a weapon. Maybe there was something scary and sinister under his ordinary surface, his air of a conventional man studying with William Bridgnorth to express himself in a noble, traditional English manner? And what exactly was Frank's connection with Merlinda? Sometimes these two turned up at different moments and left in different directions, but there were occasions they arrived and left together.

As he got out of the train at Embankment and joined the large crowd moving along the platform to the exits, it suddenly puzzled Jake to see Frank walking towards him, against this large throng of people. Surely he would be heading in the same direction as him and everyone else?

"Where're you going? Aren't we meeting here?"

Frank turned and walked for a few seconds alongside him, with the crowd.

"Hi! - yes. It's just that I – I'll have to join you in a few minutes".

"Shall I tell William? He ought to know?" Jake suggested.

"He knows. I won't be long. I've – sort of forgotten something."

It all deepened Jake's suspicions. William had stressed repeatedly that they should all arrive on time – preferably be half-an-hour early – and parade as a united group, talking together in verse. But here was one of his students taking time off for some reason before they had even started.

"See you later, then," Frank said, and walked away quite quickly up this platform, the crowd having thinned out during this short exchange. Perhaps he's not feeling well, Jake concluded; not surprising, given the heat.

"Hotter than ever," someone in front of him remarked as Jake left the station by the riverside exit. "Forecast says thirty-nine," someone else said. But the heat did not seem to reduce the energy of the Great Year Volunteers mustered outside Embankment station. Everyone in the crowd except Jake appeared to know where to go, and responded to the cheery loud-hailer instructions from the uniformed stewards. "Green passes to the left – two hundred yards along. Blue passes just here to your right. Approved Participants, to the right and *keep going* – you'll find your Top Banner about 150 yards along, end of the Main Procession."

Everyone else was able to show the passes required to admit them to the section of the Parade where they were permitted to join as reliable citizens. Jake noticed that Great Year Volunteer stewards and police mingled cordially, indistinguishable from each other with their dayglo gear and official badges and numbers. There were enough of them to achieve a quick scrutiny of every member of the assembly who did not conform to the general pattern.

"Whereabouts, sir?" a police officer asked Jake, and when Jake replied "I am not sure" proceeded to explain the different stages of the Parade. The beginning of the official Main Procession, close to

Westminster Bridge, was held in a special enclosure. Behind that came a series of equally official displays and tableaux on agreed themes, for which their creators had needed to make application six months earlier. These were the Approved Participants, and were also already assembled and simply awaiting the signal to move off. Then there would come the part to which he directed Jake, ordinary people from every region of the United Kingdom who were welcome to join in wearing smart clothes of a casual kind as long as they all looked cheerful and positive. Most would have been vetted and approved by regional committees of organisers. Everybody had to carry a certifying document, and Jake – whose smart, expensive casuals had led the policeman to think he might even be an Approved Participant – did not possess one. But it was eventually accepted he could join those people he declared he was with, waiting with an empty trolley - on the opposite pavement, overlooking the Thames.

Jake crossed over to join the small group gathered around William and consisting of – not Frank at the moment, but certainly Merlinda and a good-looking woman in her late thirties whom he believed he recognised as the student from another class met on William's doorstep a couple of weeks ago.

William himself stood between the broad trolley and the parapet above the river, talking to a man Jake did not recognise. He appeared to be receiving instructions from William, so no doubt this was Jeffrey Shanks, learning what to do about pushing the Cake all the way to Hyde Park. Pleasantly William welcomed Jake: "Saving the new contingent coming up/ From distant Somerset, we are complete."

"Then has the Cake arrived?" Jake was bound to ask, looking at the bare trolley standing here on its strong rubber wheels, smiling at Merlinda, nodding at the others one by one (his father used to nod like this at familiar customers in the store). Anna Armitage took no notice of his greeting and stared out across the water. Jeffrey, whose hand patting the rail of the trolley impatiently signified a desire to have this over and done with, had his eyes at this moment fixed on the back of Anna's head.

"It is due now," William replied to Jake's question; loud and emphatic, his manner assured, even triumphant. He had made no concessions to the heat, dressing out of doors exactly as he did in his classes at home. Not seated in an armchair, he was really very tall and broad, an updated version of an eighteenth century rural gentleman whose every word and action would be serious and important.

"Our friends in Somerset have promised me," he went on, attracting the attention of everyone within a radius of ten yards, "that they will bring a banner they have made/ For this occasion. We are in touch online, /And they have formed a 'Blank Verse Colloquy'/ To work with me in video-conference/ From Taunton, twice a week."

Merlinda turned her head and looked at William with her mouth slightly open in consternation. If this sort of arrangement worked, where was it all going? Would William be able to handle it by himself if it became the success he certainly desired and it spread to groups like this in the regions?

And here, surely, was the Somerset delegation, two men and a woman got up in clothes of an unconvincingly casual sort – frayed jeans that seemed too new, over-laundered t-shirts – carrying a banner as they made their way through the crowd in William's direction. When they reached William's party an individual who appeared to be speaking for the three of them lifted a hand to shake William's in a patently artificial gesture; nothing about his manner looked relaxed or genuine. Nor did his blank verse greeting.

"I take it you are Mr Bridgnorth, sir," he declared with an antique formality of which William might be expected to approve – but he did look slightly doubtful, confirming an uneasiness felt by Merlinda, who came to another conclusion about them. They looked too brisk and capable. All the six here today from William's two current classes were intelligent people with problems – she allowed herself this description – who thought that the disciplines and rigours of William's teachings would help them in one way or another. The new colleagues spoke William's English after a fashion, but Merlinda could not think they had submitted themselves to the same tests with the same energy and eagerness. There was brightness in their manner, but their smiles and greetings, and the speed with which they learned and repeated the forenames they were given suggested something inappropriately professional. They could be from a branch of Security, adept at changing colour to a suitable shade for any faction or tendency they were paid to snoop on, smiling and laughing too much.

Merlinda turned aside, finding an excuse to walk a couple of yards and look down over the parapet at the Thames flowing below. Her attention was only regained when William suddenly called everyone to order. The Cake was arriving. The younger driver and older passenger in the van from the bakery wore the white coats of their profession and William greeted them like old friends. Two police officers from whom they asked permission with exaggerated regard to stop for a few minutes on a double yellow line to unload their cargo, asked questions about which part of the parade the party would join.

The police quite definitely wished to know whether William could prove he had consent to add his display to the procession. William explained, gesticulating amiably with the air of someone who could only believe that the constabulary would be on his side in such an excellent cause. Yet they did not seem altogether to believe what he was telling them. One of them went onto a mobile, muttered into it and obtained a response, shook his head. "They can't trace the details, sir," he told William. But the Somerset leader stepped forward unexpectedly and said something to the officer with his back turned which Merlinda couldn't hear. And the second policeman nodded with pursed lips. A few further prods at the mobile… One or two further words exchanged… A gesture in the direction of Westminster Bridge. The bakers looked confused and frustrated.

"All I can say, sir," the senior policeman eventually said, "is that you proceed to the appropriate position at the end of the APs, and see our colleagues at that point. They'll be aware you're coming."

Had a buck been passed? Plainly William's group could proceed for now, and discover later what their fate was to be. The bakers knew exactly what to do and how to do it; they opened the back doors of the van and a crowd quickly gathered to watch them. The higher baker spoke for both:

> "As the practitioners of an ancient trade
> We come here with a sense of privilege
> At being able to participate
> In such a splendid venture."

The two police watched everything as if waiting for a palpable infringement of the law which would enable them to intervene. The younger baker climbed into the inside of their vehicle and lifted the Cake in its multi-layered covering of tissue paper out of a very big white box secured safely to the floor. Positioning himself with legs apart to achieve steady balance, the senior baker muttered to his assistant some instructions which did not sound as if they were in verse, took the Cake from him with infinite care, and waited for him to jump down.

The Cake, once set up on the trolley, could be seen to be around two feet in diameter and stood about eighteen inches tall. It had a white icing that shone over its entire surface, plus several little representations of famous poets – Shakespeare, Dryden, Pope, Wordsworth and a modern blank verse master Merlinda could not name. Had William given the bakers advice on how to design them? And the little representations of Dove Cottage and Anne Hathaway's place in Stratford-upon-Avon? Merlinda wondered what would have happened if rain had been forecast (which it was not)? Would the colours have run and the models melted? No sooner had these thoughts occurred than the senior baker, standing back from the spectacle of his work mounted for its day of fame, observed to William Bridgnorth, "I'm glad we do not need the canopy./ The forecast tells us that fine weather should/ Prevail for the whole day, sir." "So I hear," William affirmed. Then, raising his voice and his hands, he gave them all the orders for their departure: "Now, then! The time has come for us to find / Our place in the Parade. Our day begins."

When the Somerset banner was unfurled Merlinda felt certain that the group was not genuine. At the top, above its words, it displayed the cross of St George, and she knew that William would not have supported his cause with the kind of sentiment that currently implied a patriotic devotion to a certain, limited kind of "Englishness." But worse than that, the words themselves were not suitable and made the banner itself seem out of place:

> As citizens of England we come today to praise
> The great English iambic pentam*a*ter.

Nothing was right about that statement. The most obvious thing wrong was the misspelling of "pentameter". Perhaps that was due to the probable haste with which the banner was made, but it was grossly embarrassing. Inexcusable. And then the artificial, stencilled appearance of the words was in contrast to the finely embroidered slogans on other banners now coming into sight as cohorts of other exhibitors formed up to join the long line ahead. Most shaming of all was the sheer badness of the two lines as blank verse. The first had too many syllables, both lacked any rhythm. William would never have let them get away with it in a class.

He courteously asked the Somerset trio to follow his students with their banner rather than lead them. He himself would walk one yard in front, the Cake urged on by Jeffrey would come next, the other students would follow, and the banner would bring up the rear. The eyes of onlookers would thus be drawn not to that, but to William and the Cake.

At the moment they moved away Frank Winterfield was entering his block. So far his planning had been faultless. With all the main streets inside a radius of four miles closed to anything except buses – so that everyone could reach the Parade without difficulty – he had expected to be home within half-an-hour, and he was. There was no sign of life, or sound, in the building as he tried to walk normally, casually up the stairs. On the first floor landing he was tempted to abandon this entire hazardous enterprise while he was still innocent. He could let himself into his own flat, collect some overlooked item of property, leave again without putting himself at risk. But he was planning to do that as a cover anyway, after collecting the gun. He went on up to the second floor landing.

There he turned left, as he would have done on his own floor, ready to pretend, if he saw someone regarding him with suspicion, that he had made a silly, absent-minded mistake and come up too far. But he encountered nobody. "Put the yale in the lock, and pull the door by the handle towards you as you turn it," Anna had said. But for a frightening second, fitting an unfamiliar key awkwardly into a different lock gave him a painful fear that this was not the right door at all, that Anna herself had made some mistake. Then, with a tug at the handle, he did manage to turn the key, the door opened, and he stepped inside.

For a flat with the same lay-out as his own it appeared so unlike his, so alien… A stranger's furniture and proud possessions generally rendered it a completely different proposition and one that Frank didn't understand or enjoy at all. Why on earth have that peculiar hanging screen of strings of coloured beads over the open entry to the kitchen? The short corridor leading to the two bedrooms was narrower, and he experienced a moment of claustrophobia in it; Jeffrey had lined it on one side with a low, glass-fronted cabinet and ranged a horrid series of china trinkets on top. Nevertheless the open door to the first bedroom revealed something almost comparable to his own pleasant furniture (what Sara had left for him): a standard king-size bed with deep drawers underneath it, a small bedside table with lamp, chest of drawers, window onto the yard. The main difference was in the several pictures of completely unremarkable country scenes, the kind people acquired and hung and forgot.

He crossed to the window. Although the high midday sun was shining onto the room, and it was unlikely that somebody would be able to see inside it from another window or from the ground, he wanted to check if there was anyone down in the yard. No, it was empty. It should have felt reassuring, yet it didn't. He took in from this higher level the familiar sight of the yellow drainpipe on the wall of the nearest house and wondered if a prison cell would afford him such a view.

He checked such thoughts, and went round to the door side of the bed, where he bent over to pull open the drawer Anna had said contained the hidden revolver. He should feel with extreme care, she had said, between the two spare duvets, and in no circumstances take them out because they would be very hard to fit back and a "higgledy-piggledy look" would tell Jeffrey someone else had been into the drawer. So Frank pulled on the kitchen rubber gloves he had brought (not without some anxiety, in case the efficient plastic snapping sound should be heard out in the corridor) and tried to feel his way under the soft layers of the bottom duvet to identify a hard and different object on the floor of the drawer.

Wherever his hand went he felt nothing at all. He tried again, and without question there was no gun, nothing except the soft and heavy duvets (he also explored the space between them), nothing else anywhere in the drawer. Nor was there in the other drawer. Both were empty of anything except the duvets. He stood up and looked round in despair. "I don't think Jeffrey knows that I know where he keeps it," Anna had said. But Frank surmised that whether or not it was the case, Jeffrey might anyway change the hiding-place from time to time. If that were so his mission would have failed, because there were too many possible places to look in the time he had.

But he still swiftly opened each of the drawers in the chest and ferreted among socks and pants and handkerchiefs. A pile of laundered shirts on a wardrobe shelf in the other bedroom yielded nothing. Nor was the gun concealed in a pocket of any of the suits or jackets on hangers, or in any of the boots and shoes on the wardrobe floor. Obviously it was not going to be behind or under the cushions on the sofa and the armchairs in the lounge, or visible in any cabinet. There were a few books on a small set of shelves but the gun was not behind them nor was it concealed in any imitation book. In the bathroom, or the separate lavatory? No. Similarly not in any kitchen drawer or cupboard, or in the fridge, the freezer, the oven (all unlikely, but he quickly tried them). Could he have got rid of it? But Anna said it was his proudest achievement, a masterpiece of restoration. Ancient as it was, it could once again be used for its original awful purpose.

Frank had been looking for ten – no, fifteen minutes. There was nothing to do now but leave, go back, find Anna on the Fun Parade, confess failure. But he would give every room and space and corner one final look in case an idea occurred to him. Under a floorboard? He had not seen anything like an ill-fitting carpet and was not going to try to lift any of the planks on one bare pine floor.

Irrelevantly he felt a growing hunger. There was no way he was going to satisfy that by taking something from the fridge, or stealing one of the apples or oranges or bananas in a large, fresh heap on the antique fruit bowl on the lounge/dining room table, though they were more tempting than anything he had in his own flat. Nevertheless, in miserable frustration he did pick up a peach from this display – to discover that it was false, a beautiful wax imitation, as they all were. None of them was real; but the gun hidden underneath them was perfectly genuine.

He sat down on one of Jeffrey's shining dining chairs to look at the thing for a moment or two and be absolutely sure it was real. He took it in one rubber-clothed hand, then in the other. First he rested the heavy chamber of bullets in the left, then took it by its handle – keeping his forefinger away from the trigger – in the right. At the end of its butt it had a small metal ring attached to it, presumably to allow it to be hung on a hook in an armoury. Its colour, a deeply stained or weathered silver, testified to long years out of use. Gripping the handle tightly and pointing the barrel towards the floor, he rotated the chamber. Clockwise it went, with the careful movement of his free thumb, and he thought the six small bullets, all gleaming like the fresh metal they were, were unquestionably very new. Then he released a catch and the whole chamber dropped down to a reloading position. That was so much safer a position; but not how he could leave it.

My God, he wasn't going to leave it at all, was he! That was not why he had broken into – no, only entered – Jeffrey's flat to search for it.

He took out the first of two plastic bags, wrapped the weapon inside it, put the bundle into his jacket pocket and made his way slowly out again, once more meeting or hearing no one. When he opened his own front door the place as he had left it seemed to be accusing him (quite rightly) of having come in at an unusual time of day for a purpose he should feel ashamed and frightened of. Here was his own bedroom, so unlike the one he had rummaged in fifteen minutes ago, but it was not calm and reassuring, and it should have been. There on the bed was his prepared second plastic bag, containing the brand-new shoes he had bought by mail order for this enterprise. They were still in the tapioca-like folds of bubble-wrap in which they had arrived.

The old shoes he took off, and the surgical socks he had bought from a large health emporium in Harley Street (with cash, so that his credit card details would not be traced). Both shoes and socks, he assumed, carried his DNA, so it would be best to drop them into separate recycling bins on the way back to the Parade. He fitted the new shoes over a pair of old socks, not without difficulty, and slid or nudged the revolver, still in its plastic bag from upstairs, inside the bubble-wrap. The old shoes and socks went into the same carrier, but outside the wrap so that he could get at them easily when he found a bin in which to dump them. It only remained for him to get away from the block, feeling scarcely more safe than at any time in the last twenty minutes.

The bus, for once speeding up the eerily empty King's Road, took him to Sloane Square underground station in four minutes. He decided he would not go all the way to Embankment with the gun, but alight at Victoria first with the plan to dispose of it where he would be less noticeable if anyone – if any camera – were tracking him on this journey. Victoria was only one stop, but every second in a still-crowded train terrified him, as did the fear of detection by man, woman, animal or metal detector each time he passed through a barrier. He was very glad to be out into the large concourse of the main line Victoria station and mixing with the crowds, and he intended to find a bin or bins in Wilton Road or Vauxhall Bridge Road, where small restaurants would no doubt be filling numerous receptacles with quantities of uncooked or uneaten fast food. The gun could be recycled with it.

But the public recycling containers did not appear to be available for commercial users, even the few private users, in this district. Each restaurant rubbish bin was placed in an entry at the side of the premises so as not to obstruct the pavement, and in a position where any deposit of material by an unconnected individual might be noticed. Frank once heard a policeman asking, "What are you getting rid of, sir?" when a man was unloading personal detritus in a shop bin in Chelsea, and he did not want to have to answer such an enquiry. Lamely, and with growing apprehension, he went back to Victoria and boarded an eastbound train. He was trapped by his own inefficiency. Getting out twice on a very short journey would show on his transport card records; besides, genteel St James's Park would have been too quiet and respectable for his purpose. He was bound – how badly he had planned this! – to stay on the train to Westminster, join William and his companions on the Parade if he could find them, and dispose of his burden at a later time and place.

And the shoes? For the first time he realised it would be safer to dump those in a different place, nowhere near the revolver, to reduce the chance of their being associated with it if they were found. To leave each shoe in a different place would be better still. Accordingly he took his left shoe out of the bag and poked it into a corner near the carriage door as he left. The right shoe he held in his hand as an empty escalator took him upwards, setting it down two steps ahead of him as he approached the top; where, walking away, he looked back after a few yards and saw the escalator still trying to be rid of it, the shoe stuck there as the flattening steps slid on underneath it.

If any camera took an interest in Frank Winterfield and the revolver as he emerged into the daylight from Westminster tube, no immediate action occurred. Perhaps all of Security was employing human eyes only, at this moment anyway. The head of the Fun Parade was just reaching Parliament Square and preparing to turn right into Whitehall under the gaze of Big Ben – literally so, because "observers" were watching it from high up on the scaffolding that had covered the tower for some weeks before the Great Year events. The famous structure was yet another building enclosed in wrappers and waiting for something new and magnificent to be done to it over endless coming months.

Heading the procession was, as their huge and handsome banner declared, the National Great Fun Marching Band. At the moment Frank, joining the onlookers to look out for his friends, first saw this Band, they were striding sturdily and noisily ahead. But almost at once they halted when the whole Parade did, and the music stopped, everywhere. The halt into uncomfortable and unexplained silence was not for any clear reason, because the traffic lights had been taken out of service and the carriageways were empty. All Security vigilance was focussed on the succession of open-top limousines that slowly followed the band and gave members of the public here a better chance of seeing the notables striving in the heat to maintain their grins and return the waves of spectators. In something like ten seconds both sides abandoned the attempt, and silence fell on everybody. The only purpose of a Fun Parade was for those taking part to march and smile, and when that became impractical everyone was at a loss. The royal Prince and the Prime Minister, together in the back seat of the first limousine, stopped smiling and appeared to be only exchanging puzzled observations, with small unnatural head-shakings. Well-known politicians from the major parties showed an embarrassed indifference. A limousine with the two Anglican and the two Catholic archbishops sitting opposite each other was a picture of discomfort. Someone in the crowd shouted a greeting to the four famous Olympic sportspeople in the fifth, or sixth, stationary vehicle, but when the famous woman cyclist returned it with a small wave, another called out, "Go back for your bike, Henrietta!"

What could it be that was going on over there to his left and caught Frank's attention at this moment? In the direction of Westminster Bridge – on the bridge itself? A group of young people, men and women in equal numbers, the first protesters of the day – were emerging from the lines of spectators behind the waist-high barriers. Had Frank heard very much about "the Class of 21", denoting the protest movement of an iconic year? Which meant groups of that number formed to stage demonstrations at any appropriate event? He'd heard only a very little. Why should he think these young people fitted that description? Because any of them managing to scramble over the barricades was removing one layer of t-shirt to reveal a large white "21" on the dark green garment underneath.

"Twenty-oners", somebody said in the crowd. "Well – look at *them*!" called out another, whether in approval or dismay Frank couldn't tell.

Persons from the crowd, among them only a few uniformed officers but including some Volunteers, ran silently out to intercept members of this particular "Class of 21", two to each demonstrator, and manhandle them violently away. Each was taken by this mainly plain-clothes squad to a van parked on the pavement immediately under the tower of Big Ben which Frank only now realised was a police vehicle. He had been no more than five minutes standing here and watching this, but decided it was better to keep moving – and obviously make his way back up the line rather than wait until William and the others reached him. As he moved he heard a voice say, "Terrorist alert up ahead," in the voice of authority that frequently goes with false rumours.

The small cavalcade of celebrities' vehicles stretched back only to the beginning of Westminster Bridge and a little way round onto the Embankment. Behind them, scheduled to walk and perform but now standing very still, came a phalanx of "Fun Personalities from History". There were no clowns or other entertainers yet, only persons – played by actors – whom the organisers considered it would be Fun to feature. An unseen loudspeaker identified them for watchers: "Yes, that's Maggie Thatcher enjoying a laugh with Winston Churchill. And who's that pointing at us – Why, can it really be Lord Kitchener? – Yes it is! – And there's Mr Gladstone – and the Duke of Wellington just home from Waterloo… Pitt the Elder and Pitt the Younger – and take a look at old Oliver Cromwell, actually smiling for us specially for this great occasion."

Behind these notables Frank saw the first of the large teams of cheerleaders, the National Fun Maidens, who were being kept up to the mark while they waited by some light practice of their routines.

" Low – Medium – Up – Shake! Low – Medium – Up – Shake!" a loud invisible female voice commanded. On the last word each time a lake of shaken white pom-poms formed above their heads. And then – "Remember – If you drop your pom, leave your pom. Drop your pom? Leave your pom." Nothing worse than a girl impairing the smart look of the marching ranks by bending down and picking up the damaged pom, then having to scurry to catch up the others holding the vagrant article in her hand.

As Frank came eventually to the lead banner of the Approved Participants (APs) – where he could really hope to start looking out for William and the Cake – word seemed to have been passed along the line, because everybody started shuffling forwards again, tentatively at first, with pauses marching on the spot but then trundling on quite definitely in a resolute march. Here they were, the Frinton Funsters in their dance display on an open lorry, the Drummers from Devizes, and more uniformed pipe and accordion bands than it was possible to count. Northampton had sent a display of "the Laughing Boys of History", a fashion-conscious group from Stoke Newington went by with a banner proclaiming WE'RE ONLY IN THIS FOR THE JOKE. By this time Frank was back at Embankment station, where he had left William before meeting Jake – he couldn't believe this – only seventy minutes before. So William and friends must have had to move further back in the line – unless they had been forbidden to join it at all. Clowns and acrobats went by, a set of grinning Lady Godivas on horses, a sequence offering BRITS' LEISURE – IT'S FUN TO KNIT or IT'S FUN KEEPING BEES. Over everything hung an air not of pleasure but of determination. If people had to go through with this – then they would.

The procession seemed to go back beyond the end of the APs, perhaps as far as Blackfriars Bridge and beyond. Yes, there would soon be no more vehicles driven as part of the Parade, no more bands or cheerleader teams, only a line, or march, of people who had come along without official subsidy or approval, just members of the public turning out to give support – for their own causes. The Fun Parade had attracted a huge number of demonstrators from what was called "the Forgotten Nation." Maybe William could have joined those?

But he had not. Frank suddenly saw the unmistakeable tall figure pacing slowly in front of the Cake, and Jeffrey Shanks behind William wheeling the trolley and looking weary and disgruntled, and then the others. They brought up the rear of the APs – or the Somerset banner did – and between them and the completely unofficial demonstration was a ten yard gap. Frank fell in next to Merlinda, the bag with the gun hanging down from his left forearm. As they went along, the Cake, to its credit – to William's credit – attracted attention. People on the pavements behind the barriers were pointing at it, small children about to be set down on the pavement after watching everything else were lifted up again. "Who's getting married, then?" or "Leave a slice for me!" Jake and Anna, walking side by side but very separately, smiled at the watchers and returned waves. The Somerset contingent maintained fixed grimaces.

William appeared to be well satisfied by the small success. Frank mused in horror on the thought that he was parading with a man he had robbed an hour ago of a lethal weapon he was carrying in a bag in his hand. Jake said something to him he couldn't hear, on the lines of "You've made it, then?" Merlinda turned her head and considered the line behind them. The opportunity had been taken to stage a political demonstration of a kind expressly forbidden by the regulations, with banners and slogans very different from what was allowed in the official Parade. She presumed that the limited numbers of police, concentrating on protecting the notables and safeguarding the Approved Participants, had been unable to prevent it. The officers overseeing that part of the Parade – to whom William had been referred – had only admitted him to it with a surly reluctance, and then only to push the Cake along at the tail end. There was no evidence that his group had obtained official permission, but one or two (persons from Somerset) proved a valid connection with Security and the rest looked harmless enough.

The chanting and singing behind them proposed a message different from the one encouraged in front. Ahead there would frequently be a shout from a Volunteer instructed to keep them smiling: "Are we having Fun?" ("Yes!") "Fun?" ("Yes!!") "Fun?" ("Yes!!!") This part of the procession was only now turning the corner at Westminster Bridge, about two miles to go. The positive responses already sounded slack and unsure.

Frank had a fearful thought that he might have to take the revolver, moment by moment heavier and more frightening in the worn bag in his hand, home with him at the end of the day. They had covered the fifty yards from the bridge to the next corner, had gone a few yards into Whitehall, and here there was a further brief halt. To their left, planted in the crowd, were two spick and span banners, official but pretending to be spontaneous: "WHEN YOU'RE SMILING, WHEN YOU'RE SMILING" and "THE WHOLE WORLD SMILES WITH YOU." William, standing stiffly to attention while they waited, declared, "We'll soon be at the gates of government!" From among the spectators a voice called out, having read the words on the Somerset banner, "What's that then?" and another voice answered it, "What's what?" The answer came: "The great penta-mater?" Then suddenly everyone was, inexplicably, being hurried forward again. With William striding on slowly, in formal, dignified fashion, and Jeffrey Shanks taking care not to endanger the heavy trolley by pushing it forward too quickly, they fell back thirty yards behind the last of the APs, a group of burly elders who turned out to be "Sydenham Senior Morris Men". But soon they were separated from them and were caught up short of the Cenotaph and the entrance to Downing Street by the throng of unofficial demonstrators behind. They could have been taken for the beginning of their protest.

They shuffled on until they were stopped again, leaving a longer gap between them and the disappearing Morris Men, whom they could see up there, still dancing onwards. So why this pause when the road ahead was clear? William looked round to see if there was anyone with authority he could speak to. Someone from the constabulary or the "dedicated" stewards' team? This lone individual at the roadside, who could have been either – a man in black-and-yellow protective clothing who was possibly a policeman, possibly a senior volunteer? He had a radio which could have been buzzing instructions to him.

"We have to catch up with the main Parade", William said to him, pointing ahead.

"We can't allow that, sir. You must stop here", was the reply. William's face relaxed with delight at hearing a perfectly natural pentameter.

Something was going on up there and Frank realised that parked near the Cenotaph was a white police van like the one into which "Class of 21" protesters had been quite literally thrown, whatever their age, at Westminster Bridge half-an-hour ago. "But they're arresting people," Merlinda said to Frank quietly. The demonstrators behind had seen this too. There were exclamations of concern – "It's going to be like that, then!" – followed by shouts of anger and attempts to push forward which left some of them mingling with William's group. More new uniforms now appeared in front of William and formed a tight line there was no chance of penetrating or negotiating with to reach the procession ahead.

Merlinda became anxious. Could she leave their line, mix with the spectators on the pavement, work her way towards Trafalgar Square and find out what was happening at the upper end of Whitehall? She would try. One or two police looked at her as she left the group, but must have concluded she was not about to join a demonstration. As she walked among the sightseers she found their numbers had diminished; the police must have moved people along and prevented others making up their number. She tried to move casually and unobtrusively, and keep moving, because she wondered whether – over there, was that – Yes, it was Rick, prostrate and limp on the ground. Her theory was correct. This was what Rick and his friends had been planning. He was wearing the dark green t-shirt worn by others being carted, not walked, to the police van. There was, it seemed to her, no room in it for people to lie or sit, they could only stand; and hardly do that without being pressed and crushed together. In the odd quiet of a Whitehall without traffic, Merlinda Cassell heard only abrupt police interchanges, a nasty baritone laugh from somebody among this mixed collection of enforcers, then the cries and shouts of protest and distress from the persons being pushed deeper and deeper into the small space of the vehicle. Further on, there still more to be loaded because – she later heard from Rick – the law had believed that only twenty-one protesters would appear at any one point, whereas the Class of 21 Campaign had indicated that further teams of that number were welcome to join in. Some people thrown into the one police vehicle here had been there since the first wave had lain down by the Cenotaph at the moment the top of the Fun Parade, with all the notables, turned into Whitehall from Parliament Square; hence the crowd rumour of a "terrorist" manifestation halting the procession ninety minutes before.

Merlinda wheeled round and began to walk back fast. She had to do something to help Rick. In a desperate haste to have the road clear for the Parade, the police had been hurrying its grander and more acceptable sections forward out of sight of the demonstrators, arresting as many of them as they could. They had not bargained for the appearance of successive waves of 21 groups running out of the crowds all along the route – or the huge arrival of the uninvited that had joined on at the end. They panicked. Later it became known that a radio message had gone out at this time for more transport, despite reduced police numbers. But the one early vehicle was commanded not to leave until others arrived, on the grounds that more demonstrators could be stowed in it if absolutely necessary. Second and third vans took – twenty minutes, thirty, forty? – to turn up, driven in from the farther boroughs (Lewisham, Ealing, Harrow) along roads not closed for the Parade and therefore packed with traffic diverted because of the closures.

Merlinda saw a place where two sections of the crowd-control barrier had not been connected, a gap of a couple of inches. It was easy to pull open the end of one of these heavy metal fences and manoeuvre herself round it. She ran rapidly past a police cordon and out into the empty centre of Whitehall towards where the two heavy, uniformed individuals were carrying Rick towards the van. People were crammed into that so tightly they were falling out. She could hear hammering on its walls from farther inside. No one gave it any attention.

"You can't try to put him into that? You *can't!*" she ran forward and shouted, even as hands grabbed her to prevent her getting any closer. One hand was round her mouth, another on her shoulder, and for a moment she believed she was going to be cast into the vehicle herself. There was confusion around her – which she had caused, orders she couldn't grasp contradicted by others she couldn't hear. It was at this moment that the back doors of the van were finally slammed, and Merlinda saw that Rick had not been thrown into it and called out to him by name. But he was already being carted off somewhere else. Could her turning up, she wondered soon afterwards, have distracted police attention long enough to save him from being injured or killed among his companions?

She was given by one pair of police to another, with instructions, then roughly turned round and marched back to the side of the road, not a protester, not a dangerous character, just an interloper to be thrown out with a warning, too trivial to be bothered about. But in the end she was thrown, like any of the others, and landed suddenly flat on an empty pavement with no breath left, on the other side of the metal barrier with no one to pick her up.

Slowly she walked back down the pavement feeling most conspicuous. Where she walked had been completely cleared of its crowds, who had been herded away down the featureless streets leading off Whitehall. Hardly anyone would have had sight of the demonstrators, least of all of the van filled with too many of them to survive. When she reached William, the Cake, and their team – standing still and looking out of place behind the same police line – she saw her friends almost as strangers, so little could she connect them with the people and the incidents she had just observed. Jake thought she looked frightened and shaken for some reason, and there wouldn't be any asking her, yet, where she had been and what she had done in the last quarter of an hour.

Probably she said the appropriate thing to the police here: "I got lost. Can I please go back in?" They allowed her to pass, as their radios hissed with information. All at once the procession was allowed or required to move forward again, William Bridgnorth and the Cake of Celebration fortuitously heading the hundreds of well-wishers who had turned into dissidents. For a minute or two Jake dropped out to see exactly who was following them, and took a leaflet someone ran out of the march to offer him. It was topped by the headline word

FUN – but a slash deleted the "U". Below, it said, "U is not there – is U! U has been struck out. U is the Forgotten Nation." What on earth did that mean?

He had to sprint back along the moving array of protest banners, and past the demonstrators singing and chanting their own messages to counter the official mood of the day. When he reached the Cake again, with William still walking beside it in unperturbed majesty, the group had already passed the place where Merlinda had seen the demonstration. The carriageway here was empty and clear, as if nothing at all had ever happened. Passing the place now, only ten minutes afterwards, Merlinda found that alarming – the traces were covered already. She turned to Frank, wanting to tell someone. But no words came, and besides Frank's attention was occupied by the woman met sometimes at William's and reintroduced by him today as "Anna from my other class". She was asking Frank about something he was carrying in the plastic bag he had apparently gone back for at the beginning of the Parade. They were nearly at Piccadilly Circus, and Anna was walking on his other side, arguing with him. "I can't give it to you," he was insisting. But she went round to his left side and grabbed at it. He immediately transferred it to his other hand and she gave up with a snarl of disgust. What was it she wanted from Frank that was so important, Merlinda wondered? Something he could have promised her, or borrowed from her? Not *stolen* from her?

Had the front of the Parade slowed, or the later sections been hurried on by the police so that they could catch up? Because William, Jeffrey (weariedly keeping the trolley going), the rest of group, the Somerset banner-carriers – they were all now once more close behind the last of the Approved Participants. William rose to the occasion, taking advantage of the big increase in the number of spectators in Piccadilly Circus. Turning his head as he walked, he spoke his first public words on the Parade, projecting them, Jake thought, so that nearby sightseers, perhaps even spectators standing on the steps of "Eros", could hear him.

> Friends and companions in our splendid cause!
> We are, I calculate, about half-way
> To our green destination – yes, Hyde Park –
> Truly a most "historic" meeting place –
> Where we shall cut and hand around to all

Pieces of Cake in honour of our great
Shakespeare, Dryden, Pope, Wordsworth, Tennyson.
And, in our lifetimes –

But whichever name or names William Bridgnorth intended to recite next were lost. The siren on a police vehicle pressing urgently into Piccadilly from Leicester Square obliterated every other sound. A gap behind the Somerset banner was made by the police for the vehicle to pass through the Parade and drive towards a spectacle of confusion outside the "Flagship Quality Emporium of BeauCo Plc", two hundred yards down Piccadilly from Eros. No one in the procession, now a ragged line of scared people, knew what to do. A large crowd of demonstrators from behind the approved march had joined them, landing William, Cake and supporters in the middle of a very diverse crowd: Approved Participants in costumes, Forgotten Nation protesters with banners, lost Volunteers, and spectators caught up in the muddle. And an odd thing was happening in this melee: some of the later APs in the Parade were taking off their costumes, or tugging outer garments up over their heads to reveal dark green t-shirts bearing the figure 21 – and making for the doors of BeauCo Piccadilly, "the newest, grandest, most fashionable Quality Emporium in Europe."

Merlinda saw that Frank had detached himself from Anna, but what she didn't see was that, as he hurried to keep up he tried again to change the hand in which he carried the bag they had been quarrelling about – and dropped it. Its plastic handle had broken. It fell into the road and, although desperate to get it back, he was pushed forward by people walking close behind him and had no chance of retrieving it. When he turned his head he could not see where it was, and there was no space in which he could double back to go and look for it. It would carry his fingerprints and his DNA! He absolutely had to find it before anyone else picked it up.

Everyone in the group – except him – gathered protectively round William and the Cake on its trolley. When an opportunity finally came, with the line halted by the police, Frank left the others standing still in the crowd about twenty yards on from BeauCo and began to push his way back in the direction of Piccadilly Circus –only to be halted by a command from a large individual in uniform, the prelude to the appearance of a marching single file of riot police with masks and shields. Shoulder to shoulder they formed a line facing outwards in front of the BeauCo facade, and further lines seemed to have formed up at the front and back of this part of the procession, creating an enclosure in which everyone was confined.

Frank had not realised that riot police, whom he had only ever seen on television and newspaper coverage of "riots", could have different heights and widths – and, behind their shields, vulnerable faces. A few years ago he had heard an office colleague say that riot police in droves were being recruited from the long-term unemployed to reduce their numbers. Behind their disguises these men – and women – were a varied lot. Some looked bewildered by what they had to do, others had fear in their eyes. Along the lower rim of each shield was the name and logo of the company hiring them out to the authorities – Great Security Solutions (GSS). Nobody was attacking them. They presented a barrier no one was trying to penetrate because all the Class of 21 demonstrators who had planned to occupy BeauCo Quality Emporium were already inside. All the police had to do was hold the line and prevent more people from following them in.

The procession had broken up. But among the stewards gathered near the riot police line at this moment was a woman who had rescued a lost bag. One of the purposes of her being here was to see that the Fun Parade was tidy and orderly (no longer the case, but she was trained to behave as if it was). Walking alongside the Approved Participants in a supervisory capacity, wearing a Fun Parade National Office badge, she had fallen back as the well-organised middle part of the procession was passing from Whitehall into Piccadilly Circus. There she saw someone in one of the very last troupes of performers drop the plastic bag he was carrying. She didn't call out. It would be enough to grab it and catch him up if she could. So she had taken Frank's bag into her charge.

It looked like the much-handled result of ten minutes convenience shopping – or a few items being taken for recycling (true in fact). It had been overlooked by everyone as cast-away rubbish, and that offended Agatha Tenby. The Volunteers – there were several scurrying around nearby – should not allow rubbish to lie on the route of the Parade. Agatha, controller of a lot of recruiters, and organisers of volunteers, did her duty by bending down, collecting this oddly heavy item – like a lump of metal? – wrapping the broken top of the bag round the rest of it and setting off to dispose of it.

As she approached the BeauCo Quality Emporium she became aware that hundreds of people were held by the police in a space in front of it: lost paraders, protesters with more banners and leaflets, Volunteers who could not convince the police that they deserved to be let out, foreign tourists who would go home to report on the unpredictability of British culture.

She had not yet examined the wrapped-up contents of the bag. Was it really important that the owner should be sought out to have this carelessly-dropped item restored to him? Agatha, imprisoned among "the rioters", as the media at this minute were already starting to call them, began to wonder if doing her duty by this parcel was worth it. Was it necessary to carry this heavy item of rubbish, whatever it was, all the way to Hyde Park and Lost Belongings? This was how what she thought would be a trivial decision – to abandon the bag – changed the day for her, and changed her life completely. She would take a quick look to see what it was, then find a litter bin in which to leave it.

Where she stood here, about twenty feet away from the front doors of BeauCo Quality, sternly closed with riot police in front of them, Agatha removed the outer covering of the parcel and found layers of bubble wrap softening the edges of whatever was inside another plastic bag. When she pulled the folds of the bubble-wrap apart, there was Jeffrey Shanks's restored Edwardian revolver, flat and cool in her hand. Its weighty butt rested in her palm, her forefinger lightly touched the side of its trigger. She supported the barrel with the fingers of her left hand. It was a second of sheer astonishment for her, to come across such an object dropped in the road. She concluded that it would have been lost from a float in the Parade. She had no apprehensions because she could see at once that this was a preserved, cherished antique. Intrigued by it, she had these few moments in which to manipulate its movable parts and catches with her two thumbs, and turn it over, noticing with curiosity that there did appear to be bright imitation bullets, in what she believed was called its "chamber".

It was when she had raised the barrel to a horizontal, pointing position, with her left hand steadying it at breast height, that a plain-clothes Security man – one of William Bridgnorth's Somerset delegates – gripped Agatha's right wrist firmly and asked, nodding at the gun, "Excuse me – what's this, madam?"

The fired bullet created, in the Gourmet Insights window of BeauCo Quality Emporium, a small rough-edged hole and an entire surface of fragmentation; a thousand pieces would have fallen out if you had touched it. Inside, it went on to smash a finely-poised window arrangement of This Month's Seafood Illusions. The loud bang was audible both outside and inside the Emporium. But there were no more shots, which was lucky, because any worse-judged interventions from Security could have agitated Agatha enough to cause deaths or grave injuries.

It took Frank Winterfield some time to think that it could easily be Jeffrey Shanks's gun that he had heard. This theory gave him relief because the weapon was now altogether out of his hands and its firing could not be blamed on him.

It never occurred to Jeffrey that it might be his own gun because he could not know that it was gone from his flat. But every kind of rumour went round the "boxed" (once it would have been the "kettled") crowd: a Security gun had gone off by mistake, or had been deliberately fired as a warning to demonstrators; an anarchist markswoman had infiltrated the Parade to assassinate a police commander; an Islamic suicide gunman had released the first bullet in a batch of which the last would be used on himself. People immediately around Agatha pressed back from her in terror. A moving cordon of constables, in and out of uniform, surrounded her as she was dragged away distraught to the line which boxed in the crowd, and through this line, and to another inevitable white van.

Jake Coleman actually did see this happen, and recognised who it was being arrested and taken away. He did not associate Agatha with the gunshot – why should he? – and his first instinct was to struggle through the crowd and speak to the police in case he could be of any help. Within seconds he decided not to. The police taking Agatha in didn't look as if they could be spoken to.

William Bridgnorth did not at first notice that his supposed Somerset supporters had vanished. Then he saw their disappointing banner, untidily half-rolled up, lying in a gutter, and imagined the four were lost somewhere; which he did not wholly regret. He wanted to continue the journey to Hyde Park because they must already be half-an-hour late. His air of authority brought three or four people over to enquire. "I know as much as you do – and no more," he said, several times. If they did not move on soon, the entire procession in front would have begun their final displays and performances in the park. The fears of the crowd at the sound of the gunshot gave way to ordinary perplexity. Why were they not allowed to move? What was happening inside the Quality Emporium, where people with big banners proclaiming "21" were appearing at upstairs windows? Several hundred people were trapped in the street in the fiercest heat of the summer.

In the middle of the imprisoned crowd there was a mood of despairing calm as time passed – one hour, two – and police tactics became clear. People kept here, thirsty and bewildered, pursued and arrested if they managed to escape, would be deterred from demonstrating in future. Without the chance to move William and the group felt restless, even bored. Merlinda wanted to find out for herself what to expect. It was unbearable to stand here and wait; although William's ability to retain poise and dignity was incredible. Surely even he must be exhausted by this? There was no sign of movement, every sign that they would be there for hours. Or days? Merlinda noted carefully the exact position of the trolley and told William what she would like to do, with his permission. He gave it and she moved off slowly through the crowd to see what was happening for herself. She was still shaken by her earlier experience, still anxious about Rick, and it was difficult to go anywhere far among this angry and distressed mass.

Here was a woman in recommended Volunteer clothing, who surely ought to know – or have some power to do something about –what was happening. But she turned away from Merlinda's question with contempt. "Next time they can have Fun going and fucking themselves." Merlinda's feet kicked empty bottles of water. She walked for five minutes with a father looking for a lost five-year old. She read the stationary banners of numerous Forgotten Nation marchers from the north and from London: "FUN in Newcastle? Come and see", "Come and have FUN in Hackney," "The Forgotten Nation is round the corner from YOU." Then someone tapped her shoulder, lightly, a young woman she knew well, carrying a banner and accompanied by a girl Merlinda did not know at all. "What happened down there then? There was shooting?" Aurelia asked. "There was shooting but we don't know who," Merlinda replied. What else could she say to Aurelia, apart from merely confirming that fact? Aurelia had addressed her almost as if they were still companions at No.18, as if she was asking "Any milk left?" or "You late to-night?" She used the same casual tone of voice, as if nothing was any different and they would talk about all this later on at home. As Merlinda walked on, though, she did once look back, and saw that Aurelia's banner, which everyone around her was ignoring said "CAPITALISM WORKS. IT'S FUN!" with the noun in blue lettering. This had been carried along among anti-capitalist protesters who had either mocked it, or taken it as irony and let Aurelia stay with them.

Returning, Merlinda overshot the place where William had been standing but met him making his way back to it himself. He told her he had been trying with immense courtesy, she was sure, to find out from a police official how long they would be detained. None had reacted to his questions, the eyes stared past him into the crowd, the lips failed to move. They did speak in undertones to each other, and nodded and pointed and used mobiles. William said he had been informed earlier that as an official part of the Parade they were due in Hyde Park with the rest. Was this true? It produced one surly response from a speaker looking over William's shoulder as he replied: "You'll not be getting to Hyde Park today." Merlinda went back with him to the Cake through groups of people sitting dejectedly on the ground and fanning themselves against the heat with placards and leaflets.

For a few minutes Merlinda began to wonder whether even William was acquiring a perplexed and indecisive air. He contemplated his Cake, which had so far survived the heat and the rigours of the journey quite well – but how long could it last? To Merlinda it looked a pitiable token of hope ruined, a symbol not of celebration but defeat. No one around was paying it attention any more. It was old news. These people were fellow-victims, not members of the public waiting to be entertained. There it was, in the middle of its accompanying coterie, marooned and, although still beautiful, high and purposeless on its trolley, not moving forward, doing nothing. Jeffrey looked at William as if he would have a new instruction to give.

But then Merlinda looked at William and knew exactly what they should do, and stepped up close to him to speak – only for William to pre-empt her, smiling and speaking softly, with the same plan.

> "Should we not seize the opportunity
> To hold our celebration here – and now?"

With the last three words he lifted his voice. He was making it clear not only to his friends but to other people nearby that they were entitled – and expected – to listen. Anyone who ignored or doubted him would be converted by his air of conviction, good humour and irrefutable logic. Several turned towards him, managing to stand back a little, even in this dense boxed, or kettled, crowd, because this was going to be a speech and you needed to leave space between speaker and audience. During the subsequent lines the nearest formed a circle which drew others to look over their shoulders and work out what was happening.

> "Good listening friends, it was our former plan
> To hold this ceremony in Hyde Park,
> With all the other proud participants
> In this event. But our one small request –
> To make our way *there* – has just been declined,
> With no reason given. We are to be held back
> Within this space because authority
> Has so decreed, and how long we languish here,
> Denied all movement has not been made clear.
> – Therefore, dear comrades in captivity,
> I seek your kind attention to affirm
> That words can't be confined, the power of speech
> Breaks every limit. And, at this time and place,
> Not in Hyde Park, we are inviting you
> As special guests to share our sustenance
> And speak our verse, which is – as you can hear –
> The five-foot line so natural to the tongue
> That I address you in. Please understand
> Your thanks are not required, but should you wish
> To utter some few sentiments in verse
> We would allow that and be gratified
> Beyond all measure. – Let us share the Cake!

Jeffrey Shanks steadied the trolley as William opened the antique case which contained his great-grandfather's silver knife. The precision and accuracy which William had applied with smaller implements to several lesser cakes now came into action with this supreme manifestation. Skilfully he produced small square, precise piece after piece, each a full-fruit portion decorated with marzipan and icing, out of the bakers' elegant structure, manoeuvring them neatly onto cardboard plates taken from a bag on the lower shelf of the trolley.

Merlinda took them from him and Frank handed them out. Jake found the stacks of cardboard cups in the box in the same place and opened the first of the weighty litre bottles of water. It did not surprise him that Jeffery had found pushing the trolley a severe undertaking.

The Cake stood up firmly without crumbling but the time came when the figures and emblems on the top had to be presented to people near the end of the queue that had formed. "For you, Dove Cottage, William Wordsworth's home," he declared to a young woman whose t-shirt announced "TOGETHER: THE UNION". To his delight she responded with the words, "Some of the time it was, but in his youth/ He lived in revolutionary France." Even, out of the crowd in this box, came one stray dog to take a piece and be refused a second. As it turned away and was lost among the human legs milling round, Merllnda looked more closely and could have sworn it was a ragged version of Young Toby. Or the real one... A creature not arrested as so many were for behaviour noted by police who took their names when they were eventually released from open air captivity.

22

Rick kept for me something printed in a week-end political newspaper ten days later, and I passed it on to William. It was the only mention anywhere (so far as I know) of what we had done, a paragraph written by one of the regulars in a column to which he – or she – gave the title "You'd never know, but…" with the byline "Truthsurfer" underneath it:

Nice surprise to see an intriguing character from my past heading up the Forgotten Nation demo that fell in behind last Saturday's so-called "Fun Parade" in Central London. William ("Bill") Bridgnorth gave decades of dedicated service as an extraordinary local government officer – and colleague of mine – in the London Borough of Eastbridge. Then the cuts were used to impose early retirement on him. But I remember him best for his personal cause. Bill advocated and promoted the use of traditional blank verse – yes, the kind used without a second thought by people in Shakespeare's plays – as a natural mode of speaking. He and a band of followers pushed a huge Poetry Cake on a barrow up Whitehall and along Piccadilly, leading the thousands who turned out in the equatorial heat for the Forgotten Nation Campaign. When an exploding firecracker gave the Met and Security the opportunity to "box in" large sections of the march outside the BeauCo Quality Emporium in Piccadilly for six hours, Bill proceeded to distribute free pieces of cake and beakers of mineral water to hungry and dry marchers. His reward? A night in a police cell and an appearance before magistrates on Sunday morning on the obscure charge of committing "a blemish of the peace". No, I didn't know either. Apparently it's a mediaeval offence reintroduced to persecute minor political nuisances. Bill Bridgnorth was fined £500, with £100 fines imposed on all his supporters. The clever ways they devise to stamp out any kind of dissent or creativity…"

I am looking forward to going to the Lake District next week. When I was at Uni, people went to the Lakes on camping trips, but I have never been there myself. I am a bit worried in case William won't have the breath and the strength to get up Scafell and hold a seminar in honour of Wordsworth on the summit, which is what he plans to do. But that might apply to the rest of us.

If anything, the little martyrdom William experienced through his arrest and the chance to plead guilty with a short speech in verse (which the magistrate listened to with interest) seemed to bring out new passion in him. He revealed to us that he has discovered through the internet that there is something called The World Federation of Native Verse Speakers, to which people with many nationalities belong. French members use the hexameter, the six-stress line of their classical drama, and some Italians attempt Dante's *terza rima*. Both of those seem to be more difficult and less natural than English blank verse. The Italians have plenty of rhymes available, but conversation in improvised *terza rima* can be very tricky. William was thrilled to find that a party of Japanese doctors will be attending a conference in the Lake District at the same time that we will be there, and some of them propose to spend their leisure time talking in haiku. "They might give us some medical support," William believed.

We came out of the magistrates' court into the street laughing nervously – well, except for William, who was as calm as usual and looked radiant with satisfaction at having broken the law in an excellent cause.

Someone proposed we went for coffee, though when I looked round, Anna was not with us. She had disappeared from our party at the end of the Parade because she'd seen a police inspector on duty who used to be her boy friend and he had allowed her to get out of the box early. All she did after the case in court – where she sat in the public seats because although she was not one of the accused she was loyal enough to William to want to come and support him – was shout out "Goodbye" and "See you later", and run away up the street with the guy Jeffrey following her.

Therefore it was just William and our class of three people that ended up in a coffee place opposite the court building, where we sat among other accused persons and witnesses waiting to go in or relaxing after having been sentenced. We noticed that the police involved in our case were all making for the nearest pub.

It's interesting how unusual situations bring out a different side in people. In this cafe, when we'd gone up to give our orders at the counter, Jake suddenly said "This morning is on me," and I thought he meant to treat us to the coffee and snack we were having. "But you can't do all of that," I told him, looking at my watch and seeing it was 1.20 p.m. We were all asking for plenty of sandwiches, which was quite reasonable at lunch time after such an event.

"Lunch as well," Jake was insisting. I looked at Frank, and at William, and they both seemed as puzzled as I was.

"But you —" William began, and for the first time I ever heard this, he failed to complete a line he had started when he fully intended to do so. He'd realised before Frank and myself that Jake had paid the fines, for all of us. Yes, William's included. I hadn't even begun to work out how I could dare to ask my parents for a hundred pounds, so I accepted, with a bit of protest. Not that I could have refused, because Jake was determined and had fixed it with the court officials at the hearing to pay it in cash, and I hadn't understood what he was doing. He joked about having been to a cash machine on the day of the Fun Parade in case he needed to, so it was all right! The only reason I had before this for thinking that Jake could be generous was that he'd bought me a couple of juices in New Cross after our meeting at the Laughter Studio all that time ago.

Frank and I made a date to go and eat at Godneau's, two days after the court case, and talk some more about all this. But that evening I was surprised to turn the corner of the street and see him still standing outside the restaurant, because we had agreed to meet at our usual table — and besides, there was a slight shower falling.

"Look!" he said.

He pointed towards Godneau's window, and gave a shrug and stared as if defying me to explain what had happened.

The window itself was empty: no menu, no flowers, no view of the table where we had eaten meals three or four times with Godneau himself mournfully attending to our orders. Interior and owner had gone. Godneau had vanished off the face of his premises. The sense of shock was really powerful at this moment; the sadness about Godneau came later because he had begun to seem permanent. But then —

"Wait a minute," I said to Frank. "There's a notice on the door."

If I expected some information as to where Godneau might have moved, I could not have been more wrong. The notice was a formal announcement to tell everyone that the business conducted there had been closed, the company wound up, and the bailiffs had moved in. The restaurant company! I stared at the name in horror.

"That's the company I know about — I'm engaged by their consultancy."

Except that I had never had a single reply to my recent phone calls and e-mails to HandF, or to my one letter. Texting didn't produce any response either. I had completed all my assignments, and there were no more instructions for me to follow.

Out of a job after the demo, Rick offered to come with me on a visit to the office, which I had described to him, including its two directors, in almost the same detail that I had used when giving my account of it to William's class. He had the time now – as I certainly did – and felt recovered enough from his experiences on the day of the Parade; about which he said he would speak or write some time, but definitely not for the moment.

It was almost as difficult to find the place on this second visit as on the first. The alley opening unexpectedly off the Piccadilly end of Regent's Street was still as dark, the intercom and lift just as forbidding; although we were admitted to the front office quickly and this was temporarily reassuring. Maybe nothing had changed. I hadn't noticed last time a rather soiled and faded look about the large wall photograph of the City of London in which a door opened to admit me to the room where I was interviewed (was I too impressed?). But at least it was still there. The same woman sat at the reception desk.

"My name is Merlinda Cassell," I said. "I was here before, when Mr Henbrook and Mr Green interviewed me for the job."

"Yes, of course you were," she said, as if accusing me of talking down to her. I'd assumed it would be helpful to remind her. "You knew they left?"

Rick glanced at me with a smile as if to say, "Didn't I tell you?"

I shook my head. "Left? – when?" I stuttered as I asked her this.

"Three weeks ago, about. Not long after you came."

"Ms Cassell has work to report on," Rick told her. She looked up at him for a second and shuffled some papers on her desk as if he didn't need to be answered. She looked at me.

"Do you want to see Mr Whitaker?" I sensed sympathy in her manner, a very little. I hadn't the faintest idea who Mr Whitaker might be.

She picked up her phone and tapped out a short internal number.

"Ms Cassell has come," she told somebody, looking at me while she waited for a response to this information. It took ages. Somebody was lecturing her at the other end – I could hear a loud male voice but I couldn't hear any words. All the time she was nodding and saying, "Yes. Yes." At times she gave Rick and me an expression that appeared to blame us for the talking-to she was getting. But I also got the impression she wanted us to think she was doing her best. Finally, "Right away," she affirmed, and put the phone down again. "Mr Whitaker will see you for a minute or two," she said. "You can go through."

Rick automatically moved with me, as it had been implicit in our turning up there together that he would want to witness any meeting that took place. I had to look hard to find the doorknob on the dome of St Paul's Cathedral – the automatic door in my story for William's seminar being a bit of an invention! – but on grasping it I turned it in as firm a manner as I could produce, and pushed it open. We both went forward, but not into near darkness. We walked into a room flooded with afternoon light.

It was so bright that I couldn't at first see where Mr Whitaker might be sitting. It was now a wide, carpeted lounge with a profusion of tropical plants, several of them growing out of a vast water tank with big fish patrolling to and fro in bubbling depths. Then Whitaker got up behind a long desk on the right – was it the one Henbrook and Green had occupied? I didn't think so – and came out from behind it, and stood deliberately close to us in the middle of the room. He was a smooth young individual in clothes no one was ever seen wearing except in the fashion pages. He had the look of someone who could only exist in life by taking up a superior stance to others.

"Feel welcome!" he proclaimed, raising his voice on the "-come", which I suppose is the most fashionable greeting these days, replacing "Hi!" in a lot of places and turning my parents' Hullo" into the faintest of memories. There was a small cluster of armchairs round a sofa at one end of the room – no chair like the one I had failed to move on my first visit – and I thought he might be going to ask us to sit down. But he didn't.

"Things have changed?" he said.

"They have. May I ask you a question?" I said. Rick had thought I should get my words in first.

"For one thing," he continued, as if I hadn't spoken, "all the three clients they allotted to you have gone out of business."

"*All* of them? Altogether out of business?"

"Utterly altogether."

"I was advising the Laughter Studio down in New Cross."

Mr Whitaker forced an unpleasant grin.

"The applause died down and the last laugh came with the receivers."

There was a pause. This meeting was not going to last long enough to make standing up really uncomfortable.

224

"And the company that had to recruit dogs for films?"

"Don't you see them everywhere? Hungry dogs? They started drifting in without anyone having to supply them." I thought of Young Toby and his piece of cake. If it had been him drifting in on the Fun Parade afternoon outside the Quality Emporium.

"There was a restaurant chain –" Would he know anything about Godneau, whom I had grown rather fond of?

"They have gone down. But they will resurface. Restaurants always do." What was he leading up to?

All my assignments had vanished. So what about the job I thought I had, researching their areas, thinking how to render them advice in the name of Hemingway and Faulkner? What about the letter of appointment that never came, the initial payment arriving at the end of the first month? The travel and meal expenses?

"You'll see those restaurants again, under a different name," Whitaker said. But they won't be our clients. We cannot be consulted by known failures."

Rick looked at me as if prompting me to ask some of the questions I had prepared with his help.

"I saw Mr Henbrook and Mr Green when I was appointed," I began. "They agreed that I –"

"Green and Henbrook were juniors. Learning fairly fast – but still juniors. They had no authority to appoint."

"They responded to Ms Cassell's application, and they interviewed her as if they had," Rick said, "And they –"

"Part of their training. Anything else I can tell you?"

"I've got to insist," I told him, "that I be paid for what I've done. There was an understanding that – "

"Not a contract though?"

"A strong verbal indication might be regarded as a contract in law," Rick risked declaring. Later he told me that he had no idea whether this could be the case, but Whitaker – who was hardly any older than him – didn't look as if he had the knowledge required to contradict him.

Whitaker smiled, but it looked to me as if he was forcing it to gain time.

"There would have to be a witness," he suggested.

"Ms Cassell recorded her interviews, and we are recording this conversation now." All this was true; it is what has become of a world where everyone can keep visual and aural evidence of anything they want to, and for occasions when offers might be made they do keep it.

"Well I assumed that," Whitaker went on. "Some transactions are certainly validated by the trust generated in the dialogue between honest participants in the proceedings."

Here he walked away, leaving us standing alone. Did I hear him give a sort of sigh of resignation? "And on that basis–" he was now back at his desk and had opened a drawer – "I am giving you this in termination of the verbal agreement we made with you."

It was an envelope he found very quickly, obviously prepared for a meeting like this, and he came across swiftly to hand it to me. My hand shook as I took hold of it and I held it tight all the way down in the lift.

Outside, in Piccadilly Circus, I shouted to Rick above the traffic noise, "I wasn't going to argue. It might cover my debts from the last few weeks. And the Lake District. It won't go any further."

"We should have examined it properly before we left," Rick believed.

But no, I hadn't had the courage to keep us there in Whitaker's office. I couldn't wait to get out when I knew he was admitting defeat. It was enough for me to see that the envelope contained a cheque which we took it would be cashable. Can you imagine – I didn't even take it out to see how much it was for until we were in the street?

We went on hand in hand down Piccadilly in the latest ferocious heat.

"They got the window mended the same night." I nodded at the BeauCo window as we passed it. "But you weren't there to see any of that, were you!"

"No", he replied. "I wasn't. I didn't see any of it."

I go on remembering what he said next, after pausing and smiling. "But there'll be more chances."